W9-BWG-944

# FORCE COLLECTOR

Written by

KEVIN SHINICK

LOS ANGELES • NEW YORK

For information address Disney • Lucasfilm Press,
1200 Grand Central Avenue, Glendale, California 91201.

Printed in the United States of America

First Edition, November 2019

1 3 5 7 9 10 8 6 4 2

FAC-020093-19284

ISBN 978-1-368-04558-2

Library of Congress Control Number on file

Reinforced binding

Design by Leigh Zieske

Visit the official *Star Wars* website at: www.starwars.com.

Logo Applies to Text Stock Only

Dedicated to Josephine Viola.

Thanks for always listening.

# CHAPTER 1

The image was not what it seemed, but the pain was undeniable.

It hit him like the opposite of what he imagined hyperspace was like, a blinding white light streaked with black flames shooting directly into his eyes. Even with his lids shut, Karr could feel it burning his retinas. Had he not known better, he would've blamed it on a flaw in the lenses of the stormtrooper helmet he'd recently bought—Death Star era, slight carbon scoring, 7.5 grade level in the antique military guide—but otherwise not a bad purchase for fifty-seven credits. Unless, of course, it *was* responsible for the pain. But he knew that wasn't the case. Not even brand-new lenses could protect him from this agony.

As the pain bored into his eye sockets, he recalled a warning a pilot gave him once, about never staring directly into a double-haloed Tatooine eclipse.

*Good advice,* he thought as he began to lose consciousness.

Only he wasn't entering Tatooine airspace. He was entering the Force.

"Are you okay?" Karr heard someone ask in a tinny voice. Actually, it probably wasn't a tinny voice but rather a damaged speaker in the stormtrooper helmet. Maybe 7.5 wasn't an accurate grade for the piece of junk after all.

Karr was lying on his back. The floor was cold, but his face was hot.

"What are you wearing?" This time he could tell the voice belonged to a woman, but he thought that was an odd follow-up question. Usually when people came across him passed out on the floor they'd ask him if he knew his name. "Karr Nuq Sin," he mumbled out of habit, realizing only a hair too late that wasn't the question she had asked him.

"What are you wearing?" she asked again slowly, sounding more annoyed.

"Green cargo pants, blue flight jacket, desert boots, black gloves, and a newly acquired Death Star–era stormtrooper helmet. Grade level: seven point—" He stopped himself in light of the new information and reevaluated. "Six point nine."

"You need to take it off. *Now*." Her voice sounded like coins and static through the helmet, but yes. It was definitely a woman. Probably a teacher.

"School policy prohibits any student from carrying a weapon or wearing military paraphernalia," she added, probably quoting some passage from the code of conduct.

Karr wouldn't know. He'd never read it.

He struggled to his feet and searched the floor for the black glove that always landed nearby after one of his episodes. He found it and used it to salute her. "No military paraphernalia present, *sir*!"

"Except for the helmet?" She ignored the incorrect address and took the glove from his hand to inspect it.

"The helmet is an artifact . . . *sir*!" Now he was pushing it.

Namala Moffat sighed. "Just take it off." He pulled the helmet loose with a soft pop. Now she could see him for what he really was: a brown-haired, brown-eyed kid with a chipped tooth to go along with the chip on his shoulder. "Where'd you get that?" she asked.

"I got it from Janu Blenn. His great-grandfather was a service fueler in the Empire," Karr told her. "Stormtrooper, third class."

Moffat frowned. "That boy's shyer than a Snivvian at a market auction. He told you all that?"

Karr just smiled. "In a way."

In the years since his unusual abilities had surfaced, no doctor (human or droid) had been able to explain them. Episodes of blinding light and searing pain weren't exactly coveted abilities, but the images that accompanied those things were pretty cool. Most of the time. If he remembered them when he came to.

Karr didn't feel like explaining all that to the teacher, so he didn't.

The truth was that, yes, Janu Blenn *was* incredibly shy, but he was also stubborn. It'd taken Karr five whole days to convince Janu to sell him the trooper helmet after he overheard the boy relay some family lore about how his great-grandfather claimed to have had his mind manipulated by a Jedi. Karr figured he probably made the whole thing up to get a better grade on his history project, since the Jedi didn't exist during Imperial times, but he had to know for sure. Which is why he was willing to go as high as fifty-seven credits.

Of course it would've been easier to just wave his hand and manipulate Janu's thoughts like a Jedi, but Karr wasn't there yet.

Soon, he hoped. But not yet.

Which was why he needed the helmet.

When Karr turned thirteen, he started to experience changes. Of course, everyone was going through changes at that age, but unlike Zarado, whose horns started growing longer, or Lara, whose adult coat of fur started coming in, Karr began getting terrible headaches that often came with garbled visions when he touched certain things, sometimes.

"You're just experiencing growing pains," his mother, Looway, would say to him, trying to hide her concern.

"Maybe," said Karr. But unless his brain was growing beyond the size of his skull, he didn't really get it. And it was changing him. Changing his outlook. At a time when most kids felt like they could take on the universe, Karr felt doomed. And he worried that his "adolescence," as they called it, wouldn't be a phase he went through but rather his expiration date.

Eventually, his family took him to a doctor. The doctor couldn't find anything wrong with him, so they went to a different doctor. Same result. A third doctor couldn't help, or a fourth. Everybody in his family had their own guess as to what was happening to Karr and how to fix it, but it all came together in a mess of garbled noise.

One afternoon, after the same old argument about what was wrong with Karr, he was sulking in his room when he saw his grandmother standing in the doorway. She had the oddest smile on her face. Then, almost in slow motion, he saw her lips form the words, *It's time.*

"I know what is causing your headaches. It's the Force," J'Hara said as she sat on the edge of his bed, wiping the hair out of his face.

"The *what*?" he asked as if she had just diagnosed a disease.

"The Force," she repeated. "The Force is what gives the Jedi their power." His grandmother had spoken about the Jedi before, but to be fair Karr was younger at the time and she might as well have been talking about schoolwork.

That day, however, the Jedi. The Force. The war. It all sounded like one of the fables she used to tell him before bed. But it wasn't, of course. This time it was a revelation. Karr had been looking for hope. Hope that what he was going through wasn't something bad but rather something awesome. And this definitely counted as hope.

"What do you see?" his grandmother asked as she looked into his eyes. "When you get these headaches?"

"It's tough to say. The pain is so great, sometimes it's impossible to see anything. Like staring at the sun and trying to focus on the solar flares. For a really long time I saw nothing. Just felt a lot of pain. But then one day something changed. I could see and hear . . . something. Sounds? Words? Feelings? I don't know."

"That's because a new perception has come into your existence. You're experiencing a gift. Your headaches happen because you aren't finding yourself in the Force," J'Hara explained. "Once you figure it out, who knows? You might be able to learn about an object's past just by touching it. That would really be something, wouldn't it?"

"Is that what the Jedi did?"

She nodded. "Perhaps a few, here and there. Not

many, I believe. The Jedi could do all kinds of things. Maybe if you could find Jedi objects, what you learn from them could show you how to use your abilities properly. How to become a Jedi."

"How to become a Jedi." Karr would always remember the day she uttered those words. For as long as he could remember, Karr had felt as out of place in the galaxy as he did in his own skin. His family had always been tailors, middle-class workers, but Karr felt he was destined for greater things. And that day, he was learning it was true.

"Where can we find the Jedi?" he asked eagerly.

"Sadly, they haven't been seen in decades," she confessed.

"But how can I learn about the Force properly if I don't have a master?"

"*Life* is your master," she said. "Let the galaxy lead you as if you were *its* apprentice. It has much to show you."

"But if I never know when something I touch is going to give me a headache, how am I going to make it through life?"

J'Hara thought for a moment. "I will make you gloves."

After that, Karr decided to learn as much about the Jedi as he could. Through books, through stories, and if need be, through the headaches. Which was why a good part of Karr's days was spent searching for things he could touch that might shed some light on the lost masters: robes, weapons, communicators, and of course his most recent acquisition, the stormtrooper helmet.

The teacher wasn't having it. She plucked the helmet out of his hands. "I'll just . . . hold on to this, until after the final siren," Moffat said with enough authority that it would probably keep most kids from arguing. "You can have it back then."

But Karr wasn't most kids. He turned on the sly charm, or that's what he hoped it sounded like when he said, "Why don't I just keep it in my locker?"

The teacher stared at him.

He was usually pretty good about staying out of trouble, but maybe his lucky streak had come to an end. He was just about to try some other pleading approach that might let him keep his prize when a big, nasty call from the end of the hallway stopped him.

"Karr Nuq Sin is delusional!"

Both Karr and Moffat turned their heads.

A big Besalisk named Royke loomed large and loud. He was oversized in every way, even for his species. The girth of his four arms alone nearly covered the width of the walkway as he approached, and his cronies flanked him like stubby moons orbiting a grumpy planet.

Royke was a bully, a blowhard, and a snob. At best, he'd rank a mere 4.3 in Karr's quality guide.

The lumbering oaf put one of his four arms around Moffat's shoulders. "Let me help you out, ma'am. This kid is a freak. Has some sort of brain disease, so I wouldn't get too close. In case it's contagious."

Karr protested. "I don't have a brain disease. You don't know anything."

"Lurdo thinks he's a *Jedi*," mocked the Besalisk, mispronouncing the word so it sounded more like "Jedee."

Karr snorted. Royke wouldn't even know about the Jedi if he hadn't heard Karr ask so many questions about them. The Jedi were all but extinct, and unless you paid attention in history class—which Royke most certainly did *not*—most people knew very little about what they did or how important they had been to the galaxy. To Karr himself even! And that someday he would become one. They were guardians of justice, for crying out loud. The keepers of the peace—

"He even stole from his own grandmother," Royke sneered.

Unfortunately, Karr didn't feel much like keeping the peace at the moment. And as much as he wanted to be a Jedi, he figured he could probably get away with just one brawl. Historians would say he was getting it out of his system.

Moffat figured out where things were going, and she tried to head it off. "I'm sure he hasn't stolen from his grandmother. Stop antagonizing him and go back to class."

"Oh, yeah? What about those gloves? I heard him telling someone they were from his grandmother." Royke snatched Karr's glove out of the teacher's hand and flapped it around.

Karr's heart began to race. The gloves were a gift from his grandmother. Something special she had made him. Without them he felt exposed. And angry. Angry at Royke. Angry at Moffat for being so careless.

Moffat's eyes met his with a look of both irritation and apology. "Give that back to him, right now."

But Royke wouldn't. He couldn't. Not when he had an audience to entertain. He danced around the hall, singing *"Look at me! I'm Karr!"* as he waved the glove just out of its rightful owner's reach. Then the unthinkable happened: Royke jammed his greasy, pudgy fingers into the glove.

"Give it back!" Karr hollered.

"What are you gonna do? You're not a real Jedi!" He worked his hand deeper inside the glove.

"Oh, yeah?" Without even thinking, Karr stretched his arm out and used an open hand to grasp the air as if it was Royke's throat. He poured all his anger, all his grief, and all his concentration into the gesture.

The bully's laughing stopped. Then his breathing stopped. His eyes bulged from his head and he dropped to his knees, struggling to inhale whatever air he could into his quickly closing lungs.

# CHAPTER 2

Moffat yelled at Karr. "Stop that! Whatever you're doing, stop it—right this instant!"

He lowered his hand, but Royke continued to gasp and wheeze.

The teacher jumped between them and grabbed Karr by the shoulders. She shoved his arm against his side. "What are you doing to him?" she demanded, loud and scared and ready to shake him to pieces.

Royke dropped to his knees and fell forward face-first. All four of his long, beefy arms splatted to the floor, splaying in every direction.

Everything went quiet.

The scattered students who lingered in the hallway stood wide-eyed; they held their hands over their mouths and didn't say a word. No announcements blared from the headmaster's office. No doors opened, no datapads beeped inside backpacks, and none of the bully's friends so much as *breathed*.

Until Royke's big body started to shake. He was laughing quietly.

He worked his way up to a belly laugh as he rolled over and stared up at the ceiling. He pounded all four fists on the floor with glee.

At first, no one joined him. Then everyone did.

"Ha!" the bully cackled above the laughing crowd. "You totally thought you had Jedi powers!"

Moffat's face turned red.

Karr's turned even redder. "You just wait until—"

"Enough!" declared the teacher. She snatched Karr's glove from Royke and handed it back to Karr, but her expression remained stern. "Both of you, go to the headmaster's office!"

Side by side, Karr and the bully skulked toward the office, neither one speaking or trying to make eye contact. When they finally arrived, the door was closed. After a few minutes it opened and a hand waved Royke inside—leaving Karr to take a seat and await his fate.

Karr sat on a bench in the lobby outside the headmaster's office, twiddling his thumbs and trying hard to hear what was happening on the other side of the closed office door. The muffled conversation was difficult to understand, but Karr couldn't help noticing how much it sounded like a regular conversation between the Kitonaks in his biology class. He didn't speak Kitonese, of course, but there was something about their low voices and the way their cheeks swallowed the words that always made it sound like they were conspiring. Probably not a totally fair judgment, Karr thought, but then again at this school the odds were pretty good that most students were up to no good. Just like the odds were pretty good that Royke was behind that office door convincing the headmaster that *Karr* was the one to blame for all the commotion.

From where he was sitting, Karr could see across the lobby and into the teacher's lounge. In there, Moffat worked at a table—reading through a database that was probably filled with job listings for some different career path. The trooper helmet rested beside her screen. She had won the argument as to where it would stay for now, but Karr had gotten what he needed from the object—confirmation that Janu Blenn was either lying or misinformed. Karr had seen no Jedi in his vision, only the blurry images of the Death Star and an explosion. Whatever he was meant to get from the vision was still unclear. It hadn't shown him any Force wielders, at least none that he was aware of. But still, the eyes of the mask stared back at him from across the way as if they were angry. As if he had stolen something from them. And in a way, he had.

Karr ran his gloved hands along the curve of the bench, wondering if he should add his mark to the graffiti he found there. *The Hutts are nuts! Oktar is a Yak face!* and his personal favorite, *Don't look away, you'll never win, if you leave your lunch by a Gamorrean.* That one would be tough to beat.

Maybe just his name and the date? It would be proof someday that the sure-to-be-famous Jedi Karr Nuq Sin had been there. What's the worst the headmaster could do to him?

He pulled a small knife out of his pocket and was busy scratching his first initial onto the bench when a side door slid open.

Kragnotto, the Ankura Gungan teacher in charge of the science program, led a Mirialan girl into the room by her arm. He was hauling her a little too fast and a little too rough to actually be helpful, and she was not playing along very well—dragging her feet and generally making the teacher work for every bit of progress.

When they reached the bench, he thrust her toward

it. "You waits here! And the next time meesa find you rummaging through meesa things," he said, his cheeks shaking and showering anyone within a meter radius with spittle, "yousa gonna get more than just detention."

The girl smiled like she didn't care. Maybe she didn't.

The Gungan left the way he'd come in, letting the door slide shut behind him. Karr kept his head down, minding his own business. He didn't need extra trouble. He went back to work on his carving like he hadn't seen a thing.

But after a few seconds, the girl spoke. "Seriously?"

Karr glanced up. He was the only person she could possibly be talking to. "Seriously . . . what?"

"Are you really writing your name on the bench?"

He held up the small knife and wiggled it for show. "No, I'm *carving* it on the bench."

She rolled her eyes. "Leaving graffiti on a seat while you wait for detention? Isn't that a little on the nose? We get it, you're a rebel. For your next trick, maybe you could break a window or play some music super loud. That'll show 'em."

Karr had no response. Wasn't picking a fight with

someone you don't know also a little on the nose? But from what Karr knew of the Mirialan species, their skin was usually green like hers or pink, not green or pink with flushed red cheeks, so clearly she was fuming about something other than Karr's petty vandalism.

Karr had seen Mirialans before, but something was different about this girl beyond the flushed cheeks. Was it her eyes? They were sparkling blue, but almost more than sparkling. Glittering. And did they have specks of gold in them? Maybe. He had never been so close to a Mirialan before, or stared so long at—

"What are you looking at?" she barked.

"Uh, nothing," he said as he went back to his amateur artwork. There was definitely something different about her, but he was not about to look up again to find out.

He was just starting to make good progress on the *K* when she asked him, "What did you do?"

"Huh?" He chanced a glance at her.

"What. Are. You. Here. For?" she said slowly, as if teaching him the language.

Karr tried to make his answer casual. "Oh . . . I tried to choke someone using just my mind."

The girl eyed him suspiciously, like she didn't quite

believe him but she kind of wanted to. "You used the Force to choke somebody?"

Now she had his attention. "You know about the Force?"

"I'm not an idiot. Do you really have the Force? Did you really choke somebody?"

"I said I *tried* to."

It was her turn to scowl at him. "So you *don't* have the Force. Do you even know what it is?"

"Um, of course. It's an energy field created by all living things."

"Yeah, yeah," she said with a flap of her hand. "Binds the galaxy together and all that. Why is it everyone always says the same thing about the Force? Makes you wonder how true it all is, doesn't it? Like that's all anybody knows, because that's all somebody wants us to think."

Karr was stunned. He almost never met anyone who knew about the Jedi, much less had an opinion about them. "What are you talking about? Why would you think it isn't true? You can read about it in history archives. Some of them. A little bit."

"You can read about Sith Lords, too. But nobody believes in *those*."

Karr remained silent.

"Besides," she continued, "I've been on Merokia for about three days, and I'm already pretty sure I've seen all the archives this planet has to offer."

"What's that supposed to mean?"

"It *means*, there might be a more boring, pointless planet somewhere out there in the galaxy . . . but I wouldn't bet any credits on it. I guess that's what happens when your planet is so close to the Unknown Regions and so far from the Core."

Karr didn't disagree with her, but the judgment still stung. "Then what are *you* doing here?"

She withdrew to her end of the bench, like a kleex retreating into its shell. "My father moved us here for work. I had to leave all my friends behind," she complained, mostly to herself.

Karr nodded like he was sympathetic to her problem, but he didn't really have any friends to miss. If he disappeared the next day, no one at school would even notice he was gone, or wonder where he went.

"I can't believe it took me three whole days to get detention, though. I must be losing my touch."

"Wow. You must be . . . fun. So where did you move here from?"

"CeSai," she replied.

Karr had never heard of it, but he didn't want to say so out loud. Otherwise, she might think she was right about his home planet being a nowhere planet, in the middle of no place. Merokia wasn't perfect, but if you weren't local you didn't get to complain about it. "Oh, yeah," he nodded, and then he lied. "I hear it's nice. Is that where you learned about the Jedi?"

Smugly, she said, "It's where I learned they're a big fat hoax!"

"No way, the Jedi aren't a hoax."

"How do you know? Have you ever seen one?"

"I've never seen a rancor, either, but I know that it's real. The Jedi kept the peace in the Republic," he said, echoing his grandmother's explanation of their role in the galaxy.

She scoffed. "The Jedi were a story the Republic made up. They used it to keep order in the galaxy—and by scaring everyone with the idea of a magical army of space wizards."

Karr didn't even know where to begin. "*Um*," he said forcefully, ready to launch into a full-length lesson on the strengths and virtues of all things Jedi, "actually, the Jedi were around for thousands of years! Why would the Republic invent a fake magic army when they already had a real clone army?"

Carefully, as if she was being very patient with someone who was very slow, she said, "Exactly. Isn't it funny how the Jedi went away when the Clone Wars ended? The Republic didn't need them anymore, so they let them . . . I don't know. Fade away, or whatever."

"That's not true!"

"Okay, then what happened to them?"

Karr didn't have a good answer. "I . . . I don't know. But that doesn't mean they never existed."

She shrugged and leaned back, folding her hands behind her head. "Just trust me on this one."

"Why would I trust you? I don't even know you!"

"Good point." She leaned across the bench and offered him her hand. "I'm Maize Raynshi."

Karr grudgingly held out his own. "Karr Nuq Sin."

But she didn't shake it. She used the grip to pull his hand closer to her face. "What's with the gloves, Karr?"

"They protect my hands."

"Well, yeah," she said. "That's what gloves *do*. I mean, why are you wearing them indoors?"

"So that I can control my abilities."

She folded her arms. "Your totally real choking abilities? Those must be *amazing* gloves."

"I . . ." He paused. He barely knew this girl, but he barely knew just about everyone, so it didn't matter anyway. He told her the truth. "Sometimes when I touch things, I can see the past. I mean, the past of whatever I'm touching."

Maize cackled wildly. "Bantha fodder! I don't believe you. Show me."

Karr tried to retreat. "I can't just do it on command."

She grabbed his gloved hand again. "Come on, what do you see in *my* past?"

"It doesn't work that way. In fact, I'm not sure it works with people. I think it has to be an object. Like an item that's witnessed something big."

Maize let go of him and scanned the room for something that might work. Seeing nothing with potential, she reached into her bag and pulled out a small metal drafting tool. "Tell me about this," she said, holding it out to him.

"What is it?" asked Karr.

"I got it from my dad."

"Is he a Jedi?"

"No, you nerko. He works for the First Order. . . .

Wait a minute." She withdrew the object and held it close to her chest. "Aren't you supposed to tell *me* what it is?"

He sighed and removed his right glove. "Fine. Give it here."

He took a deep breath . . . closed his eyes . . . and took the tool with his bare hand. In an instant, his blood pressure skyrocketed—like every drop in his body shot to the top of his head and then had nowhere to go. The pain pushed against his skull until he screamed at the top of his lungs.

Then he did the exact opposite of what a boy his age should do to look cool.

He passed out.

# CHAPTER 3

He'd only just met Maize, but he could already pick her voice out of a crowd. This time, she was the one who was kneeling beside him, shaking him. "What happened? What did you *do*? Come on, Karr—get up!"

For a few seconds, his ears worked better than his eyes.

He and Maize weren't alone anymore; he could hear several accents and dialects in the lobby around him and the sound of people arguing about what to do. He opened his eyes and learned that he was the center of attention for the second time in half an hour.

He blinked hard, trying to get his eyes to work right again.

Maize asked him, "Are you okay?"

"Yeah," he muttered. "I just need a minute."

He could see Maize then, and he focused on her face to calm himself down. Although from his point of view, she was either kneeling above him, looking at him upside down . . . or else her head had come loose from her neck and she was speaking through her—

"Tattoos!" That was what was different about Maize, he thought as her face came into focus. Most of the Mirialans he'd met had facial tattoos, but Maize didn't.

"What do tattoos have to do with anything? Are you okay?" she asked.

"Uh, sure," replied Karr, feeling caught again. "Why?"

"Because you cried out in pain and then passed out on the floor," she shot back.

"Oh. Yeah. Right."

Karr had done that so many times that he had forgotten how scary it could be to people seeing it for the first time. One guy told him it was like watching a space slug give birth to triplets. Another said it was like he was wrestling some invisible entity. What nobody had ever said, though, was that it was like he was a Jedi. But he hoped that it was just because they'd never seen one.

"Are you going to get up, or what? You're making everybody worry." She sat up straight, cross-legged, so she wasn't hovering over him anymore. "That was scary!"

"Sorry. I'm fine. Don't worry."

From his position on the floor, Karr stared up at

all the gawking faces. The most concerned-looking face belonged to the Ovissian headmaster. Maybe it was because he was interested in the boy's welfare, or maybe he was worried about how this would affect the school, but most likely it was because he stood next to Royke, who didn't look concerned at all.

"Loser," the Besalisk muttered.

The headmaster said, "Let's get him to his feet."

"Yeah," echoed Royke. "He's got detention coming!"

But lucky for Karr, detention was the last thing on anyone's mind. The headmaster inclined his four-horned head and asked, "Are you okay?"

"I'll survive. I always do."

"We should still contact your parents," he said. "You need a doctor."

"Sure," said Karr, even though he knew that doctors would be no help. "Actually, we have a medical droid on hand for whenever this happens. These seizures. They've been happening off and on for years. I can just call Arzee. He'll come check me out."

The headmaster agreed and helped him to his feet. "I do remember reading something about that, in your file. Go ahead and call your droid. Okay, everyone. Let's give him some air."

Karr activated his comlink. "Arzee-Seven? I had another seizure."

"I'm sorry to hear that, sir," said the droid. "I'm on my way."

When everything was settled, the headmaster instructed everyone who hadn't fainted dramatically to get back to class.

"I should probably wait outside," Karr said, hoping he was about to get away clean.

Maize piped up. "And shouldn't somebody go with him? Or something? In case it happens again. He's in a very fragile state, sir."

The Ovissian thought about it. "That's not a bad idea."

"*I* could go with him," she said. "Mr. Kragnotto already yanked me out of class anyway."

"Is that all right with you, Karr?"

"Uh, sure."

He came to a decision and nodded. "Then get home safely, and we'll see you again when you're well."

"Wait a second!" cried Royke. "He's not getting detention? That's nexu dwang!"

Maize flashed him a rude finger gesture as she left the building by Karr's side.

On their way out, Maize said quietly, "You said you could see the past when you touched things. You didn't say anything about falling to the ground, screaming."

"I didn't? Well, sometimes I fall to the ground, screaming. Now you know."

The family speeder appeared in the distance, and soon Karr could see the familiar figure of RZ-7 in the driver's seat. Medical droids didn't usually drive, but it wasn't so weird that anyone said anything about it as the speeder pulled up to the school—where an assortment of other vehicles was already parked. The area was dotted with all sorts of landspeeders, large and small. The only thing they had in common was that they were all kind of beat-up. Most of them were either secondhand vehicles or they belonged to teenagers who were still getting the hang of driving.

"Hey, Karr! I heard you died today," someone said. It was a Togruta hanging over the side of his speeder. "Too bad I heard wrong. . . ." He laughed as he zipped away.

Maize turned around and shouted, *"E chu ta an do padda-mames!"* at the retreating vehicle.

"Did you just say—"

"Something about his mother, yes. My father had

some business dealings with the Hutts. It's a wonderful language for swearing."

He nodded, impressed. "Thanks, I guess. That was . . . great. No one ever stands up for me, especially not at school. I hope you don't regret it later."

"I never regret *anything*."

The idling landspeeder sputtered a bit, suggesting it needed a new coil driver but also drawing Karr's attention to a potentially awkward problem. "Oh, no," he said with embarrassment. "Arzee brought the two-seater."

With surprise, she asked, "How many speeders do you have?"

He cringed. "Um . . . just the one. But it only has two seats, so . . ."

Maize laughed. "Don't worry. I'll sit on your lap."

He blushed all the way down to his toes. "I'm really sorry there isn't more room, but . . . I mean, *you're* the one who offered to see me home." As Karr crawled into the passenger seat, he gestured to the droid. "Anyway, Maize, this is Arzee."

The metallic blue driver gave her a nod of acknowledgment. "It's a pleasure to make your acquaintance, madam."

"Same here." Maize climbed in and sat on top of Karr's thighs, wrapping her arms around his neck.

If RZ-7 had any eyebrows, he would've raised them. "We'd better get you home, sir. You're turning all red."

"Just drive," Karr grumbled.

Maize ignored his blushing and his awkward grip on her waist. "So!" she said brightly to RZ-7. "You're a medical droid? And they make you drive, too?"

Karr answered for him. "Yes. I mean, no. Between you and me, he's not really a medical droid. I built him, and I don't know anything about medicine—so neither does he."

The droid revved the engine, and the speeder lurched along. "He doesn't know much about driving, either!"

It was hard to talk in an open-air vehicle that was zipping through the desert, but that was all right. Karr didn't know what to say, anyway—but whenever they slowed to make a turn or wait for a train, Maize peppered him with questions.

"What do you mean *you* built him?" she shouted over the speeder's hum and the rumbling of the train.

"I made him from parts I found, here and there. He's working with the circuitry of a protocol droid, the hard drive of an astromech, and the casing of a medical unit. But what he's really good at is getting me out of tricky situations."

"You're just lucky the headmaster didn't ask him for his evaluation."

Karr laughed. "Arzee can't evaluate anything bigger than a splinter in my finger. I built him to be my friend, not my nurse."

"Well aren't you handy."

The train was slow to get out of the way, so Maize had time for one more question. "I never asked you how you got your crazy ideas about the Jedi."

"*My* crazy ideas?" he sputtered. "Their story is—"

"Their story is a mess! Nobody agrees about who they were or what they could do, and there's no proof they ever existed at all! The stories are lies, and that's all there is to it."

RZ-7 revved the engine and ducked the speeder around the last train car.

"My grandmother told me about the Jedi, and she would never lie."

"Then she's crazy and wrong, that's all. I'll tell her myself, when I meet her."

The road opened and the wind picked up, so Karr had to yell to be heard. "You can't! She's dead!"

"Free your mind," J'Hara said to Karr. He tried, but his inside voice couldn't be quieted. He was seventeen years old and his thoughts revved at a pace usually reserved for the engines of cruisers. Though he had practiced this many times before, he still couldn't quite get it right. Still couldn't move the object. Was it him? Was it his teacher? J'Hara had never truly explained how she knew so much about the Jedi, and he began to wonder if she knew what she was talking about. He was growing restless and impatient. This would probably go quicker if he had a real Jedi to train him, but of course there were none. They were gone. If they even ever existed at all. All he had was his grandmother. All he had was her word. And it was beginning to wear thin.

Of course, Karr loved his grandmother. She was the light in his universe, but even so, there were days when his recent cloudy disposition would block that light. He had been working with her for a few years, and yet he felt no closer to becoming a Jedi than to becoming ruler of the galaxy. He was of the age where adults stopped appearing as adults and started appearing as peers. Flawed peers. And in moments of discontent, Karr would notice the cracks in a lot of J'Hara's stories. Like how a Sith Lord could live to over five hundred years of age or how the Jedi could move objects or make people believe things using only their minds. Were they meant to be fables? Larger-than-life lessons merely intended to make an impact on the listener? Because if so, there was a word for that: *myths*.

But they were also written about in history archives, so this confused him. Maybe the truth was somewhere in the middle. Perhaps the Jedi were wise people who had radical ideas of peace and were also good at wielding lightsabers. Maybe the idea that everyone was connected through an energy field was just a hopeful fantasy. Maybe the Jedi were just really good at convincing people of that.

"Try again," his grandmother said.

Karr sighed. "It's not working."

"It will," she said with her usual confidence.

"You always say that, but it never does. Maybe you're wrong. Maybe I don't have the Force. Maybe I have some sort of tumor or something that's giving me these headaches and we're wasting time with this when we should be finding a cure."

"That's your mother talking."

"We've spent all this time learning about the Jedi and yet I can't do anything they can do. I can't make anyone say what I want them to say. I can't fight someone using just my mind."

"Of course you can't," she argued. "And why would you want to? That is not the Force. Those are by-products of playing with the Force. You're looking at it the wrong way. A Jedi does not want to fight. Jedi are the peacekeepers. They do what they do."

"Well, what I wanna do is give up!" he shouted as he threw the cup across the room, half hoping his grandmother would yell back and fully hoping that she would finally reveal some last hidden secret that would solve all his problems.

But J'Hara did not take the bait. "I understand your frustration, my boy. I can't claim to fully know what you are going through, for I am not like you. I do not possess any ability with the Force, but I am versed in it, and I am doing what I can to help you find your way."

"But *how* do you know about the Force?" he asked.

For a moment her gaze went elsewhere. Inward, almost. And then she replied, "Like you, I found it around me. I asked questions. I was open to it. Do I have all the answers? No. Do I know more than most? Maybe. And so together we will take this journey and perhaps . . . find something wonderful."

Karr took a beat before asking the question he hadn't had the heart to articulate any earlier. "What if I don't want to be on this journey anymore?"

He was almost afraid to look at J'Hara for fear he might have hurt her feelings. But when he did lift his gaze, he saw that she had the expression of someone who had been expecting that question for a long time. She turned to walk away, throwing out a casual, "You must do what you feel is right with the Force."

Karr grunted. Sometimes her serene personality had a way of enraging him. But he agreed to humor her one more time. One more time so he could justify abandoning all hope. "Fine! I'll try to levitate it again."

"No," said his grandmother, quickly turning back to him. "You're angry. You want to destroy something. Very well. Destroy it! But do it from a place of calm. Not anger. Visualize it. Crush it."

Karr looked at the cup on the floor. It hadn't cracked when he threw it across the room and that worried him. Just his luck that he picked the toughest cup in all the galaxy to try to crack.

"Picture it," his grandmother said. "Use the space around the cup to tightly condense your grip around it."

Karr looked at the cup. Then he closed his eyes and raised his hand. Concentrating. Using the Force. Focusing on the space around the cup. But it was hard. Harder than he wanted it to be. Harder than it had a right to be.

"Concentrate," said his grandmother again. A word he had begun to hate.

*Concentrate!*

He clenched his jaw tighter, but for every breath that seeped out of his mouth, a measure of doubt seeped into his brain.

*Concentrate!*

Karr couldn't help thinking of all the holes in her stories. The confusing timelines, the convenient connections . . .

*Concentrate.*

The description of powers that no one had ever seen with their own eyes. That no one could attest to.

*Concentrate.*

The stupid act of trying to use imaginary powers to crush a stupid cup! She told him tales of Jedi levitating large objects, and yet he couldn't even levitate a cup! Why? Because they were myths! They weren't real! And he was no Jedi!

*Concentra—*

Karr spun toward his grandmother with an anger that he didn't know had been festering for a few years. *"I can't do it!"* he screamed. *"I'm not a Jedi!* There are no Jed—"

But when he looked at J'Hara, the old woman was grabbing her chest and falling to the ground. "Grandmother!"

J'Hara winced in pain and grabbed the nearby tablecloth, dragging it to the ground, plates crashing beside her. The sound of shattering glass confused Karr, since that was what this exercise was all about and yet something had gone horribly wrong. "What have I done?" cried Karr as he ran to her side. "I'm so sorry! I'm so sorry!"

The old woman looked up at him weakly, but as always it was she who comforted him.

"You didn't do this, Karr. There is nothing to be sorry about. I am an old woman and this is the way of things," she said, gasping for air. "I'm glad I had the honor of showing you who you are."

Karr's mind raced as he tried to figure out some way to help her. But she didn't seem to want help. She seemed proud. She seemed happy. At peace.

"Don't be sad. Continue your training. Go out in the galaxy to learn your place in it. I will still be on this journey with you."

And with a smile, she quietly passed away.

Part of Karr knew that it was just J'Hara's time to go. But he felt responsible. Had she spent so much energy on him that it weakened her? Had she devoted all that time to training him for nothing? Karr couldn't live with that. And he became more determined than ever to prove that his grandmother was right. That he would become a Jedi.

# CHAPTER 4

Karr opened the front door and leaned inside.

"Hello?" he yelled, hoping that no one would respond. If no one was home, he wouldn't have to explain why he was back from school in the middle of the day, or who Maize was, either. The place always seemed a little empty with his grandmother J'Hara gone—less like a home and more like a plain old house—but just this once, he was glad for the silence.

"Come on in," he said to Maize.

He led the way directly to the living quarters, skipping the kitchen in case his mother hadn't heard him come in. There was always a chance she might pop up out of nowhere to embarrass him with affection or worry.

They were just getting settled when an older boy stepped into the living room. It was Karr's brother, Trag, passing through. Trag was prepared to ignore whatever his little brother was doing until he saw Maize.

"Who's this?" he asked.

"A friend."

When Karr didn't volunteer any further information, Trag looked Maize up and down, shrugged, and retreated to his bedroom.

"Let me show you something."

Before Maize could either agree or protest, Karr pushed aside a curtain in his own bedroom to reveal a closet full of seemingly random objects from all walks of life: belts, staffs, blasters, comlinks, helmets, and more—all of it meticulously cataloged. Scribbled on the walls and shelves beneath the objects were erasable flimsiplast notes with dates, like he'd been trying to map out a whole galaxy using just this oddball collection of stuff.

"Whoa!" she exclaimed. "Did you do all of this?"

He couldn't tell if she was impressed or horrified. "Yeah." He cocked his head toward the shelves that held his treasures. "And some of these things have shown me their past."

Maize took a closer look. She gently picked up a kloo horn and turned it over in her hands. "How does it work?"

"Well, you've seen it in action. Sometimes I touch something and everything gets loud and . . . and both bright and dark at the same time. It's hard to explain. It's sort of like being on fire, but then other things come through: voices, pictures, colors—and then . . . then I black out."

"Sounds horrible."

"It is, sometimes," he said. "I'm still not sure what causes the flashes, but they're always something big. It's almost like some objects are witnesses and they want to tell me what they saw. Does that make sense?"

Maize looked at him blankly, so he decided to keep talking.

"Like this, for example," he said, picking up a mouthpiece that looked so old it definitely shouldn't go in anyone's mouth. "This is an A99 aquata breather that belonged to a fishing merchant. The guy who sold it to me said that the merchant got it from a Jedi that used it for marine reconnaissance. I'd hoped it would show me something about the Jedi, but no matter how hard I concentrate, I can't get it to zap me with a vision. So either it didn't experience anything big—"

"Or the guy was pulling your leg," she interjected.

"Pretty much."

"There's a lot of people out there who will take advantage of you, Karr."

He ignored her and moved on. "But this, on the other hand . . ." He held up a wooden staff, or at least part of one. The top was a silver handle that looked like it had been smoothed in a furnace. The bottom was shattered and fragmented, indicating that it had been longer in its heyday. It was completely blackened and charred, but something kept it from crumbling.

"The first time I touched it, I passed out, fell down, and chipped a tooth." He flashed her an oversized, slightly jagged smile. "I thought for sure it must've belonged to a Jedi, because it affected me so strongly, but in the vision, at least from what I could tell, the owner didn't wear traditional Jedi garb and I didn't see a lightsaber anywhere. What's weird, though, is that he clutched the staff as if it was one . . . and I swear I could hear him mumbling about the Force. And he was in the middle of what I think was a big battle."

Maize gave him a sideways glance. "You hear what you wanna hear, I guess."

Karr took slight offense. "Maybe. But I don't always see what I want to see, otherwise I would've seen a Jedi by now, wouldn't I? Anyway, I think that's when I understood that the items that give me visions always show me things that are significant. *Important*," he added, having found a better word. "Fortunately, the Jedi have seen a lot of action, so I search for their things specifically—with the added hope that I can also get a lesson out of the deal—but sometimes I'll reach for random things as well just to see if they can show me anything."

"So you still haven't seen any Jedi then? In life or in your visions," she said.

He deflated a little. "No. But they were real."

"But you can't prove it," she countered.

"I don't need to prove it. I know what's true, and I don't care if you don't believe me," he fibbed. "I swear there's something in me that guides me toward this stuff. And it can't just be an unhealthy interest!"

"If you say so."

Maize slowly walked around the room, running her hands over a few objects as if checking them for dust. She stopped when she spied a datapad on his bed, the screen still faintly glowing. She picked it up and read aloud, " '*Antique Military Collector's Guide*.' What did this tell you?"

"That I've been overpaying for this stuff," he said with a laugh. "I only got it a month ago, and I've been spending too many credits. Now I know better."

"You bought all of these things?"

"No, not all of them. I found some. People gave me some. And yeah, I bought some. After a while I realized I might have some luck looking through junk shops, or bartering with pilots and tourists. Now this handy guide lets me know what something's worth before I lose too many credits."

Maize stood with her hands on her hips. She paused and took everything in one more time, as if she was a judge about to present the award for Best Jedi Museum. Then, with an air of authority, she said, "I think you're crazy."

Karr was about to argue with her again until he saw the smirk on her face. "I'm just teasing you. Sort of," she added, sitting on a chair in his room. "Look, the truth is, I only know what I know from my family's experience. CeSai did really well under the Empire. Then the New Republic kicked the Empire out, and there was no one left to run the planet. Everything fell apart. As for the Jedi, who knows who they were or what they did. I've always assumed it was folklore, but"—she looked at him with a glint of adventure in her eyes—"prove me wrong."

Karr liked the challenge but knew it was a difficult one. "If I could find one, I could ask him. But they all disappeared after the Clone Wars."

"Well," Maize continued, "if you're going to ignore the fact that they never existed, you might as well move to the next theory, which is that they were all killed by the clone troopers."

"But that doesn't make sense to me. Maybe the clone troopers could've killed some of them—but they couldn't have gotten *all* of them. We're talking about Jedi Knights, the best fighters in the galaxy. All these battles across the galaxy: Saleucami, Cato Neimoidia, Mygeeto, Kaller," he recited, counting them off on his fingers. "We're supposed to believe that the Jedi coordinated an uprising . . . and then they were immediately wiped out? No way. I don't buy it."

She crossed her arms, then crossed her legs, too. "If they ever existed at all, there would be some sign of them, somewhere. Whole societies don't just disappear into thin air."

A light went on in Karr's brain. He couldn't believe he'd never thought of it before. "They do if they're Tusken Raiders."

"Tusken Raiders? What's a Tusken Raider?"

"The guy who sold me that set of goggles over there"—he flapped his hand toward a shelf with a label that read *Neuro-Saav TD-series electrobinoculars*—"he told me a story. At some point in time, due to shifting winds and soil erosion, the Sand People of Tatooine needed to migrate to a different part of their home planet. So a small tribe of them set out to find a better place where they could establish a new colony and be joined by the others at a later time. The group traveled for months before finding a spot that worked for them. But the trip was so long and supplies were so low that a lot of the tribe got sick. With very little food left, the older members convinced the head of the pack to go back to their original homeland and return with food and other necessities. And so he did. He left behind thirty males, seventeen females, and nine children, including his wife and daughter, and promised to return the following harvest with more people and supplies. A whole season passed before he could return, but when he did, he found the settlement empty. No signs of anyone. His wife, his daughter, the entire tribe . . . gone."

"Invaders?" asked Maize.

Karr shook his head. "No sign of any. Legend has it there was nothing left at all, except a drawing of a mysterious figure etched on a stone," he said, making his voice sound spooky.

"Who was the mysterious figure?" she asked. "The one responsible?"

"Nobody knows. But no one person could have taken down an entire village."

"So what's your point?"

He shrugged. "Sometimes things just can't be explained."

Maize stared blankly at Karr. "I can't decide if you really do have some incredible power . . . or if you're just good at telling stories."

"You don't believe me?"

"What? It's a lot to wrap my mind around."

Karr changed his approach. "I get it. You need facts. What about your dad's drafting tool. Don't you want to know what I saw?"

Maize blinked her eyes with recognition. Clearly, with all the commotion that followed Karr's collapse, she had completely forgotten to ask. She slid farther back in her seat. "This oughta be good."

"I'm not putting on a show, I'm just telling you what I saw. Let me hold it again." He wiggled his fingers toward her, signaling her to throw it to him.

"Go for it." She reached into her pocket, pulled out the tool, and tossed it to him.

It bounced against his chest, but he caught it with both hands and held it up to his forehead, trying to remember what he saw the way you try to remember a dream. If he could recall the image without having to pass out again, then all the better. Karr kept his eyes closed and held the tool close. "This was interesting," he said. "It was definitely part of something big. I saw . . . stars, and so much darkness, it felt like death. Does that mean anything to you?"

Maize rolled her eyes. "Are you seriously trying to tell me that it came from the Death Star?" she said, meaning the Empire's space station of long before. "My dad was never on the Death Star. He was a little kid when that thing blew up."

"I didn't say it *came* from the Death Star. Everything felt . . . cold. Covered in ice and snow." He squeezed the tool tighter and concentrated, but then he mostly saw a man—probably the one who'd given it to her. He took that guess and ran with it. "Your father has bright blue eyes, and he looks . . . younger than people think he is. He has a gray suit, and . . . and . . . black hair. He's human. You're only half Mirialan."

When Karr opened his eyes again, he saw Maize standing before him with her mouth open. Unconsciously so, he imagined, because no one would choose to look so taken aback. But what really distracted him from her gaping expression was her eyes. He had noticed them earlier, of course, but they were different now. And for the better. There was a hint of what might actually be admiration in them.

"That was . . . impressive," she said. "Or else a really good guess."

It was enough. Karr would take victories with Maize where he could find them.

# CHAPTER 5

The next day at school, things got bad and strange.

Or badder and stranger than usual, considering that school was Karr's least favorite place in the universe. He'd grudgingly finished two of the day's six classes when he heard his name called over the building's intercom, summoning him to the headmaster's office.

"Perfect," he griped. His classmates giggled.

His teacher, a Givin who was leading the class in calculus, shrugged and waved at the door. "Go on, then."

He picked up his datapad, stuffed it into his bag, and slipped out of his desk. "What did I even *do* this time," he muttered to himself—leaving off the question mark that should've gone at the end.

The teacher muttered something vague in reply, but the door shut behind Karr before he could catch it. He didn't care, and it didn't matter. He had three minutes and counting to answer the call before it came again.

If it came again, it came with detention.

With the looming threat of spending even more time in the headmaster's office, he hustled down the empty hall, zipping his bag and tucking in his shirt as he went—his shoes squeaking on the polished floors with every rushed step.

He palmed open the door that separated the school's public corridors from the administrative offices and once again sat down on the bench and stared at the door to the headmaster's office. He was alone, right where he'd been around the same time the previous day. Making a habit of it.

He wouldn't mind making a habit of seeing Maize, but this time she failed to appear. She was either behaving herself in some other classroom or doing such a good job of being bad that no one had caught her yet.

Karr figured the odds were about fifty-fifty either way.

He felt around on the bench until he located the first letter of his name, etched there the day before. Since he didn't know how long he could expect to wait for whatever scolding or punishment was coming, he considered finishing the job, but before he could fish out his little knife for another go at graffiti, the headmaster's door slid open.

The Ovissian headmaster . . . was not alone. He was joined by Tomar and Looway Nuq Sin. Karr's parents.

All three of them wore somber expressions.

Karr's stomach sank. The last time his mom and dad had shown up at school, it was to tell him that his aunt had died. He didn't know any other old people now that his grandmother was gone, so anybody else's death would be a real shock. His brother? His uncle, on the other side of the planet?

"Is . . . is everybody okay?" he asked.

Looway caught on quickly, but she was careful when she replied. "No one is hurt or anything like that, but we need to talk."

The headmaster gestured into his office. "Please, come inside."

Karr looked over his shoulder but saw no one to rescue him from whatever dire news he was about to get. No sign of any other teacher, no hint of Maize, no comforting beeps from RZ-7. He stood up straight, slung his bag over his shoulder, and sighed. "Let's get this over with."

They all retreated into the office, and the headmaster closed the door before taking his seat behind a big desk. When everyone was settled, he folded his hands and let them rest on the gleaming surface in front of him. "Karr, your parents and I have been having a conversation."

"About me?"

"About you," his mother confirmed. "We've been so . . ."

"Worried," his father offered.

She continued, "Yes, we've been worried about you, dear. Ever since your grandmother left us, you simply haven't been yourself. Your headaches have gotten worse, and we all know they're happening more frequently. Yesterday alone, it happened twice!"

"I know, but I'm learning . . ." He stopped. What could he tell them? He'd tried the truth before, but it'd never worked. His grandmother had believed in the Jedi, but no one else in the family did. "I'm learning to live with them."

His mother smiled warmly and patted his knee. "You've been very brave, Son. But we've finally heard back from the specialist you saw last month—the one who came in from Chandrila. It took a long time to go through all the test results, but now we have some . . ." She looked up at her husband, but he didn't finish the thought for her, so she kept going—even though she didn't sound terribly confident. "We have some answers, and we have a plan."

Tomar confessed, "You'll probably like part of it, but you might hate the rest of it."

Karr sighed. "So . . . give me the good news first, I guess."

"The good news," his mother repeated. "Well, you hate school, don't you?"

"This one," he admitted, avoiding eye contact with the headmaster.

The headmaster sighed. "I realize you've had your difficulties, especially with a death in the family."

"My mother," Tomar said. "His grandmother. She lived with us. She and Karr were very close."

The headmaster bobbed his horned head with sympathy. "It must have been a hard time for everyone, to be sure. And now *this*."

Karr sulked. "Now *what*? I believe I was promised some good news."

His mother pressed onward. "Yes, and the good news is—after the end of this term, you won't have to go to school anymore! Not this one, at any rate. You want to leave it so badly, and you've had so many fainting spells, we've realized that it's just not safe for you to attend here any longer."

"Wait. What?"

His father hastily chimed in, "You'll be joining my brother at the trade school in Taeltor Province, where you'll learn to take things a little easier."

He was stunned and not at all happy. Neither one of those pieces of news sounded particularly good. He felt like he'd been lied to. "What? You can't . . . you can't do that. You can't just send me away because I have headaches."

The headmaster unfolded his hands and leaned forward, the upper and lower horns on his face coming closer. It was probably meant to be a reassuring pose, but it mostly felt threatening. "That's not what's happening here, young man. Your constitution is not suitable for all the . . . excitement. That's what your doctor said."

Karr turned to his parents. "I get picked on a lot, but that's not what causes the headaches. Or the fainting."

Looway looked at him with wide, damp eyes that were sure to spill over with tears any second. "But dearest, that's exactly it. The stress of it all. That's what the doctor concluded—and he's the foremost expert in the sector."

"I don't care who he is. He's wrong. Grandma said I have the Force, and I believe her!"

"Even if we believed that—and we *don't*," his father was quick to add, "there are no more tests they can give you. You've been checked over by every capable physician and droid we can afford, and this is your diagnosis."

"My diagnosis is that I'm weak?"

His mother shook her head. "Your diagnosis is that you're sensitive. You've been complaining about this school since your first day. I thought you'd be happier to hear that you don't have to finish your term."

"I *am* happy about that part!" he insisted, even though he was thinking of Maize. "But how is this better? Taking me out of one school and putting me in another one? What makes you think that'll be any better, or make me any happier?"

Tomar shrugged. "At the new school you won't be so alone. Your uncle will be there to look after you, and you won't be surrounded by a bunch of other immature children. Most of the people at the trade school are older than you."

"Yeah, because it's supposed to be a school for adults, not for kids!"

The headmaster replied, "Between us, we've pulled some strings. I know that your family business is, perhaps"—he hunted for the right words—"not your truest passion. But we all believe that it will do you good to focus on doing substantial work. Something with your hands, something that you can concentrate on without distraction."

His father said, "You're nearly a man now. It's time you learned how to do more than sew a straight seam or judge the quality of fabric. You've learned everything you're going to learn at home, and you hate this school. You're miserable here, your health is in jeopardy, and it's time to try something else—so why not bring you up to speed on the finer points of the tailoring business? It might not be your favorite thing, but you have a knack for it. With more focused training, you could be truly great. Imagine it—creating your own clothes, to your own preferences, for your own clients! You could be the youngest shop manager on the planet!"

"Sounds thrilling."

"I know you're only being rude, but I'll be happy if

it bores you. You need to be a little bored. I honestly think it will do you good. It'll help settle your mind," he said with finality. "I've talked it over with Cornell and he's made all the arrangements. You're very fortunate that he's such a good teacher and the school holds him in such high regard."

*"Fortunate,"* Karr grumbled bitterly.

The Ovissian settled back into his chair. "Yes, *fortunate*. The doctors feel that your headaches will subside and your fainting will diminish—if you can only find a quiet routine to occupy your time. And I agree with them."

"I'm being punished for being different. That's what this is."

"No," he insisted. "You're being given an opportunity to find happiness and stability elsewhere. Let's not mince words, Karr: you don't make much trouble, but you certainly receive plenty. This school isn't always the gentlest place, and I'm aware that we have students who are hard on the younger, smaller—"

Karr sighed. "Weaker. You can just say weaker."

"We don't think you're weak," Looway assured him.

"You think I'm useless."

At last, she started to cry. "Please don't be like this. We only want what's best for you, and you haven't been happy here."

She wasn't wrong, but he wasn't happy with the idea of leaving, either. He only had another three semesters before he completed all his terms. He would have options in other careers, if he went looking for some. Jobs that could get him off Merokia in search of his true calling: being a Jedi. Surely he could suck it up that long, couldn't he? Especially if he could convince Maize to hang around.

Maybe it wasn't rational, and maybe it wasn't fair—but now that he was being given an escape pod, he didn't want to leave at all. He knew his way around, and he had even managed to make a friend. A pretty friend. A friend who thought he was a little weird but didn't treat him like he was stupid.

Someone he could really connect with.

Eventually. He was fairly sure.

The headmaster and his parents tried in vain to convince him that he was looking at this all wrong, but it didn't work. In the end, when he was sick to death of hearing them talk about him, and around him, and over him, Karr grabbed his bag and hopped to his feet.

"You said I have until the end of the term, right? Then I still have classes here, at least for another couple weeks—so let me go. I need to get back to calculus."

His dad called his name, but Karr didn't look back. He let the office door slide shut behind him. Back in the lobby, he opened the door to the hallway with his bag and his shoulder, and he darted into the hall before anyone could stop him.

It was very quiet out there.

He'd been in the office long enough that classes had changed, and the students were mostly seated at their desks, pretending to listen to whoever was talking and wishing they were somewhere else. The corridors were silent except for the echoes of his own squeaky footsteps and a dull throb in his ears that turned out to be his own heart beating too hard because he was too angry.

He automatically started toward his correct classroom, but he didn't want to go in there. He wanted to run and scream, and possibly break things while he was at it. There had to be another way.

His steps slowed.

They said he didn't make much trouble, but what if he did? What if he made *real* trouble? If he got arrested, would they kick him out of the trade school in Taeltor Province? It would embarrass his uncle, but Karr barely knew the guy. He was a lot older than Karr's dad, and mostly they only saw each other at holidays or funerals.

He wondered what kind of minor crime he could commit. It couldn't be too big or too destructive; he didn't actually want to hurt anyone. Perhaps if he broke some school property, or vandalized something bigger than a bench in the administrative lobby. Yes, maybe vandalism was a good place to start.

His mind was wandering in the direction of "light arson, maybe" when he heard something shatter nearby. He backtracked, listened hard, and heard something else break. Something was going down in the science lab.

He crept up to the door and looked in through its window.

Inside, he saw Maize. She was mad. Mad enough to break things.

Another glass beaker went spinning, and Karr ducked away, even though there was zero chance it was going to hit him. It smashed against the wall, and when the last pieces had tinkled to the floor, he knocked on the door—carefully and loudly enough that even an angry girl with a room full of breakables might hear it and recognize a friendly gesture. Then he palmed the door control.

"Hey. Um . . ." A long, clear test tube hit the floor near his feet, and he cringed. The glass missed him but not by much. "Hey, Maize, could you . . . could you *not* do that?"

She froze. "Karr?"

"Yeah, hi." He stood up straighter and let himself inside.

"Get *out*." Maize sniffed and wiped her nose on her sleeve. She'd obviously been crying, and she was obviously trying to pretend otherwise. She stood in the middle of a war zone, surrounded by broken glass—and behind her there was a table with two lit burners blazing away. So Karr wasn't the only one contemplating arson. It was just one more thing they had in common.

"Are you all right?"

"I said, get out."

"I know, but I don't want to. What's going on?"

Her hand flexed around a measuring glass. Karr thought maybe she was thinking about throwing it at him, but she put it down instead—hard enough to crack it on the counter. "My dad got reassigned this morning. One of the big First Order ships sent a shuttle for him and took him away, and now we're stuck here without him! I don't even know when he'll be back."

"Didn't you just move here?"

*"Yes!"* she shouted. With a sweep of her arm, she knocked the thick glass cup off the table. It hit the floor with a tinkling pop and split into three pieces. "We could've just stayed where we were!"

"Did you even get to say goodbye?"

"No! He was gone when I got up. It's almost like my mom doesn't even care—she just sent me off to school as usual like nothing happened, but it happens all the time. I'm so tired of trying to hold on to him. Why can't we just find a place to live?"

"You can . . . you can live here, though. Even if he's gone."

"Here? This is nowhere! You know it better than I do. Now I'm stuck here, probably for at least another term of school, and it's all stupid, it's just *stupid*." She was crying again, her bright blue eyes sparkling. "Nothing personal."

"It's fine." He laughed awkwardly, quietly. "It's

almost funny. I just found out a minute ago that I'm getting sent away, too."

She paused and frowned. "Oh, that's right. I heard your name on the intercom. I wondered what that was about. Now you're leaving me, too? Great. Just great."

"Well, now you know. My parents are sending me off to a trade school. It's a long way away."

She wiped her nose again, this time on her other sleeve. "Do you want to go there?"

"No."

She thought for a moment. Karr could practically see the wheels in her brain suddenly working at twice the normal speed. "What if I went with you? It can't be any worse than here."

He sucked in his breath. Was that even an option? He didn't think so. "You're supposed to finish your terms at a school like this before they let you in. But I have this uncle who's getting me in there. It's a long story."

A chime at the door distracted them both. They watched as the door slid open and Namala Moffat peered inside. She took one look at the mess and the two kids who'd apparently caused it, rolled her eyes like she was exhausted, and said, "Stay here. I'm getting the headmaster."

Feverishly, Karr began working on his story. There'd been a groundquake, that's what he'd say. A very small, localized quake. No, there'd been an explosion! Someone left an experiment unattended; that's what did it. He had to think of something. Even if he'd actually been planning to wreak some havoc, and even if he couldn't stay there with Maize, he didn't want *her* to get in trouble. What if she got expelled before he transferred to his uncle's school?

He'd never see her again.

The wrinkles on Maize's forehead said that she was still thinking hard, too. Her eyes were clearing up. She was looking at him in a way that was partly thoughtful and partly scary. "I've got another idea. You don't want to go to the other school. I don't want to be at this one. Maybe we should just . . . go somewhere else."

"Like where? Like *how*?"

An alarm went off. It wasn't a loud, scary alarm—it was a quiet series of beeps that meant someone was in trouble and teachers were being summoned. Maize's maniacal grin grew wider with every chime. "Like, *anywhere*. Like, my dad's ship—that's how."

"What? No way."

"They picked him up with a shuttle; he won't need the personal ship the First Order gave him until he gets back, and that won't be for months—at *least*. Unless I get into trouble bad enough." A bright, wicked smile spread across her face.

"Do you even know how to fly?"

"Yeah, I can fly," she said with confidence that wasn't quite contagious. Karr wasn't sure he believed her, but he really wanted to. "My dad's been teaching me, and anyway, you can bring your droid. He can fly, right? Isn't that one of the things you said he could do?"

He was pretty sure that he'd never said any such thing, but he was too caught up in the moment to correct her. "Sure, he can fly. Sure, we can . . . we can do this," he said, warming up to the idea. "I'll call Arzee—he can get here in a few minutes. Before my parents can even make it home, probably."

"Do it. Call him, but . . ." The alarm was picking up, its frequency rising. Footsteps pattered in the hall outside. "Have him meet us at my place. I'll give you the coordinates. And lock that door," she commanded.

Karr punched the appropriate button.

Maize ran to the nearest window and jacked it open. She held it up for Karr, who scrambled to her side.

"Are we really doing this?" he asked, one leg already over the ledge and one leg still clinging to the windowsill.

She pushed him the rest of the way, and as he toppled into the bushes, she said, "Yeah, we are, so come on. Let's go find someplace exciting."

# CHAPTER 6

Maize lived near the school in a neighborhood of nicer housing that was usually occupied by government officials, so Karr thought her dad must be somebody pretty interesting. When he asked, she told him, "He's a diplomat who specializes in technology systems. He helps big First Order engineering projects stay safe, and he negotiates fallout from security breaches."

"What does that even mean?"

She shrugged. "When *our* spies get caught, he helps them hide what they found. When *their* spies get caught, he finds out what they learned and keeps them from sharing it."

"He plugs holes in security walls. Got it."

"Close enough, yeah." She entered a combination on a keypad, and the front door opened. "Let's make this fast. My mom will be back around midday, so we don't have long to grab what we want and get out of here."

Karr wanted to follow her to her room, but he stood awkwardly in the middle of the living area instead—looking around at the tasteful art and furnishings that suggested more money than he'd ever had. Or seen. Or heard about. It wasn't that the place was fancy. It was all the clean lines and smooth surfaces, all the missing dust, the absent dirty dishes and sewing scraps. This was a house with a cleaning staff.

When Maize returned with a bag slung over her shoulder, he asked, "Do you have any credits? We should probably have some, right?"

"Way ahead of you." She patted the bag. "Now where's your droid?"

"He'll be here any second."

It was more like thirty seconds, but Karr's family landspeeder chugged up to the house, looking a little tragic next to the nicer homes and vehicles. "Hello, sir. I brought the things you asked for," the droid announced as the kids climbed aboard.

"Great, thanks, Arzee."

"And where are we going now?"

"To the spaceport," Maize told him. "And hurry it up."

"Are you taking a trip, madam?"

Karr answered that one. "We all are, buddy. I'll explain on the way."

By the time they reached the lot where Maize's dad had parked his company ship, the droid was all caught up and mostly on board. "But, sir," he said at a volume that could be considered a whisper, "I am not programmed with the necessary—"

Karr stopped him and responded in an equally hushed tone, "You can pick it up as we go. Maize knows how to fly, and she can teach us." He hoped.

The ship was a smallish First Order yacht called the *Avadora*, and it looked rather like a silver kitchen utensil whose function Karr could only guess at. It was pretty and shiny, and probably cost more than the town he'd grown up in, but, hey—he needed a ride off Merokia and he could certainly do worse.

The ramp lowered, and Maize strolled inside like she owned the thing. She practically did, as she reassured him on the way to the cockpit. "Nobody needs or wants this ship until my dad gets back."

"And you said that could be . . . months?"

"I'd be real surprised if it was any sooner. Sometimes he's gone as long as a year. Hey, droid," she said to RZ-7. "Buckle in over here, if you're my copilot."

"Yes, madam, but I may need . . . time to configure."

"Configure away. Karr, there's room for you over here, too."

He squeezed in and latched himself to the seat, exchanging worried looks with RZ-7, who bravely returned his attention to the task at hand.

"Everybody ready?" she asked

Karr tried to sound game. "As ready as I'm going to get."

"That's good enough for me," she mumbled.

"Are they just going to . . . let us leave? Without paperwork or . . . ?"

"Yeah, my dad has priority clearance. No one will bother us. Watch." She flipped some switches, closed some hatches, and ignited the engines, and the *Avadora* lifted smoothly off the landing pad—taking to the sky and shooting past it with ease.

Before long, they were paused in orbit and Karr was silent, staring down at the only world he'd ever known. It was mostly brown and red with desert dust, but streaked with blue where the oceans surged and lakes pooled between the mountains. From up there, it seemed much bigger than it'd ever felt when he was standing on its surface. He'd hardly ever flown anywhere before, much less beyond the atmosphere, but he lied when Maize brought it up.

"I like the view better up here. Have you ever been to space before?"

"A couple of times. But it's been a while," he added, before she could ask for any specifics. "I forgot how . . . um . . . quiet it is, up here."

Together they admired the faint glow of the atmosphere beneath them. "Yeah, it can be. So where do we go now?" she asked.

"Now?"

"We have to go *somewhere*, and I'm open to suggestions. What have you got?"

He scratched at the back of his neck. Now that this whole "running away" plan was really underway, he wasn't sure where to take it. "We should definitely go looking for Jedi artifacts," he said.

She rolled her eyes. "I thought we wanted this to be a *successful* mission."

"Well, where do *you* want to go?" he snapped defensively.

She thought for a moment. "I don't know. Whenever I complain to my dad about the number of times we've had to move, he says the same thing: 'When my job is done, I promise we can move wherever you want. You'll have the entire galaxy to choose from.' " She said it in a lower register, imitating her father's droll delivery. "I know it's just a dopey response meant to shut me up for a while, but I keep thinking I should learn more about what's out there. That way I can hold him to his word and have an answer the next time he says it." She leaned back, putting her feet on the console and her arms behind her head. "So if you want to go looking for dead-wizard loot, I guess I'm down with that. I'll expand my horizons, get out of detention, and definitely get my father's attention. Lead the way," she said, gesturing at the vastness of space outside the cockpit window.

"Hm. Okay. Well . . . we're not too far away from Utapau, are we?"

She thought about it, doing math or consulting maps in her head. "In the grand scheme of things, no—it's not that far. We can get there fairly fast in this thing. Do you really think you can find any trace of the missing laser-sword goons on Utapau?"

He wanted to tell her to call them by their rightful name, but she was the pilot, so he kept his protests to himself. "The *Jedi*," he said pointedly, "fought alongside the clone troopers on Utapau. It was one of their last known battles. Maybe we can find somebody who remembers something."

"What, like leftover clones? Those guys don't live very long, you know."

"Maybe we'll find somebody else, then. Let's try it and see. I've got a good feeling about this."

"You do?" she asked dubiously.

"Yeah. I'm getting a headache just thinking about it."

"And that makes you happy? All right then, let's do this. My dad is going to be so *mad*."

Karr couldn't tell if the idea worried her or thrilled her. "What will he do, when he catches you?"

Maize cocked her head, adjusted her grip on the throttle, and turned to the navicomputer. "Who says he's going to catch me?"

Karr smiled. "I bet they wouldn't make a Jedi go to sewing school."

"Is that where they're sending you? I thought you said it was a trade school."

"Sewing is a trade. It's the family trade, actually. They want me to skip the final terms and go straight to making clothes for fun and profit," he said, putting a lot of sarcasm on the last part.

"Like your gloves?"

"Like my gloves."

She programmed the coordinates for Utapau and sat back in the pilot's seat. "You really hate the idea of being a tailor?"

"Yeah."

"Are you any good at it?"

He nodded grudgingly. "Yeah."

"Maybe someday you can make clothes for me."

He blushed all the way down to his shoulders. "Aw . . . you could afford something nicer than I could make."

"So what? I'd rather have something from a friend than from a store. Anyway, hold on—we're ready for hyperspace. Next stop: Utapau."

She submitted the course, pulled the throttle, and the stars stretched long and thin across the blue, cold ocean of hyperspace.

On the way, Maize figured out that she wasn't dealing with two of the galaxy's most gifted, experienced pilots—not that she was one, either. She mainly knew the basics, but she taught Karr and RZ-7 what she could. The droid, for his part, found the cruiser's programming tutorials and busied himself with the finer points of space travel.

"Once I have all the schematics uploaded, I ought to be able to manage this craft without any difficulty. In case you were to become incapacitated, Captain."

She nodded. "Captain. I like it."

"What does that make me?" asked Karr.

The droid answered, "Excess baggage?"

Karr laughed. "Okay, hotshot. Don't get too comfy in that seat."

When they finally emerged from hyperspace, the planet Utapau loomed before them—a sphere of light green spaces and pale brown swaths, with little blue to break it up. Here and there, lights flickered beyond the sharp shadow of light, but there wasn't much to see from so far away. Caught in orbit were nine moons—dancing gracefully around the planet and one another.

Maize announced triumphantly, "We're here! Now where do we go? It's not a huge planet, but it's still . . . I mean, it's a *planet*. If your headaches are tingling or whatever, give me some further direction." She pulled up a data stream with general facts about what could be found on the surface, plus cities, towns, settlements, and outposts.

"That's not how my abilities work, exactly, but I'm

not against going with a strong gut feeling, either." Karr watched the information scroll and concentrated. This was the planet where General Grievous was killed, effectively ending the war. He'd learned about it in school and considered himself a bit of a history buff as far as the Jedi were concerned. Did any one location call out to him? It looked like a list of place names and dry facts, and he couldn't tell what was important and what wasn't.

Then he saw Pau City roll up in the stream. "Wait! Stop, right there."

She paused the screen. "What? What am I looking at?"

"Pau City—that's where it all began. The Battle of Utapau. Let's start there."

"It says here that it's just a big hole in the ground." Maize picked up the location anyway. "Are you sure about this?"

"One hundred percent," he lied through his teeth.

"Fine, then that's where we're headed. I hope you're happy."

"So happy."

"That makes one of us."

He laughed. "Oh, admit it. You're having fun, too."

"I admit nothing!" she declared, but she did it with a smile.

When they reached their destination, they were both overwhelmed. Up close and personal, the city was both more and less than what they'd expected, and wind whipped across the planet's surface. It was all they could do to stand upright, bracing themselves against the gusts, blinking until their eyes watered.

"Boy, you weren't kidding. When you said 'hole in the ground' I thought you meant it as an expression."

"Nope," she said. "It's a literal sinkhole. All the cities here are, I think."

Karr stood between Maize and RZ-7 beside the *Avadora*, which they'd parked beside the gaping circle that disappeared toward the planet's core. "Why'd you set us down here?"

"Because it's one thing to leave your home spaceport with your dad's ship, and another thing entirely to show up on a distant planet with a First Order yacht that doesn't have a flight plan." Maize busily read up on the place, her fingers swiping down a ribbon of information on a datapad. "It's definitely a sinkhole, and there's a whole city down there. Wow. I've never seen anything like it."

Karr squinted down into the dark. "It goes on *forever.*"

"No, just eleven levels. Let's go check it out."

"Maybe we should look around first?"

She shook her head. "No way. It's too windy up here, and I've already got a shirt full of sand. Let's go."

He let her take the lead, not because he felt any personal squeamishness about heading underground into an alien civilization . . . or exactly because of that, but he wasn't about to say it out loud.

The city's levels were their own neighborhoods, according to Maize, who could read and walk and talk at the same time, much better than Karr ever could. Up top were the government officials, and below that the richest residents—and so forth, and so on. Near the bottom were the produce levels that kept the city fed. Turbolifts connected the levels, moving citizenry up and down as needed.

"What's at the *very* bottom?" he asked.

"Mines, apparently. They excavate all this stone. No, wait. Not stone. It's fossilized bone. That's their main building material. Sounds like quite an operation, and there's a lot to see and do. You're the one who's all plugged in to the telekinetic laser knights. You tell *me* what happens next."

The city pulsed and surged around them, occupied mainly by local Utai with elongated bald heads and bulging eyes, and Pau'ans, lanky gray humanoids. But there were enough off-worlders that nobody looked at the teenagers with too much more than a curious glance. Humans abounded, along with droids from every corner of the galaxy, Weequays, Rodians, Sakiyans, and a number of other species. Below the brightest, cleanest top levels with the most expensive dwellings and shops, the markets and merchants were hopping, and a dozen languages were spoken on each block.

"Are we going to wander around all day, or . . . ?" Maize hinted.

RZ-7 tried, "Perhaps I could make some suggestions."

"I'm thinking, I'm thinking."

An enormous, sharp-skinned lizard-like creature squawked and dodged a city maintenance droid. The creature wore a saddle and a rider—who began swearing at the droid in some dialect Karr didn't understand.

"Over this way—there's got to be *something*." He hoped

he was right. He could feel his heartbeat nervously pounding behind his eyeballs by the time he pointed out a secondhand store wedged between a mechanic's workshop and grocery that specialized in some indigenous cuisine that smelled like berries and raw seafood. It made him want to puke, but he restrained himself and concentrated on the issue at hand.

"A junk shop, sir?"

"Junk shops are gold mines, Arzee. Watch this: I'll prove it."

A big, beefy human was leaning against a wall, smoking some unknown substance from a pipe that was almost as long as his forearm. He snorted in Karr's general direction and asked, "What are you calling *junk*?"

The boy cleared his throat. He backed away. "Um. Nothing. Sir."

"You called it a junk shop." He bobbed his chin toward the little storefront.

"No, I called it a gold mine. If you heard the bit about the junk shop, you must've heard . . . the part about the gold mine. I'm sorry, I'm not trying to offend anyone. Is it . . . is it *your* junk shop? I mean, gold mine?"

He laughed, and it was a big sound to match the man's size. "It's mine, all right. My wife doesn't like it when I smoke in there, and I wanted a break. The climate control's not working and it's hot inside, even with the fans running."

"It's a little warm," Karr agreed, trying to be pleasant—since his first interaction with a local had turned out to be an accidental insult.

"It's too warm. Because of the springs," he added. "Another level or two down. Sometimes the heat, it comes up and makes everything sticky. Now what do you want from my junk shop, boy?"

"He doesn't know," Maize said.

"Just looking to browse? I can live with that. Maybe you'll find some treasure yet." He finished another long draw from his pipe, then tipped it over and stepped on the coals to snuff them out. "Come inside, and let's see what you find."

Inside was a jumbled, tumbled wonderland of confusion. All the way to the ceiling, rows of shelves were stacked—each one weighed down heavily enough to sag. At a glance, Karr saw books and scrolls and musical instruments, toys and weapons and games, tack and harnesses for work animals, communication devices and screens and computational boards, tins and bins and buttons, lamps and survival gear and bottles of vintage alcohol no one in their right mind should consider sipping.

The merchant squeezed back behind the counter and settled into a large round seat with cushions that had molded themselves to his considerable shape. “I’m Sconto, my friends. What brings you all the way to Pau City, and what do you hope to find here in my shop?”

“I don’t suppose you have anything left from the Clone Wars?” Karr asked.

The man smiled at them. “Are you kidding me? I’ve got the best thing to come out of the Clone Wars . . . me!”

# CHAPTER 7

Maize's eyes widened. "You fought in the clone wars?"

Sconto let out another belly laugh. "Not quite. My *father* was a clone."

It was Karr's turn to be amazed. "Seriously?"

"If my mother can be believed, and I have no reason to doubt her."

"But I thought clones didn't live very long. You must be . . ." Maize quit before she could speculate.

Sconto didn't offer her an age, only a wink. "I'm about as old as I look. Either my non-clone blood won the fight, or else I got lucky—and I didn't inherit their sad, short life span." If he was telling the truth about his father, then he must be in his late fifties.

Karr beamed. Leaving Merokia was already proving helpful. "Then if your dad was a clone trooper, you must know about the Jedi," he prompted.

Sconto's expression fell. A blank look replaced his wide smile.

Karr could see Maize was about to laugh, thinking

she had found someone who shared her disbelief, until she noticed that all the good humor had gone out of the room.

"Don't talk to me about Jedi," Sconto said, his cheery demeanor taking on a hardened tone.

Karr chided himself for being so carefree about his quest. He forgot that the galaxy was a big place filled with big opinions, and many didn't line up with his way of thinking. "I'm only asking as a history buff. I'm trying to find—"

But the man cut him off. "My father was killed in those wars. Gone before I ever met him. And I don't think I need to tell you who I hold responsible?"

"The Jedi," Arzee said enthusiastically, as if answering a bit of trivia.

Karr winced, wishing he had programmed the droid to understand when a question was rhetorical.

"War is an ugly thing," Sconto continued. "Both sides think they're right, and many lives are lost because of it. You can't argue with fighting for what you believe in, but . . ." He paused as if he was tempering his anger again. "Betrayal," he bellowed. "To turn on your fellow soldiers in arms, to cheat and strike like cowards! That's just . . ." He searched for the worst word he could think of. "Disgraceful." Then he spit on the ground as if the word wasn't enough.

Everyone was a little dumbstruck, but Maize couldn't help breaking the silence.

"The Jedi really existed?"

"Absolutely," he said with bitterness. "There were tons of them. But now they're all gone. Of course, their legend has grown beyond their power by now. It happens that way sometimes, with heroes and villains alike. The truth is never as simple as it seems, in history books or anyplace else. The Jedi were a bunch of power-hungry renegades, a few of whom might have had *some* sort of abilities." He waved a hand dismissively. "But at the end of the day, they were violent traitors, and the clones were right to put them down."

Maize decided to try a little diplomacy. "We're not interested in politics," she confessed. "We're just here as part of a school project."

As his mind caught up to hers, Karr added to their cover story. "A history project!"

Sconto began to see clearly again. "School, huh?"

RZ-7 agreed. "Yes, sir—my young friends here are working on a special assignment, outside the classroom. Directed study, that's what they call it."

Karr nodded vigorously. "We're researching the effects of the . . . the fall of the Republic on planets like Utapau."

"Or Mirial!" Maize agreed, offering up the planet from her own heritage. "You know, out-of-the-way places that were abandoned after all the fighting, and no one stayed behind to clean up the mess. We're going there next, but Utapau was closer, so we started here first."

Karr adored and admired her lying skills, and he tried to keep up. "We live on Merokia, and this is the nearest location of a big battle. That's why we're here in your amazing shop, and not rummaging through some dusty old library—we're supposed to use primary sources, like interviewing people who survived, or cataloging items that were used in the fighting. That kind of thing."

Maize capped it all off. "It's for extra credit."

Sconto softened again, and the pleasant shop owner they had originally met stood before them once more. He clapped his hands as if restarting the scene. "You've come to the right place, for sure! You're welcome to interview me, of course, and I have . . . oh," he said, his voice trailing off as he dragged the chair on its rusty wheels, running his hands over the stock behind the counter, "so many odd little things that might serve you. Let's see what I can find. . . ."

He shoved his fingers into crevices and corners, pulling out recorders, helmets like the one Karr had surrendered to his teacher, belts, gauntlets, cuffs, custom parts for strange weapons, small books and assorted manuals, keys in every shape and size, and the preserved skeleton of a small animal that once might've looked something like a tooka cat.

One by one, he lined things up on the countertop.

Karr quietly removed his right glove and tucked it into his pocket, and Sconto kept talking.

"Here we have a small control panel, the sort used for door locks or portal seals. I am told that it came from the second Death Star, but it's hard to say for certain. It might have come from a similar installation, or it might not. Over here, this is a set of Old Republic glasses, made for the galley of a large warship that still flies, I'm led to understand. Someone told me it was converted to a hospital ship that travels the galaxy on mercy missions, but you couldn't prove it by me. And this"—he indicated another mystery panel covered with circuitry that could have performed virtually any function, on any ship or in any home—"this . . . all right, I'll be honest. This one came from a hand-drying device that was installed in a washroom facility on board a personnel support craft. They can't all be exciting, but every scrap that survives is meaningful, you understand? Everything that lingers and can be held, or touched, or repaired . . . it has value to someone, someplace."

"What about that?" Karr asked, pointing to a staff that reminded him of the one he had back at home, in his collection.

The shopkeeper exclaimed, "Ah!" and grasped the stick in his hand. "Good call. This baby comes with some *authenticity*." He rotated the staff to reveal a name etched into the side.

Karr tilted his head and read the name aloud. " 'Medon'?"

Sconto waited for a bigger response, but then confessed, "Yeah. I wasn't sure who that was, either, but then I looked him up. And if it's who I think it is, this staff belonged to *Tion* Medon, the port administrator here in Pau City back during the Clone Wars."

"So he saw some action?" Karr asked.

Sconto shrugged. "It's possible. I wish I knew for sure if it was his, because it would fetch a nice price if so, but unfortunately Medon isn't as rare a name as I'd like it to be."

Karr was only halfway listening. "Sir, could I . . . touch it? I'd be real gentle. I don't want to break it or hurt it, I swear."

Sconto handed it over to Karr. "Since you're such good students, I suppose I could allow it. You want to record it, yes? For your project?"

"Yes!" both kids said together.

From the bottom of her bag, Maize produced an imaging unit as proof of their good intentions.

"Very well, here you go. Please be careful, though. It's pretty fragile and I'd hate to have to call your parents for money, should you cause any harm."

Before he even reached for it, Karr knew he'd gotten lucky. The piece was definitely old, and his skin was on fire before his fingers were fully around it. Then, as he stared at it with something like delight—and something like terror—he gently squeezed.

There was a flash. There was darkness.

There was a blurry image. Karr tried to focus,

but it was no use. And in some ways the fog added to his terror. He saw a lanky figure dressed in reddish brown. And though he couldn't make out the face, he most definitely saw jagged teeth and bleeding eyes. Karr tried to convince himself that the eyes weren't really bleeding—that it was just a normal Pau'an—but he couldn't be sure. It was almost enough to make him let go of the staff back in the real world, but before he could react, the Pau'an blurted out, "Greetings, young Jedi. What brings you to our remote sanctuary?"

Karr quickly turned to see whom he was talking to, wondering if his body was turning in Sconto's shop, as well—when, suddenly, he saw him! A man wearing, from what he could tell, a brown belted robe. An actual Jedi Knight. At first, Karr couldn't hear him—but his voice came in very clear, very suddenly: "Unfortunately, the war."

Karr wheezed and blinked furiously. The image skipped and jumped in time.

"With your kind permission," the Jedi continued, "I should like some fuel and to use your city as a base as I search nearby systems for General Grievous."

"He is here," Tion Medon whispered as he stepped

closer to the Jedi. "We are being held hostage. They are watching us."

For a moment, Karr thought Medon was referring to him. But the image jumped again.

"Tell your people to take shelter," said the Jedi. "If you have warriors, now is the time."

More sputtering. Karr desperately held on to what he could. Everything was becoming fuzzier. His vision skipped in and out, went black for a second, then returned.

The Pau'an bowed to the Jedi, steadying himself with the same staff Karr was currently holding. As the port administrator turned to leave, Karr heard another figure ask him, "Is he bringing additional warriors?"

Medon responded, "He didn't say," and crossed once more to the exiting Jedi in a conspiratorial fashion. "Master Kenobi," he whispered as he approached his ship. "General Grievous is a force to be reckoned with. Will you be bringing additional troops?"

The image of Kenobi flickered, and his voice went in and out. Karr tried to stay in the vision. ". . . rest assured . . . necessary arrangements. General Skywalker and I dueled with him . . . planning accordingly."

The world around Karr sparkled and hummed; reality went in and out of focus, trading places seamlessly with the psychic mirage of the Jedi Master from long before.

He wanted to know more, wanted to stay in that world forever, surrounded by what he imagined were thousands of Jedi. But he also wanted to make sure he didn't faint or fall—or break the staff that meant so much to the shopkeeper.

"Son, are you all right?"

"Karr? Karr, come on—snap out of it!"

"Sir? Do you require medical attention at this time? Here, sir." RZ-7's voice cut through the static. "Let me help you sit down. There you go, that will do."

Karr allowed himself to be lowered to the floor. Maize's small fingers pried his away from the staff, and she handed it back to Sconto—who appeared genuinely concerned. He'd come around from behind the counter, and he hovered nervously above them.

"I'm sorry," Karr gasped. "I'm so sorry, everyone. It's nothing, I'm fine. I swear, I'm fine. This happens all the time. I'm only . . ."

"He has thin blood," the droid informed the shopkeeper. "A tragic condition, but you see, that's why I travel with him—for his safety, and the safety of others. He will be fine. Please give him a moment."

The big man fidgeted nervously. "What does he need? What can I do?"

Maize patted Sconto's arm. "His medical droid will take care of him. Please don't worry. He needs some food, that's all. I'll take him . . . around the corner. There was a place, wasn't there? He'll be back to his old self in no time."

"There are many places in this district, though only a few have food he could eat. Here, let me go get you something. . . ."

"No, no. Please don't go to the trouble. Thank you for your time," Karr said, struggling back to his feet with the help of his droid. "You've been very helpful. Maize, did you . . . did you take any pictures of the staff?"

"Oh, yeah, I'll do that right now," Maize said, capturing some shots with her imaging unit.

Before they could shuffle out together, Karr paused. He turned back to Sconto and said, "Sir, thank you for letting me hold your artifact. It's quite a find. And if you ask me, it definitely belonged to Tion Medon. So make sure you price it accordingly."

The shop owner looked at the staff with new eyes. He didn't have to believe the boy, nor was there any reason he should, really, but Karr sensed that he did. "Thanks," he said with a smile. "I will."

Everyone else chimed in, thanking the shop owner profusely, and backed out of the crowded little store as fast as they could without raising further suspicion.

Karr's head was still ringing a bit from the blackout, but when they were back on the street, he couldn't contain his excitement. "I saw one! I saw a real Jedi!"

"What? In a vision?" asked Maize.

"Yes. From the staff. And he was everything I imagined he'd be. The robe and the . . . well, all I could make out was the robe, but it was definitely a Jedi. The administrator addressed him as one."

"Wow," said Maize. "And here I thought it was enough you found someone to confirm the existence of your crazy crusaders"

"You can't call them that anymore," Karr said with exuberance. "Because we found proof! And because I saw one." He was so excited that he began to feel lightheaded again. "Whoa."

RZ-7 steadied him. "You've experienced a lot, sir. Perhaps we should get some food in you."

"Yeah, I think food might help."

RZ-7 said, "The Pau'an diet isn't likely to agree with either one of you. Let's try the next level down. If nothing else, we should find a cantina or something that caters to off-worlders."

Soon enough, they found a small, dark diner that catered to a wide variety of travelers. They squeezed into a booth at the back and sent the droid up to the bar with credits and loose instructions to order something edible.

The diner was busy, and the drinks were flowing—but no one offered the teenagers any, and neither of them pressed their luck by asking for anything they shouldn't be able to buy. Karr's brain was bouncing around in his skull, and his hand felt hot where he'd held the staff. He was deeply relieved when his droid returned with large mugs full of water and the promise of runyip cheese and crackers to come.

He downed half his mug in a few seconds and felt a bit better right away, but the aching fog of the vision still lingered. He rubbed his eyes with the back of his hands and tried not to moan.

"So what did you see, exactly?" Maize asked him.

"Are you going to be all right, sir?"

He answered RZ-7 first. "I'm good. This one wasn't so bad, actually. I didn't faint all the way or anything!"

Maize poured some of her own water into his mug to top it off. "That is great. Were you able to get anything else from the vision? Or just confirmation?"

He beamed at them both. "I got *names*."

"Names? When I gave you my father's drafting tool, you mostly mumbled about what he looked like. You got names this time?"

"Two of them. One was named Kenobi and the other was General . . . Skywalker, I think!" he said excitedly.

At the next table over, an Utai in a municipal jumpsuit barked, "Skywalker?" and several heads turned—including Karr's. "That's a name you don't hear every day, not anymore."

Karr swiveled on the rough seat cushion. "You know that name?"

Several others murmured, "Jedi, yes, hm."

The city worker nodded, his bulging eyes bobbing on his face. "Old stories, that's all."

"Not stories!" someone else at the table argued.

"Everything's a story, eventually," the first Utai protested. "So long as someone lives to tell it and someone lives to hear it. Same for the Republic, same for the Jedi, same for all of us one day, if we're lucky."

Quietly to Maize, Karr said, "More proof they were real."

The native heard him. "Real, yes. That's not a question. Were they good? Were they bad? Were they wrong?"

"Were they all destroyed?" Karr asked quickly, before the philosophy lesson could progress any further.

The Utai shrugged. "Who can say? Maybe they simply left. There's no telling. Not now, not here. But!" he said with a lifted finger. "Do you know what I heard? There is a story that is still told, around campfires and on long trips through space: It is said that Luke Skywalker—at the Battle of Jakku—he used the Force to reach into the sky and pull down the Empire's ships! The battle's victory belonged to him, that's what they say."

Karr's eyes were wide. "*Imperial ships!* Are you telling me that the Jedi existed after the Clone Wars?" He was used to no one on Merokia knowing anything about the Jedi—or even about galactic history, really—so the revelation that there might be Jedi still alive stunned him. "That would make Skywalker incredibly old, if he lived through the clone *and* civil wars," Karr noted, thinking again how maybe he was wrong to question some of his grandmother's tales.

"That's how I heard it, anyway. That's how the New Republic won the Battle of Jakku and ended the war with the Empire. I'm sure someone who lives there could tell you more than I know, though. Visit the outpost at Niima and try your luck."

Karr fully expected to look back at Maize and see her rolling her eyes again, but she didn't. She looked at him instead and said, "Let's go find your Jedi!"

# CHAPTER 8

Once the gang was refreshed with water and cheese and a weirdly flavored soda that Maize had insisted on trying—and then immediately dumped out—they all headed back to the ship to plan a new course. Karr's headache was all but gone, replaced with excitement. Somewhere on Jakku he would surely find more Jedi artifacts. It was like the Force itself was guiding him! But when he said so out loud to Maize, her enthusiasm began to wane.

"Maybe. If we're lucky."

But he wasn't in the mood for any pessimism. "I know we don't have much to go on, but any lead is better than no lead—and I'm going to follow this one. My grandmother was right. Practice and persistence pay off. I'm getting better at this."

The droid agreed. "It's true, sir. And I'm saying that as a high-ranking member of the medical field."

Karr laughed at the droid's attempt at humor. "I'm pretty excited about how well that last trip went."

They emerged from the shadow of the sinkhole and returned to the *Avadora*, which was waiting for them right where they'd left it. It was a little warm inside from sitting out in the sun, but Maize started up the life-support systems and got the temperature down in a matter of moments. She found the coordinates for Jakku and began to program them into the ship's navicomputer.

"Everybody buckle up. We'll clear the atmosphere, hit orbit, and then make the jump to hyperspace—so we can get a few hours of sleep. It's past our bedtime already, and it'll be a while before we get where we're going."

Karr checked the ship's console data. "It's past our bedtime?"

"Uh-huh. It's past mine, anyway. I don't know about you, but I could use a nap."

"Does this thing have"—he looked around—"living quarters?"

"It has a couple of pullout beds and a facility for washroom business. That's about it. This isn't a long-haul passenger transport. It's meant to be comfortable and fast. It's not meant for weeks of space time. Arzee?"

"Yes, madam?"

"You'll keep watch for us, won't you?"

"Absolutely. Get some rest, and I'll finish configuring my pilot protocols so I can fly the ship. If I must. Without assistance. For emergency purposes, you understand. Should you or Karr become incapacitated."

While RZ-7 made the jump to hyperspace, the kids tucked into their respective sleeping nooks and the lights dimmed. Karr hadn't even realized how tired he was, but it'd been a busy day. Maybe he should contact his parents and let them know he was all right. Maybe they didn't deserve to know just yet. Maybe they could worry, and that would teach them something about packing up their children and shipping them off to the far side of their home planet against their will.

"For my own good," he muttered.

"What?"

"Sorry. Just talking to myself."

With a yawn, Maize said, "That's silly. I'm right here. You could talk to *me*."

"About what?"

"Tell me . . . tell me a bedtime story," she said with another yawn, or it might've been a sigh. "Tell me about your grandmother. She sounded nice."

"She *was* nice. She's the one who told me what my abilities are, and she helped me learn about them. She taught me how to go about controlling them."

Maize giggled. "Are you sure she was qualified? I mean," she added fast, before he could object, "how bad were your visions before she started teaching you? Because I've seen a couple of them now, and they look awful."

"They're not awful. Okay, they're *kind* of awful. But it was worse when I didn't know what caused them, or what they meant, or how I could avoid them. Trust me, Grandma was the first to admit she didn't have the Force, but she believed in it. She *wished* she had it. And maybe she wasn't the most likely tutor, either, but she cared about it. Cared about me. Even though I possessed something she never would. Sometimes I think that's more important, because she didn't take it for granted. And when she saw it in me, she did her best to help me reach my potential." Karr paused. He hadn't expected to reveal so much, but Maize had that effect on him. "Anyway, she also made me the gloves, and that helped a lot. Someday, I hope I can get good enough to feel things and understand them clearly without the headaches and fainting."

"And your grandmother thought you could? Someday?"

He nodded, even though Maize couldn't see him in the dark. He said, "She always believed in me. More than my parents ever did."

"I know how *that* feels."

"Yeah?"

"Well, sort of. My dad's gone all the time, and I don't think my mom is very interested in me."

"What makes you think your mom isn't interested in you?"

"I don't know," she said sleepily. "I think she believes I have more in common with my dad than I do with her. That there's a natural bond between us that she'll"—she yawned—"never have."

"Is that true?"

She turned her body away from him and faced the wall. "Who can tell? He's never around long enough to find out."

"That's funny, because you and your mom look so much alike I would've guessed you have more in common with her."

"How do you know what my mom looks like?" she asked, turning her neck to look at him.

"There were some holos in your house. You're the spitting image of her. Minus the tattoos, of course."

Maize groaned and turned away again. "Ugh. Don't get me started on the tattoos."

"Why not?"

"Because that's all she ever wants to talk about. She comes from this very . . . let's say traditional family with some strong opinions about Mirialan customs."

"Which involve getting tattoos?"

"Yeah. It usually happens after you've completed a certain"—she yawned again—"task or . . . achievement or . . . something." Karr could hear her drifting off. "Just more status symbols if you ask me. That's all she cares about. I told her I wasn't interested, but that if I ever did decide to get one it would only be on half my face, since I'm only . . . half . . . Mirialan."

The words barely escaped her lips before they were replaced by snores.

Karr smiled. If someone had told him a week before that he'd be running away with a weird rich girl from another world, he wouldn't have believed them. But there he was—scared, excited, and worn-out—almost entirely because of her. And he wouldn't have it any other way.

"Wanna hear more about my grandma?" he said

jokingly to no one. And though no one answered, he decided to think about her anyway.

"What do you mean I'm supposed to clear my mind?" fifteen-year-old Karr asked his grandmother curiously. "Isn't that a bad thing? I mean, why am I going to school if it's better to have an empty brain?"

J'Hara had been winding a ball of yarn when their conversation began, and now she was using it to explain meditation to him. "The brain is like a sponge, Karr. It can absorb a lot," she said as she squeezed the blue mound of dyed bantha fur. "But sometimes it becomes too saturated with superfluous things."

Karr wondered if he had just cleared the part of his brain that knew what *superfluous* meant. Off his look she added, "Unnecessary. Frivolous. Unimportant."

"Like how fast the Incom T-85 X-wing can go?"

"Exactly. But by clearing your mind, by quieting your thoughts, you allow your brain to open up and become receptive to things you didn't even know were out there."

"Like the Force," he said, less as a question and more as proof of his eagerness.

"Like the Force," she repeated with a smile. "Shall we try it together?"

Karr nodded as his grandmother joined him on the floor, crossing her legs as a silent suggestion for him to duplicate.

"Is this how the Jedi meditate?" he asked.

"People can meditate in all sorts of ways, but yes, I'd say there's a good chance the Jedi approached it this way. Now let us close our mouths and open our minds."

Karr sat next to her in the same position and watched as she closed her eyes and rested her hands on her knees. She took a deep breath and let it out. Karr did the same.

After a few seconds of silence, Karr said, "It's tough not thinking of anything."

He looked to her for a response, but there was none.

The two remained in silence for another beat.

"I can't help thinking I should have gotten a pillow to sit on."

Without opening her eyes, J'Hara whispered, "If you feel regret, you are living in the past. If you spend your time worrying, you are living in the future. Try to be in the moment. In the here and now."

Karr closed his eyes again.

After another few seconds he asked, "Where am I living if I'm hungry?"

J'Hara exhaled as if she was giving up.

"I'm sorry," Karr said, noticing his grandmother's frustration. "I keep trying to be open, to think about the Force, but all I keep seeing is what I think lightsaber battles would look like."

"You'll get there," she said wearily. "Just . . . keep practicing. Practice and persistence pay off."

"I will." Then, as if the idea to ask for guidance just struck him, he asked, "Grandma, what do you think of when you think of the Force?"

The older woman looked at him with surprise, and then he watched as her gaze went inward. A tear rolled down her cheek. "It's best not to think of anything. Free your mind," she said. "The Force is not something you can hold on to. It's something that flows to you, through you . . . and away from you."

He didn't remember falling asleep, and he was very confused when a pillow hit him upside the head.

"Get up, already. You've slept long enough, and we're almost to Jakku."

"What?" Groggily, Karr pulled himself out of bed. "I mean, ready when you are, Captain."

"I like that. Keep calling me that," she said with a smile.

"I'm gonna."

When the *Avadora* dropped out of hyperspace, a message popped up in the ship's communication log. Maize saw it, pulled it up, and then deleted it almost immediately—before Karr could even see what it was.

"What was that?" he asked. "Was it important?"

"Nope. Just my mom."

"Is she mad?"

She shrugged. "Who cares?"

"What did she say?"

"Other than 'Maize, what do you think you're doing?' . . . I don't know, and I don't care. That's why I cut it off. She'll be fine," she said with a flap of her hand. "She's always fine. She'll go get a new pair of shoes and forget all about me. I'm surprised she hasn't done it already."

"She's your mother."

"That doesn't mean she cares," she said, her mouth set in a hard line. Then, to change the subject, "Look, there's the old Hutt outpost the Utai mentioned."

He hurried over to the viewport like he could see the outpost from space. "Niima?"

She showed him a holographic map. "Right here." She indicated a few dots on a desert sprawl. "I hope my language skills are as good as I pretend they are at school."

"What? I thought you spoke Huttese."

"I speak a little bit of very rude Huttese, but I hope I won't need it. Let's park this bird and see what's going on down there."

A short time later, they stepped into the blast furnace of a stark, beige world of sand. The wind blew hard and hot, dragging small grains into their eyes, their clothes, and in RZ-7's case—his joints and circuitry.

The droid observed, "This is . . . less than ideal, sir."

The sky was a vivid pale blue, so bright it was almost white above them—and the heat was dry but persistent. Karr practically felt his eyeballs shriveling as he stood there. Maize didn't look too much happier, and the droid was doing his best to keep from appearing miserable. "How far are we from the outpost?"

Maize squinted down at her handheld map/comm device. "It's right over there."

"That's a sand dune."

"On the other side of it, then. Come on. The sooner we find it, the sooner we can get out of here. This place is no fun."

"It's a desert."

"Yeah, exactly. There's not much to do in a desert. Not much that's fun, anyway." She wrapped a light scarf around her face to keep out the tiny, needling grains of sand and led the way forward, trudging against the wind.

Karr and RZ-7 fell in line behind her, neither one prepared to argue.

Maize's map was right, and on the far side of the sand, a small settlement was nestled in the shelter of a crescent-shaped dune. It consisted of a handful of buildings, a smattering of marketplace shops and stalls, an awning-covered blockhouse that looked like the center of operations, and a large Hutt-style gate that announced, yes, this was a town—and furthermore, everyone should beware of entering it on anything less than business, with anything less than polite manners.

"It's *definitely* Hutt," Karr said.

But Maize was staring down at her datapad, to which she'd downloaded all the information on the settlement she could find. "Says here it *used* to be Hutt, and now it's not. Hutts set up shop before the Battle of Jakku, but it doesn't look like they stuck around very long." She lifted her eyes and looked around, but seeing nothing to snag her attention, she looked back down again. "Supposedly there's a lot of old weaponry—and ships and things left over from the battle. People salvage that stuff for a living."

"I don't see any."

"I saw some downed Star Destroyers when we entered the atmosphere. Those ships alone must keep the scavengers busy."

"You figure they would've picked them clean by now."

She shook her head. "Clearly not. If they got everything, nobody would be here anymore. Nobody stays anywhere if there isn't any money."

He elbowed her. "Hey, look over there."

"At the junkyard?"

"Yeah. Look at those giant tarps. I wonder what's underneath them."

"If I had to guess I'd probably say . . . junk."

"Funny. I'm going to guess . . . ships." He stepped past her, into the lead. "Let's see what's down there. With your knowledge of Huttese and my knowledge of the Jedi . . . we'll find out about the legendary Skywalker as quick as a Teek on a shopping spree."

RZ-7 mustered enough enthusiasm to say, "Yes, perhaps we'll be back on board the ship and into the cool, sand-free void of space before we know it!"

Karr said, "You two are killing me."

And maybe it was true, but they followed him anyway—down the dune, past the blocky gate that announced NIIMA OUTPOST, and into what passed for a town square.

It was more of an oval than a square, really, and not terribly well populated. A handful of merchants sold strange bugs grilled on sticks; others offered the local version of ale or a thick, dark liquor that smelled like death in a cup. The whole place felt fleeting and temporary, like no one actually lived there on purpose—and no one wanted to stay there any longer than was absolutely necessary.

The blockhouse squatted thick and plain at the center. The droid made a beeline for it.

"Arzee, where are you going? I want to get a look at what's under those tarps!" Something at the back of his mind kept telling him the ships were important.

"If I may suggest an alternative, sir . . . let's visit the fellow in charge of what's under those tarps. This is a junkyard, and you had such marvelous luck in the junk *shop* . . . let's see if your luck holds. Also, if we go to the trouble to introduce ourselves, there's less of a chance we'll be shot on sight for trespassing. If, in fact, this settlement is managed by the Hutts."

Maize said, "I told you, it's not. Not anymore."

"All the more reason to tread carefully," said the droid. "Do you really want to anger anyone who sent the Hutts packing?"

"Good point, Arzee," Karr said. "All right, let's visit the man in charge."

"Or the woman in charge."

"Yes, Captain. Or the woman in charge."

Karr and Maize stood side by side in the shadow of

the Hutt gate, crossing their fingers and working up their courage while the pretend medical droid sauntered toward the blockhouse, and whatever fortune waited within it.

# CHAPTER 9

A short line had formed outside the blockhouse. Karr, Maize, and RZ-7 joined it. The others were mostly human, with a few Teedos scattered about, and all of them had the ragged, secondhand look of folks who scavenged for a meager living. Most carried armloads of metal scraps pulled from ships that had crashed and burned more than a generation before. Everyone looked hot, hungry, and broke.

"Um, excuse me," Karr said, in an effort to engage a tall, thin man who'd joined the line behind them. "Could you tell me . . . what's this line for, exactly?"

"We're all here to see the blobfish," he said, low and quiet.

Maize turned around and asked, "The blobfish?"

The man said, "Shhh! It's not his name. Unkar Plutt, that's him. You're in *his* town now."

"Is he a Hutt?" she wanted to know.

He shook his head. "No, all the Hutts are long gone."

"Is that good or bad?" She craned her neck to see around the people in front of her.

"Take your pick. It's about the same either way."

When the gang got closer to the front of the line, they learned three things: One, the scavengers were mostly queuing up to swap their findings for small food packets. Two, Unkar Plutt was a cheapskate. Three, there was a reason everyone called him the blobfish.

He was big and wide like a Hutt, but the resemblance mostly ended there. The junk boss of Jakku was a Crolute—a humanoid species that was much more likely to be comfortable in a wet environment than living on a desert planet. His limbs were thick and doughy, and his face was flat and saggy. He looked like he'd be happiest sitting on a log in a boggy marsh—or better yet, underneath one.

His gummy fingers counted out food rations and collected offerings with surprising speed. "Three quarter portions," he said as he plopped the rations on the counter in exchange for the scavenger's finds. The creature scowled, but took it. Karr didn't know anything about this planet's currency, but even he felt that was a small amount to get for what the scavenger had just hauled across the desert.

Karr approached the window, and the Crolute opened his hand. "What have you got?" he asked, barely looking at Karr. Then his tiny, deep-set eyes narrowed even further. "Hey, I don't know you. This is my concession stand, not my charity drive. Get out, all three of you. Unless you have something to sell, I have nothing to give."

"We have credits," Maize said. "We're here to buy, not sell."

It might've been her confidence, or her clothes, or Plutt assuming that the upper class were usually easy marks, but the Crolute begrudgingly gave her his attention. Karr didn't know why the merchant chose to believe her, and he didn't care. He was just happy he had stopped yelling at them.

"Yes, sir," Karr added. "We're looking for *Jedi* artifacts, specifically. Possibly even from the end of the Galactic Civil War," he said, his voice going up at the end, hoping the blobfish would understand his meaning and reveal what he knew. But when he didn't, Karr added, "We were told that if we wanted to find quality merchandise anywhere in this corner of the galaxy, you were the fellow to see."

Unkar folded his sausage arms across a hanging

breastplate that clanked when he moved. "The Jedi have been dead since the Clone Wars," he said as a matter of fact, but then teased, "I *might* be in possession of some of their wares, however." Karr was thrown by the Clone Wars comment since he had hoped to hear more about the Jedi Skywalker pulling ships from the sky, but he was happy they had access nonetheless. "But if you're lying about your financial situation," the merchant growled, "I'll make up for it by sellin' your hides." Then he barked something to the rest of the line in a language Karr didn't recognize.

When he looked at Maize to see if she knew, she only shrugged at him.

But all the other scavengers wandered away as they'd apparently been commanded, and Unkar Plutt reached up to pull down a metal screen that closed the vending window. "Get over here," he told them. "Come around back, and you can look through my *serious* merchandise. I have two or three things in mind that I think you'll like, yes. Items beloved by the Jedi, carried by Jedi. Even used by Jedi during the Clone Wars, if the stories are true!"

Maize made eye contact with Karr, showing him

a little eye roll that said she didn't believe Plutt for a minute, but she played along regardless.

Around the side of the concession stand there was a door. Their host opened it and waved them all inside, chattering as they joined him in the dark, stuffy space. "Most of what's here on Jakku comes from the battle between the New Republic and the Empire. I had no great love for either side myself, but I owe them something, I guess. They left so much carnage in their wake. Such vast machines of war, wrecked and abandoned as if they're worth nothing. Well. They're worth a great deal, if one knows how to sell them in pieces and scraps."

RZ-7 led the way with flattery. "You clearly run a thriving establishment. You must be a tremendous businessman." The Crolute stared at RZ-7 as if he had just noticed him. He looked him up and down, then said, "How much you want for the droid?"

RZ-7 gasped.

"He's got some interesting hardware. For a medical droid," Plutt said pointedly, with what seemed like a knowing glance.

"Uh, no," Karr stammered. "He's not for sale."

"Bah!" The blobfish stormed ahead, his body swaying from left to right.

Plutt showed them to a round stockroom that was full of shelves and ladders, with lights hanging from cords to illuminate the lists, charts, and inventory forms that hung on the walls.

Karr made appreciative mumbles, and Maize did the same. Then she said, "You must send a lot of your stock off-planet, don't you? You can't possibly keep it all here."

"No, I don't. But I am more than a merchant—I am a collector. Sometimes I collect for myself, and sometimes I hang on to special pieces I think might find a home with someone wealthy down the line. And some of the things I take from others in trade, I keep here. Things from before the Empire. Items that are precious only to the very few."

He flashed them a sly-eyed look, the kind that communicated almost out loud that he thought he'd found just the right suckers with just the right purses.

Maize didn't see it, but Karr did. He knew that look. It usually came from clients who were about to ask for a discount or complain that the price for their new suits had been inflated or whine that they would need to defer payment, just this once. It was the look of a man who didn't merely love money—but would cheat to get it, or to keep it.

As quickly as Karr had seen the look, it disappeared when the big, soft fellow turned his back and began to search his rows of stock. Some of the shelves had labels, and some did not. Some had notes slapped on them that declared a piece reserved, or already sold and waiting for pickup. Unkar Plutt skipped those and reached to a second shelf—climbing up on a footstool and then a ladder until he could pull down just the right object for his audience.

"Here it is. The thing I wanted to show you."

When he stepped down again, he was holding a ship's throttle controls—just the lever and its casing, all its wires capped off and tucked into a housing block it sat on like a presentation stand.

"What's that?" Maize asked, eyes wide.

"It came from one of the Republic ships—a small flier that crashed somewhere after a conflict with the Separatists. Probably flown by a Jedi. When someone from off-world brought me this to trade, I knew it was special. Didn't even realize what he had, the fool."

"Can we touch it?" Maize was the one who asked this time.

Karr did not. His fingers didn't want it. Nothing about the throttle lever struck him as passingly important in any sense. It took all his energy to hide his disappointment.

The merchant handed it to her with something like reverence, or perhaps fear—like it might explode if it was handled too carelessly.

Maize turned it over in her hands, poking at the buttons on the left-hand side of the lever and gently tweaking the caps on the wires. "This is actually pretty cool," she told him. "Do you know who the ship belonged to?"

"I told you, it was a Jedi pilot," he said, but something about his tone of disinterest said that he might not be telling the whole truth. Or any of it. "There were a handful of them, at least. More than that, perhaps—who can say? But the price is not a trick or a joke. I know what it is worth, and I will accept no less."

"Of course not. We would not dream of haggling," said RZ-7, before remembering he probably shouldn't be calling attention to himself.

"Speak for yourself," Karr told him.

Plutt harrumphed. His arm flab jiggled, and his

breastplate rattled. "No negotiations! My stock is rare and priced accordingly. You can either afford it or you can't. Don't waste my time!"

Only then did Maize notice that Karr hadn't yet tried to touch the throttle casing. "Karr, don't you . . . don't you want to take a look?"

"Uh, yeah. Sure. Give it here."

He slipped off a glove, took the object in his hands and pretended to get thoughtful. He turned the item over, looking at it from every angle. From the corner of his eye, Karr could see Plutt scrutinizing him as much as he was scrutinizing the throttle. Suddenly, a low electronic chirp caught everyone's attention. Both Karr and Maize looked to RZ-7, but the droid didn't seem to be the source. Unkar Plutt gave a grunt of dissatisfaction and pulled a handheld communicator from his belt. He held it up to his mouth and said, "Hold on," before turning to the kids and grumbling, "Don't go anywhere!"

He turned toward a door that was partly hidden behind a tall metal ladder on wheels. He pushed the ladder aside and opened the door to reveal a small office, barely any larger than the cockpit of the *Avadora*.

He wedged himself inside, leaving the door open a crack so he could keep an eye on his guests as he conducted whatever shady business he was involved in.

Maize whispered to Karr, "You must really be getting good at this. You didn't even flinch when you touched it!"

"That's because there's nothing here."

She frowned. "Nothing? Not a tingle? Not a twitch?"

"Nothing. It didn't witness any important events. I doubt it was even used by the Republic. Actually, nothing in this storeroom looks like anything that would help us. Let's go back to the junkyard. I want to look around there, instead."

"What do you expect to find?" she asked.

"I don't know." He cocked his thumb and pointed in the direction he meant. "I've got a feeling, though. Let's go see. Everything in here is just . . ."

Unkar Plutt emerged from the tiny office. "Just what?"

"Just . . . out of my price range," Karr tried.

"Then make me an offer."

But all Karr wanted to do was leave. "It's okay. We're good. It's just not what I was looking for."

"Don't insult me, boy! I'm losing money talking to you. I shut my stand to show you that throttle because I thought you were a serious collector."

"Look," Maize interrupted. "If my friend says this isn't what he's looking for, it isn't what he's looking for. Don't take it personal. It's not an insult. We're just looking for some very specific items."

Karr said, "Yeah, and this isn't one of them. But we'd still like to look around the outpost, if that's all right with you, sir."

"Bah!" Plutt threw his arms up and tossed the datapad onto a nearby shelf. "If you don't like what I'm offering, then you're not welcome to any of it. Get out of here. I have scavengers to feed, and if you're bringing me nothing and buying nothing . . . you're no use to me."

Before he could get any more insistent, Karr, Maize, and RZ-7 darted outside into the punishing desert sun. The door slammed behind them.

"Perfect," Maize muttered.

But RZ-7 disagreed. "On the bright side, miss . . . Mr. Plutt has now secured himself indoors, and we're interested in what he keeps *out*doors." He popped his head toward the open junk lot.

"Let's go see what we can find," Karr said. "But let's stay off his radar, if we can. Let's split up while we're looking. If anybody finds anything interesting . . . whistle or something."

The droid was on board. "Very good, sir. How about this?" He then emitted a high-pitch whistle that caused everyone in the area to look and even a few animals to stagger in pain.

Karr lowered his hands from his ears. "I'd suggest about a thousand decibels lower, but you've got the right idea."

With that, Karr pulled his scarf up over his head to protect it from the sun and also to cover his face—as if Plutt wouldn't know him if he saw him sneaking about beneath the tarps. It made him feel like a spy on a mission. Was that what this was? Well, it was fun to pretend, and he needed to stay out of the Crolute's line of sight.

With his hands clasped together, Karr playfully raised his index fingers to form the image of a blaster. He dramatically checked left, glanced right, and when no one seemed to be looking his way, he made a mad dash for the nearest tarp, pretending to evade enemy blasts along the way. When he was safely protected by the flaps of the first ship, he looked up to see the undercarriage of a quadjumper, its hull cracked, its heat-shielding tiles popping loose and falling to the sand.

Karr pulled off one glove and raised his hand to touch the ship, but he felt absolutely nothing except for warm metal and peeling paint.

Onward to the next one.

Somersaulting in the sand to the imaginary sound of ship's fire, Karr weaved and dodged his way to the second tarp, when he suddenly heard a whistle. He excitedly scanned the horizon only to find a baffled Maize staring at him and gesturing as if to say, *What the hell are you doing?* Karr just grinned as he ran off to the next tarp, but it was only the shell of a Taylander shuttle. It'd been totally gutted inside, and no one would've ever mistaken it for an interstellar ship, much less one that had once been piloted by a Jedi. Time for the next one.

"Third try threads the needle," he whispered encouragingly to himself. He still saw no sign of Unkar Plutt at the head of the line of scavengers that had reformed over at the concession stand, so he took a deep breath and sprinted to the farthest tarp covering the largest craft. As he picked up speed he realized how good it felt to exercise his legs after being in the close quarters of the *Avadora*. Reaching his destination, he congratulated himself on avoiding the dozens of spies he imagined were after him and rested his hand on the nearest surface to catch his breath. But instead of calming down, his breath quickened. Even through his glove he could tell this was something worth checking out. He slowly raised his eyes to glance at the treasure before him: a Corellian freighter.

By the time he caught his breath, he knew he'd hit the jackpot. He couldn't explain how he knew, but he did. This ship was special.

From underneath the tarp and the craft's body, it was hard to see much more than a vaguely circular shape with two points sticking out at one end—but he found the hatch and worked it open. It dropped with a hum and a grind, and when Karr stepped onto the ramp, he felt ready to jump out of his own skin.

He jammed his right hand back into his glove and tried not to touch anything.

He turned back to where RZ-7 and Maize were crouched, back beside the Hutt-made gate that marked the entrance to Niima Outpost, and whistled. *Come on,* he mouthed when he caught their attention, gesturing with both hands that they should join him.

When the coast was clear, they did. They ran up beneath the tarp, ducked under the ship, and hopped onto the ramp—where Karr was waiting.

"Are you okay, sir?" asked the droid in a soft digital voice.

"I'm great. Look at this ship, Arzee!"

Maize was less than impressed. "This isn't a ship. It's a wreck."

"True," Karr agreed. "But the prize is somewhere inside."

# CHAPTER 10

Karr led the way into the belly of the ship. It wasn't exactly what he'd expected, and he tried very hard to keep from feeling disappointed. The interior was grimy but mostly intact, and it looked exactly like the kind of small, slapdash craft that had been popular a generation before . . . but these days, it probably couldn't hop between two planets in the same system without blowing a circuit. Not without a lot of help.

It wasn't the rust, because there wasn't much. It wasn't the dated equipment or the exposed panels or the strange stains. It wasn't even the stale, warm smell of something dark and dry and abandoned.

Or maybe it was. Maybe it was all that, and then some—a once proud craft, left to rot under a canvas sheet in a nowhere outpost on a desert planet. Nobody cared about any of it anymore.

"It's my prognosis that it's . . . an unfortunate craft, in an unfortunate state—if we're being honest, sir," RZ-7 said.

But Karr was too wound up to wind down. "Maybe, but can't you feel it?"

"Feel what?" Maize asked, exasperated.

"I can't describe it. It's something in the air. No, in the ship itself. Think of all the things it must have witnessed! It's like . . . it's like it wants to tell me all about it."

"You can't be serious."

Arzee said, "Sir, it's quite dark in here. Let me see if I can turn on the lights."

Karr said, "Careful, though. And quiet. Don't do anything that'll catch anyone's attention."

Maize wasn't worried. "We'd need fireworks to get anyone's attention around here. Don't get too worked up about it."

Karr ran his gloved hands across every centimeter of the place. "I wonder where it's been, and what it's carried. I wonder who its pilot was. Maybe it'll tell me." He began slipping one hand out of its glove.

Maize shook her head. "It looks like an old spice freighter to me. Arzee, can you find any evidence of what this thing used to carry?"

The droid was silent for a few seconds. "I will look,

madam. Although with so many cargo holds, one would imagine it could smuggle just about anything."

"That's not helpful, Arzee," she scoffed. "Although he does bring up a good point, Karr. Maybe whatever you're looking for is hidden away in here somewhere, in a secret compartment or something. Otherwise, why wouldn't scavengers have picked this ship clean? Unless it's so old that nobody wants it—not even for parts," she said, answering her own question.

"It's probably still here because of the Force." Karr bounced happily from place to place. "My grandmother used to say that the Jedi were good at blending in and looking unthreatening, just like this ship. It looks useless and old, but we found it here, intact, because Unkar Plutt couldn't convince anybody to buy it. Even in bits and pieces. *That* was the Force at work."

"You sure about that?" she asked.

Karr stopped his exploring. "Do you *really* think that guy wouldn't have sold this thing—whole or in parts—for two credits and a glass of sow milk?"

Maize thought about it, her head bobbing from left to right as she pondered the possibilities. "You have a point."

"I always do!"

"You *sometimes* do," she said, but he was already gone again.

Karr went deeper into the ship, opening cabinets and sticking his face under consoles. He ran his fingers along empty shelves and tried every lever, every button, and every switch. But nothing turned on, no lights lit up, and nothing happened.

Maize caught up to him somewhere around the central sitting area, where he was lifting cushions off a bench seat and kicking anything that looked like it might open if he tried. "What are you looking for?"

"Anything."

"That's not helpful."

"I'm not asking for help," he said from under a holochess table. "I'll find it myself. It's around here somewhere, I can *feel* it."

"Feel *what*?"

"This. I think." He crawled out from under the table, but hit his head on the underside and dropped what he was holding. "Ow!" The item rolled across the floor.

"I've got it." Maize stopped it with her foot. When

Karr climbed to his feet, she nudged the object in his direction with her toe.

"Thanks! I'm glad it didn't break. I couldn't hold on to it. I tried, but even with the gloves it was difficult." He picked up the orb at his feet. It was gray, dotted with silver circles. He held it with a squint, struggling to keep control.

His head was spinning and his eyes were watering, but he wouldn't put it down.

"What is it?" Maize asked again.

RZ-7 caught up to the pair of them. "Sir, what did you find?"

"I have no idea!" he said merrily, poking and prodding it. "But I know it's important!"

"Okay, so tell us what you see. Concentrate, or whatever it is you do."

"I am, I am," he assured them.

He hugged the thing between his leather-clad palms and concentrated as hard as he could. Then he pulled off one glove and gingerly touched the orb with his fingertips.

The dark ship's interior, lit mostly by RZ-7's buttons and the weak yellow safety lights that had come on when the ramp dropped, grew darker still. It went black, and no matter how hard Karr blinked or how closely he looked, he saw nothing at all except darkness, and then brightness, and then . . .

When he opened his mind's eye, Karr noticed he was still on the ship. Was the vision not working? Normally it transported him to a different time and place, but he was still beside the holochess table.

Suddenly, a blue lightsaber sliced through the air, erasing any doubt in his abilities. Whatever the orb had witnessed, it had witnessed it on that very freighter. Karr tried to focus on the face of the person wielding the lightsaber, but his talents weren't that honed yet. Was it a Jedi?

"Now that you're comfortable holding the lightsaber," he heard someone say, "why don't we move on to technique?" Something about the voice pinged in Karr's head. He knew it from somewhere but just couldn't place it. Karr followed the voice until it led him to a different figure. He couldn't see that one's face, either, but the man was wearing a flowing robe. Now *that*, Karr thought, was definitely a Jedi.

"You're not going to make me fight you, are you?" said the person waving the lightsaber.

The man in the robe laughed. "No. But we should work on your connection to the Force."

A nearby golden blur—a droid, maybe?—asked, "May I be of any assistance, Master Kenobi?"

*Master Kenobi?* Karr did a mental double take. No wonder the voice sounded familiar. It was the same Jedi he had seen in his earlier vision.

Kenobi responded, "No, Threepio. Young Skywalker here must do this on his own."

Skywalker, too! This was too much of a coincidence. They must have been two very important Jedi to come up twice in his visions. And to think they once stood on the very spot Karr was standing. Although much earlier, he imagined, since Kenobi seemed to be training Skywalker and he had not yet become the *General* Skywalker of the Clone Wars vision.

Karr watched as Kenobi crossed to something that had caught his eye. He pulled from a compartment the very orb Karr was holding. For a moment, Karr felt he was sharing something with the Jedi Master. Not just the vision. Not just a lesson. But a connection.

"Try and defend yourself against this," Kenobi suggested.

"What if I can't?"

"The bigger question is, What if you can? Besides, it's a training remote. It is equipped with nonlethal blasters specifically for those who wish to practice. I'm guessing our pilot handles that blaster better than we imagine."

"Unless this belongs to the Wookiee," Skywalker joked.

Kenobi smiled as he tossed the remote into the air. "Focus."

Skywalker faced off against the target as it hissed and darted across the room. With each dodge and swing, Karr couldn't help copying the Jedi in training, almost as if he was waiting his turn.

Until something stopped them both.

Kenobi reached for his chest and looked for a place to sit down. Skywalker retracted the lightsaber.

"Are you all right? What's wrong?"

"I felt a great disturbance in the Force. As if millions of voices suddenly cried out in terror and were suddenly silenced."

Then, just like those voices, Karr's vision was silenced.

When his eyes were working correctly again, he saw that RZ-7 must've gotten a few more lights on. The room was brighter, and tiny rows of secondary indicator lights blinked softly on standby. His head was splitting, but he didn't care—not at all. He grinned from ear to ear.

Maize stood above him. She smirked and put one hand on her hip. "You look pretty happy for a guy who just fell and hit his head."

"I hit my head?"

"On the seat," she said, cocking her head toward the bench.

He climbed to his feet. "I didn't feel it. How long was I out?"

His droid supplied, "Nine point zero two seconds. Approximately."

"Worse than my reaction at Sconto's, but definitely worth it," Karr said.

"If you say so," Maize said skeptically. Satisfied that he wasn't going to die or anything, Maize slid onto the bench seat and put her feet up on the rounded table between them. It was bolted to the floor. Her boot heels scraped the top, but it didn't wobble.

"The first time I fainted, I was out for ages. My parents thought I was dead."

RZ-7 backed him up. "You're on a strong upward

trajectory, sir. You've emerged from your trance after nine seconds with a smile. This is your most successful vision to date! Assuming that your head doesn't explode within the next hour."

"I don't think it's actually going to explode. It just . . . kind of feels like it." He rubbed at his temple and tried not to groan.

"Was it worth it? What did you see? Did you get anything new?"

He flung himself onto the seat beside her. "Totally worth it! I got those names again. The same ones as before."

"Skyhopper or something?"

"Sky*walker*," he corrected her with an eye roll. "And Kenobi. But it was earlier."

She asked, "What do you mean?"

"Skywalker wasn't any kind of a general in this vision. And he didn't seem to know much of anything about the Force. He was . . . training. Like me, in a way. Only he had a true mentor. A real Jedi to show him the way."

Maize could see Karr's spirits dampening. "Maybe," she added. "But you know what he didn't have? A cool friend helping him find what he needs by flying him around the galaxy."

Karr smiled. "That's true."

"And you'll get there. Just give it time. We've really only just started if you think about it."

Karr realized Maize had a point. If that same struggling Skywalker went on to become a Jedi who could pull ships from the sky using only the Force, then maybe there was hope for Karr yet.

# CHAPTER 11

All three explorers ducked out of the freighter unseen, brushed off some of the sand, dust, and grime they'd picked up along the way, and headed back into Niima Outpost to see if anyone knew anything more about Skywalker or Kenobi. Briefly, they split up—RZ-7 opted to try his luck with a few other maintenance droids; Maize poked around the market; and Karr visited the food stalls, where he chatted up absolutely no one who had anything useful to share.

"This stinks," he complained to no one in particular. The outpost wasn't very big, and there were only so many people to pester. "A man pulled ships from the sky!" he yelled. "How is it nobody knows anything about it?"

No one was within earshot, and no one answered—but a soft ruckus began to rumble through the crowd. People were chattering nervously. A few folded up their booths at the market, rolling up rugs and shutting cabinets full of food, stashing supplies and hanging signs that said *closed* in half a dozen languages.

Something was happening.

Karr shielded his eyes and squinted across the bright, dry landscape. The blockhouse shutters were open for business, but the line there had thinned. A little side landing where livestock and droids were corralled, sorted, and sold had become very quiet except for the nervous grunts of happabores.

"Stop it! Get off me!"

It was Maize.

Karr panicked, scanning the scene for her—then following her voice as she continued her shrill, angry protests. When he finally caught up to her, his heart sank.

She was being dragged away between two First Order stormtroopers.

They completely ignored her kicks, shouts, and thrown elbows, hauling her out of the outpost and toward a ship whose hull poked up beyond the far side of the nearest dune.

How had he not heard it?

How had he not seen the troopers?

He meant to rush to her side, but RZ-7 swooped in to stop him. "Sir, you can't help her now."

"I have to try!" He flung himself across the market, through the line at the blockhouse, and straight into the back of the nearest soldier—who stumbled and let go of Maize's left arm. "Let go of her!"

Maize took the opportunity to lob a well-placed knee at the crotch of the trooper who held her right arm. He twisted fast enough to miss the worst of it and tucked her loose arm behind her back so he could hold her pinned.

She couldn't do anything but writhe and swear.

The other trooper found his feet and gave Karr a shove. "Buzz off, kid. This isn't any business of yours."

"She's my friend!"

"*And* our ride home . . ." noted RZ-7 in a too-loud whisper that only Karr seemed to hear.

Maize reared up and bowed her back, trying to pop loose of the soldier's grip, but she couldn't get any traction. "My dad sent them! They want to take me back!"

"No," Karr said to the galaxy at large. "No, you can't take her. She's with *me*."

"You want to come with her?" said the man snidely,

his voice rendered fuzzy and digital by the helmet.

Karr was about to reply that he didn't think he had a choice, considering it was her dad's ship that they'd commandeered to get the adventures underway—but she stopped him by yelling, "No!"

She and Karr locked eyes, and she glared like she was trying to communicate with him telepathically. Through her teeth, she said, "Then you'd have to leave your ship here. They're only here for me, not you! So get on your ship and get out of here."

Confused, he asked, "What?"

"You still have research to do. Items to . . . to touch, or whatever. Dead enchanted space knights to track down. There's no reason for you to come back to Merokia. You can *fly around the galaxy* without me," she said pointedly, flicking her eyes toward where they'd parked the *Avadora*.

They hadn't come for the ship; they'd only come for Maize—that was what she was trying to tell him.

Karr flashed a look at RZ-7, wondering if between them they could actually pilot the craft without her. The droid shrugged, then nodded.

"Hey, guys, let me go—just for a second, would you?" she pleaded with the troopers. "Hold a blaster on me or whatever you feel like you have to do, but let me give them something. Please? It's important."

"Fine, just for a minute—but," he added into her ear, "no funny business. We know all about you, kid. If it were up to me we would've stunned you and dragged you back by your feet, but your dad is a big man in the First Order, so you'd better thank your lucky stars for that." He let her go and took a step back so he could focus his blaster on her.

"Oh, I *do*," she said sarcastically. "Every day, on every planet I've had to live."

The other one aimed his blaster at her, as well. "Yeah, well you ought to. He's probably the only reason nobody's fired you out of an airlock yet. Now say your goodbyes, or whatever you need to do. But make it quick."

Maize straightened her jacket, adjusted her pants, and brushed imaginary stormtrooper contamination off her shoulders like so much dirt. She walked up to Karr and looked deep into his eyes. *Is she going to kiss me goodbye?* he wondered suddenly. He certainly wasn't expecting that. Especially not in front of First Order troopers. Then she dug into her satchel and rooted around until she'd found what she was looking for: the small holocommunicator she'd used at Sconto's. "Take this," she told him as she pressed it into his hand. "You can keep me posted on your adventures."

"Right," he said, adjusting his expectations. "Keep you posted."

"And . . . I guess . . . you can reach out to your parents, if you want to. I can pass any messages along, and hey—it might keep them from sending jerks like these guys after you."

"I promise you they don't have access to . . . to"—he looked at the two heavily armed and armored troopers—"guys like this. They'll just worry and complain, they won't try to retrieve me."

"Well, okay, but you should keep this anyway."

"For you?"

"For me." She nodded. "If that's enough."

He nodded right back at her, a little harder and a little more enthusiastically. "Sure, it's enough. I don't want to lose touch with you. Ever."

She raised an eyebrow and grinned. "Ever? Don't get ahead of yourself. You're always getting ahead of yourself. . . ."

"You know what I mean," he said, embarrassed.

"Seriously, check in with me every now and again—please? So I know you're alive and nobody's zapped you or . . . fired *you* out of an airlock."

He vowed, "I will. Every night. Twice a day. However often you want."

She laughed and stepped back, holding out her hands to the stormtrooper, like she expected to have her wrists cuffed. The trooper responded, "Now who's getting ahead of themselves?" as he grabbed her by the arm.

As he marched Maize off toward the dune and the ship behind it, the other trooper looked back over his shoulder and said, "Good luck, kid. With friends like her, you're going to need all the luck you can get."

Karr watched them leave.

With every step, the knot in his stomach tightened.

When they were gone, and when he could hear the whirring, revving sound of the First Order shuttle's engine, he turned to RZ-7.

"Arzee, what do we do now?"

"Keep moving forward, sir. Until we find what you need!"

"I agree," he said with confidence.

Then the droid added, "Or until your parents successfully rally the authorities to come and find you, like the First Order came for Maize."

"My parents don't have the resources to drag me home, but you're right. Eventually, her dad will remember the ship—or somebody else will. That's when they'll come for me."

The droid didn't argue. "Then we must use the time we have to do what we can."

"Did you have any luck? Did you learn anything about Kenobi or Skywalker?"

"None of the local droids I spoke to had any ideas," he said. "I suppose you had no luck, either?"

Karr watched the ship that carried his friend rise and take off. In a moment, she would be gone. Now more than ever he wished he had the power to pull ships from the sky the way Skywalker was rumored to have done. "No luck yet," he said. "But I'm not leaving until I find something."

He then turned and headed for one of the market stalls, scanning the different inhabitants for anyone who looked like they might know something or who at least could be trusted. His gaze fell on an old woman who gave him a smile that was missing a few teeth. Her skin was tanned to a dull, dry brown, and her eyes had the sunken, bloodshot look of someone who was permanently dehydrated. Karr got the impression she either was a thousand years old or had at least been there long enough to see a few things.

"Ma'am, may I ask you a question?" The woman nodded at him while keeping her smile. "Do you know anything about a Jedi named Skywalker who supposedly pulled ships down from the sky during the fight with the Empire here?"

The old woman nodded.

Karr's excitement skyrocketed. "You do?" He turned and called to his droid. "Arzee! I found someone!"

As Arzee's feet shuffled quickly through the sand, Karr turned back to the old woman. "I can't tell you how happy I am to meet you. My name is Karr."

She took his offered hand and continued to smile. "What's yours?" he asked. But the woman only nodded and smiled some more.

Karr started to feel a tinge of concern. "Do you know what I'm talking about?" he asked. More nodding. Now he had an idea where this was going. He gave a skeptical look to Arzee before asking the old woman, "You wanna buy a star? I've got one I can sell to you real cheap." She nodded again and continued to smile, which caused Karr to stop smiling. Clearly this woman was nuts.

From the next stall over Karr heard cackling. He turned to find the laughter was from some sort of humanoid species he wasn't familiar with. The being had a large, almost octagonal head, but only a small portion of it was taken up by a face. And Karr might not have even noticed his hands if the tall and slender being wasn't pointing one of three digits directly at the old woman.

"You're wasting your time with that one," the being said. "Been here a little too long, if you know what I mean?"

"That's what I was counting on," Karr said, knowing that wasn't what the being meant. "You don't know anything about a Jedi that pulled ships from the sky, do you?"

The humanoid pushed air through his lips in a way that seemed to suggest disbelief. "I don't know about that, but I've got one better." He leaned in and locked his narrow blue eyes on Karr. "I know of a Jedi that was pulled *from* the sky!"

RZ-7 and Karr exchanged glances. Clues were

clues, and at this point they were desperate for anything. But before Karr could say anything, the droid beat him to the punch. "Tell us."

The being craned his tapered neck left and right. Karr couldn't tell if he was being secretive or just struggling with the weight of his own head, until he began speaking in a hushed tone. "There's a desert moon that orbits Oba Diah. I'd tell you its name, but I doubt it has one. What it does have, however, is what makes it so intriguing: the crashed ship of a Jedi Master."

Karr's skepticism had not left him since the incident with the old woman. "When did this happen?" he asked.

"Long ago. Back before the Clone Wars."

"How do you know about it?"

"I know, because my family was responsible. As Pykes we deal in, well, let's just say . . . spice trade. But that's not where our talents end. And when a plan was devised to take down a certain Jedi Master named Sifo-Dyas, the Pykes were the ones recruited."

"I don't believe you," Karr shot back. "Jedi Masters are incredibly powerful. You couldn't—"

"Go see for yourself if you don't believe me," the Pyke insisted. "While I wasn't there personally, I am a descendant of the ones who performed the deed. The ones who blew his ship *out of the sky*." He emphasized the last four words.

Karr almost felt like this guy was trying to pick a fight.

"Why are you telling me all of this?"

The Pyke tilted his head a bit. It was a question he wasn't prepared for, but Karr could see him searching for the truth nonetheless. And after a moment he said, "Pride, perhaps? The Pykes defeated a Jedi Master."

"As the Jedi are most likely all dead now, it seems to me the Pykes aren't the only ones who have that distinction," RZ-7 observed.

The Pyke glared at the droid. "I'm not talking about the clone troopers taking out those traitors. You asked me why I shared this? That is why. Besides, it was long ago. I cannot assure you what you will find if you search the moon of Oba Diah. But sometimes the most valuable thing to remain . . . is the tale to be told."

"I plan on it," Karr said almost as a threat.

"Do it," the Pyke demanded. "Go to the moon of Oba Diah. Scream your questions to whatever corpses you find there, or whatever wreckage is left. But remember this: The reason you and the Jedi are both there is because of a Pyke. And if you're not careful, the Pykes will be the reason neither of you leave."

"Is that a threat?"

"A threat is not necessary. Oba Diah and its moons house many criminal outposts. Heed it only as a warning."

And with that he turned and drifted off among the various tents and vendors.

RZ-7 asked, "Are we really going to Oba Diah, sir?"

At first, Karr hesitated. Then he said, "You bet we are!" He mused for a moment more and then mumbled, "Spice trade. Didn't Maize say the ship we saw might have been a spice freighter?"

"Yes, sir. And I did discover traces of spices remaining in the hold."

"It's not much of a connection, but if there's nothing on the Oba Diah moon, we can at least follow the spice route. If that ship we were on was shuttling Jedi along its path, we might be able to find something. If not, we can always go home and break Maize out of prison. Start all over again." He clutched the comm device in his pocket.

But the droid didn't think it'd be so easy. "Sir, when we return to Merokia, you'll be sent to the trade school—and I daresay there's a chance that Maize will be sent to a reform school, perhaps even on another world. Did you hear those troopers talking about her? She must have a record already."

"She also has a father who doesn't mind using First Order resources to bring her home. If he wanted to send her away to some boarding academy for young criminals, he could've done that a long time ago."

The droid nodded and walked along beside him, and when they got back to the ship, they spent another hour or two between them—making sure they had a good, solid idea of how it worked. Maize had told them everything she knew, and she'd flown just fine. Surely the pair of them could do the same.

"I've updated my navigational protocols to the fullest extent possible," RZ-7 assured him.

"And I was listening really hard when Maize was talking."

The droid dipped his head. "I bet you were."

"Very funny. I can't help it if we get along really well."

"I was just making the observation that if you were searching for the romantic in you as opposed to the Jedi in you, we'd have already accomplished our mission."

Karr laughed. "I guess we would have. But then again, where's the fun in that? Now let's fire this baby up!"

The droid positioned himself in the copilot's seat and buckled in.

"Will do, sir. And I've already located the coordinates of Oba Diah and its desert moon."

"Excellent!"

Karr slipped into the pilot's seat. He wasn't 100 percent confident in his skills, and he didn't know if this quest would ever amount to anything, but he couldn't deny that it felt important. Was he in control of his destiny? Maybe, maybe not. Was he in charge of this very fancy ship? For the moment, yes.

He'd never in his life felt so free.

He'd also never felt more frightened or more lost, but he wasn't alone and he had the *Avadora*'s maps to guide him.

"Let's go, Arzee. Let's see if we can find a lone Jedi, lost on a moon with no name. We can do that, right? It's not a feather in a sandstorm, is it?"

"Not at all, sir," the droid replied.

Karr knew it was a lie. But he let it go. "This is going to be amazing."

"Indeed, it will be, sir. But soon, you should get some rest. The galaxy is large, and you are only human."

Karr didn't want to rest. He wanted to continue adventuring—but the droid was right, and Karr was exhausted. So after they successfully launched the ship into the atmosphere, which was no small feat considering its novice pilots, he decided it was time to nap and to dream. And to remember.

"I hate him!" Karr cried as he ran into his grandmother's room.

"Who?" she asked, putting aside the pattern she was working on.

"That stupid Zabrak! He broke a wing off my ship!"

"Calm down. A fourteen-year-old boy should not be crying over toys."

"It's not a toy," he argued. "It's a model replica of a B-class X-wing. And it took me forever to put together."

"Regardless, if you are to be trained in the Force, you must learn to detach from your feelings."

"I'd rather detach his arm from its socket."

"Karr!" his grandmother scolded, causing him to respond with a quick, "Sorry!"

"In the Jedi Order, attachment and possession are forbidden."

"The Jedi can't play with toys?"

She laughed. "That's not what I meant. The Jedi believe that attachment and possession could lead to jealousy . . . and ultimately the dark side of the Force."

Karr dropped the model ship as if he expected it to give him a disease. "Oh, no! I didn't just get the dark side, did I?"

"No," J'Hara said comfortingly. "But you need to focus on what's important in life."

Karr looked down at the model ship, which was now missing both wings thanks to him. "I guess I can do without a crummy spaceship."

"Yes, but it does not just apply to material items. It applies to living things, as well."

"People?"

"If need be, yes. And for that reason, Jedi are not allowed to marry."

Karr stopped what he was doing. "They can't marry?" This had never occurred to him. Not that he had anyone in mind, of course. He barely had friends as it was, and the one girl he sort of liked was a Twi'lek who wouldn't give him the time of day. But it was worth noting. "So they don't have family?"

J'Hara swallowed as if she was about to say more but instead just shook her head.

"Wow, that must be tough," he said. "Family is important." And though he said the word *family*, it was clear that what he really meant was J'Hara. Someone he could rely on. Someone who looked out for him.

Karr had always considered himself to be a loner, a kid who didn't need friends, but he was realizing that the term *loner* didn't really apply if you also had a sweet grandma who made you gloves. Did he have it in him to be a true loner? He would have to if he was to become a Jedi. That was what this was all about, wasn't it? What his grandma was helping him achieve?

"But even Jedi need friends, don't they? Wouldn't you wind up loving the person who taught you about the Force? About how to use it? It's a little confusing."

"You're not the first one to think that," she said. "And you're right, the relationship between master and apprentice is a strong one, but it only goes so far, in order to minimize the emotional loss when the master is no longer needed." J'Hara reflected on what she'd just said. "Although I'm guessing that was accomplished easier in theory than in practice."

"I agree," Karr admitted. He couldn't imagine what he would do without his grandmother. Would he ever find someone to replace her? No, *replace* was the wrong word. Would he ever find someone who would relate to him the way she did? Who could make him smile like she could? He didn't know. But those weren't questions that had to be answered. Yet.

# CHAPTER 12

By the time Karr and RZ-7 emerged from hyperspace, they found themselves on the Kessel Run, a specific route usually used by smugglers to transport spices to unsavory customers.

"I feel we might be out of our element here, sir," RZ-7 said.

"All the better. We already know what we know. Let's start learning things we don't know."

"I'd like to point out, sir, that I am fluent in many languages, but in none of them does that make any sense. Also we're coming up on Oba Diah and its moon."

The two travelers pored over the maps they were able to download. Not a great deal of survey work had ever happened on the sad little moon, and enough of it was classified by various militaries over the years that it all felt woefully incomplete.

"But look, right there. That's a canyon, right?" Karr stared closely at the holomap.

"I see cliffs, yes. I think?"

"Well, the rest of the planet is as smooth as an Umbaran's scalp, so let's start there."

The droid hesitated. "What about the criminals that Pyke warned us about? Do you think this is one of their settlements?" He indicated a little encampment a few klicks to the east.

Karr enlarged the map as big as he could make it. "I can't tell. On these images, it almost looks abandoned, doesn't it?"

"Let's hope it is. If it's not, this trip may not go as smoothly as the others have so far."

He tried not to let the dire possibilities dampen his spirits. "Let's set down on the other side of the canyon. Even if it's not an empty settlement over there, maybe no one will see us."

"Very good, sir, but let's be careful. This will be your first landing."

"I hear that any landing you can walk away from is a good one."

The droid said, "I tend to set a higher bar, but I guess that is true. However, if we can't also *fly* away from this landing, it'll mean we've crashed on a desert moon that might be abandoned or might be crawling with criminals."

"I hate it when you're right. Your diagnostics are up to date?"

"Yes, sir."

"And I've read every manual I could find in this thing, so between us, we're about as prepared as we're going to get."

"Very confidence-inspiring, sir."

"Thanks, Arzee. Now submitting coordinates to . . . a spot that looks like it might be a decent place to set down. I guess."

Ten minutes later, the *Avadora* dropped with only a couple of bumps and bounces at the bottom of the canyon's north edge—in a clearing that once might have been a waterway or might have only been a wide, shallow sinkhole that settled into dust.

"That was . . . not as smooth as I had in mind, but we can walk away—so I'm calling it good." Karr unbuckled himself from the pilot's seat and stumbled before getting his footing. The ship had landed on ground that wasn't quite level, and the boy was rattled from his first experience bringing a starship to a planet's surface.

Even a week before, he would've never dreamed it was possible. Now he was chasing Jedi rumors from system to system.

Even though he was still frightened and permanently overwhelmed, he grinned from ear to ear.

"Systems seem to be sound, and no damage is reported from the engines or shields, so I'd call it a success, as well." The droid unfastened his safety belt and wobbled, then steadied himself. "Scanning for fragments of heavy metals, or other signs of wreckage."

"Cross your fingers for Jedi remnants, not weird crime-family business."

"If I had traversable phalanges, I would absolutely do that."

Karr laughed. "You know what I meant."

"I did. And the ship's scanner has picked up evidence of a crash, I believe. A few klicks to the west of here."

"Seriously? Is it the shuttle?"

"Unclear, sir. I'm detecting pieces of metal, but nothing large."

Karr sighed. "Well, let's go find what we can. It's odd but I almost wish that Pyke was wrong."

"I understand, sir. He did have a little too much

exuberance in his family's achievement. But if we do find something that connects to the Jedi, then it's a win-win."

"True, true," Karr replied as he strolled down the ramp.

Outside, the air didn't feel too different from Jakku—hot, dry, and flecked with blown bits of sand and gravel. But the canyon offered a little protection and a lot of shadow, so it wasn't quite so bad as the desert land from which they'd come. At his hip, Karr wore a canteen he'd found in the ship's tiny galley area that didn't remotely qualify as a kitchen; on his face, he had a protective visor he'd found stashed under a seat—so the glare didn't blind him. He'd taken every precaution possible, but it still didn't feel like enough.

He set a beacon so he could find his way back and set off, with the droid moving cautiously behind him—bringing up the rear and watching for trouble.

For about an hour they poked through dusty channels, hiked up piles of rock that'd slipped down the canyon walls, and found a number of dead ends with nothing to recommend them at all. They hadn't seen any sign of other people, either—of any species or potential moral alignment.

For all Karr could tell, the whole moon was deserted.

"That isn't true, sir—there are small communities, here and there. Silicate miners, mostly."

Karr's lips were dry and cracking. He tried not to lick them, but it was hard. He pulled off his gloves and stashed them in his pockets; it was too hot to wear them, and there was nothing but sand to touch, regardless.

"I'll be quite content if the planet is bereft of dangerous criminals."

"Yeah, me too. Hey, what's this?" Karr stopped at the edge of a large trench.

"A geological feature of the moon?"

He shook his head. "No, look. It's like a drag mark etched into the stone. Like something big scraped along right here. Could have been yesterday, could've been a hundred years ago, but it's the only sign of disruption on this whole eroded planet, so let's follow it."

"Very good, sir. You may be right, and it can't hurt to look."

"Unless we find dangerous criminals."

The droid said, "Let's not tempt fate, shall we?"

"No fate-tempting, right." He walked along the

side of the trench, stomping through the upturned soil beside it. "Look!"

"What have you found there?"

He pointed down at a twisted panel of metal, wedged into the dirt. "That's definitely wreckage from a ship!"

"Oh, definitely. Yes, sir," RZ-7 said, in a tone that suggested he would roll his eyes if that was an option.

"I mean, it *might* just be trash, but it's probably not. Looks like a piece of heat shielding to me." He poked it with the toe of his boot. When the droid didn't argue, he left the scrap and started to jog. "Hey, there's a pile of rubble over here."

"Be careful, sir. You don't want to start an avalanche."

But Karr was halfway up the slippery hill of rocks and gravel, kicking down pebbles as he scaled the hill. Either he wasn't worried about falling, or he was too excited to care. "Arzee, I found it! I found . . . *something*. . . ."

The droid attempted to hike the hill, but stumbled and slipped. "If you don't mind, sir, I'll stay here and keep lookout."

"Works for me! You really ought to see this, though."

"Take some measurements with your recorder, if it's that important."

"Left it in the ship," he said, then hopped down the other side of the embankment.

There, sticking out of the sand, he saw a triangular piece of metal a bit taller than he was, casting a long, straight shadow in the sand. The metal shard had been broken off of something larger during a terrible crash—that much was clear. Here and there smaller pieces of wreckage dotted the landscape, but except for the big sharp piece, everything he saw was small enough to fit in a satchel.

"Do you see the shipwreck, sir?" RZ-7 called out.

"I see small metal pieces," Karr said. "That's all, though. If there's anything bigger, somebody's already carted it off."

Shuffling sideways on the steep grade, he crept downward. He slipped, fumbled, and rolled until he was flat against the biggest piece, standing straight up like a weird obelisk. "This thing has been here a long time!" he called, in case RZ-7 could still hear him.

The droid shouted something back. It sounded encouraging, not alarmed, so Karr didn't ask him to repeat it.

He saw a series of numbers on the metal shard's exterior, but he couldn't read them clearly. He used his sleeves to rub away the grime and found traces of red paint, along with what he assumed must be the shuttle's signature. 775519. If only he had a database of any kind, he could check the numbers to see what larger craft had sent the shuttle, and when, and why. But he had nothing but guesses.

Around the field of debris he paced, crawling and climbing, examining each piece and discarding it. Then he saw a slightly bigger chunk. A corner of one, anyway; the rest was buried in the sand. He approached it curiously and gave it a gentle kick. It didn't budge. It was heavy, and after a few minutes of digging with his hands, he realized that he'd found a small storage locker.

He heaved it up out of the hole, wishing RZ-7 was there to help. The back was ripped where the bolts that had held it inside the ship had sheared off. The locker had been jerked right off its mount and thrown free.

He pushed his visor up onto his forehead.

"A ship crashed here, and somebody took the wreckage away, but they didn't get everything," he said, trying to sort through his thoughts. "A Jedi flew this craft. Or rode inside it." When he said the words out loud, they sounded true. "Where did he sit? Where was he going? Why was he going there? Why did he crash here?"

Was he really shot down, or did the craft experience some kind of mechanical failure?

Karr had no way of knowing. He could barely fly anything, even the ship that had gotten him that far. Any effort at diagnostics would be useless. "At least the *usual* kind of diagnostics," he mumbled.

He pulled his trusty little blade from a pocket and began to pry at the warped metal. After three or four tries, it popped open with a creak and a groan. Inside, he found a tangle of loose wires that connected to nothing at all, and an empty life-support pack. At first, he didn't see anything else, but something told him to keep looking.

So he kept looking, pushing aside the wires and trash until he saw it: a roundish, palm-sized device made of a dully gleaming metal.

His eyes widened. He held it up to the light to get a better look, and when he was sure, he hollered out to RZ-7. "I've got something! I've really got something!"

# CHAPTER 13

While he waited for the droid to successfully traverse the sand, Karr turned the little device over and over in his hands. "Do you still work?" he asked it, and then felt kind of stupid. It couldn't answer him, even if it wanted to. It did not light up, hum, or produce any helpful images. "Arzee!" he shouted again.

The droid answered from much closer than Karr expected. "Right here, sir. Apologies, it took some effort to come this far."

"Look what I found!"

"A holoprojector? Very good, sir!"

"It was hidden, or maybe it just got tossed into the cabinet when they crashed. It's not working, though. Do you think you can help?"

"Sir, I will do my best to try."

While the droid poked and prodded the silent little unit, Karr peeled off his gloves and very gently touched the edge.

*Zap.*

Loud noises. Tumbling, rolling through the sky.

He jerked his hand back.

"Sir?"

"It's fine." He tried again. This time he saw things falling and heard lasers firing. Everything was out of control—sparks were flying, metal was squealing and bending. Emergency lights were firing, and alarms were wailing.

Then he saw him. A figure trying hard to fly the ship. The pilot wore a Jedi robe, and for a moment Karr reflected on how lucky he was that the Jedi wore such attire. At least it had always helped in identifying them in his visions.

But now it was too much pain. He felt the faint coming just in time to let go of the device and sit down. He drew up his knees and let his head fall down between them while he tried to catch his breath.

"A bad one, sir?"

"Real bad. The crash . . . all I can see is the crash."

Just then, a gritty grinding of tiny gears grunted from the holoprojector. Both Karr and RZ-7 jumped back, surprised.

"Sir, I think there might be some life left in the unit after all. Hold on, let me see. . . ." He tinkered and tweaked, and a faint blue light flickered weakly to life.

"It's working! You did it!"

"I do my best, sir." He pried open a small panel that had been gummed shut with sand. Another light came on, which then produced a tiny hologram.

It was pale and weak and riddled with static. But it played.

From what he could tell from his vision, the Jedi in the hologram and the struggling pilot were one and the same. He looked like a man who'd taken a beating, and he rocked back and forth in an effort to hold his footing. "This is Master Sifo-Dyas, en route to the desert moon that orbits Oba Diah. I'm with . . . with"—an explosion rocked the ship, if that's where he was recording the message—"Silman, flying emergency survival capsule number seven-seven-five-five-one-nine, and our long-range transmitter has been knocked out. We're under attack by the Pykes, and I'm preparing to jettison this projector in hopes that it will be found and—" The next few seconds were garbled.

"Oh, wow, Arzee."

"Indeed, sir!"

Sifo-Dyas came back into focus. "And the truth is,

we won't make it out of this alive." He looked exhausted and frightened, but determined. "If that's the case, so be it. But there are things that mustn't be lost. This is what it's come to—and I want . . . I want everyone to understand that I've done my best. Some may disagree with my methods, but these are desperate times and someone, somewhere should know: as you are aware, I have seen a vision of the future that I feel warrants an army. You've disagreed with me, but I felt I had no choice. Therefore I have ordered one: a clone army from the Kaminoans. Something must be done, and I made that decision. It may haunt me, and"—more static, garbled shouts from someone else in the shuttle—"or then again, maybe I won't have to live with that decision very long at all."

"Oh, wow . . ." Karr said again.

Sifo-Dyas faded out, then faded back in again. To whoever else was on the shuttle, presumably this Silman person, he called, "Hurry—we can't take another hit like that!" Then, to anyone who might find the message and hear it, or to the Jedi themselves, he added, "Come find me!"

The transmission went dead.

Karr was stunned. Elated. And numb. "Arzee, that was . . . that's a . . ."

"A Jedi Master, yes, sir."

"Not a vision," he was quick to specify. "Not a blurry feeling, but my first sight of an actual Jedi." He waited a moment to take it all in.

"It's happening, Arzee. I'm making a connection. First through the headaches, then by sharing the same space with Kenobi and Skywalker on that ship. And now laying my eyes on an actual Jedi."

"What's left?" asked the droid.

"I don't know. I'm not sure, but I keep feeling . . . they . . . they might still be alive, somehow. Somewhere."

"They will remain very much alive as long as you remember them, sir."

"That's true, Arzee, but that's not what I mean. I can't explain it, but I feel I'm going to meet one."

"Probably not Sifo-Dyas, I'm afraid."

"No, most likely not him. But maybe Sifo-Dyas knew Skywalker! Or Kenobi! Maybe he worked with them, or fought alongside them! And did you hear the bit about the clones? Is that true? Do you think it's true?"

"That they were created by a Jedi? I am unaware of any evidence to the contrary, and this tragic recording is evidence in favor of the story." As RZ-7 said this, the briefly revived old holoprojector fizzed and popped, and its lights went entirely dead. The droid regarded it sadly. "It's a pity we can't salvage the rest of the message, but I think that might be the last bit of life it had. Still, it did the job."

Karr nodded. "Sifo-Dyas must've made that recording just seconds before the shuttle fell out of the sky." He shuddered to consider it.

"I guess that Pyke was right, after all."

"And we practically watched his last words." A swell of emotion filled his chest. Again, he was so close to a real Jedi that he could almost touch him. He was standing in the wreckage of the very shuttle the man had ridden down from space, and he'd watched some of his very last moments alive. Which made Karr remember the Pykes again.

"Let's get out of here before any of those criminals show up," he said, sounding as exhausted as he felt.

"Good idea, sir. Where shall we go?" the droid asked as they hiked back through the canyon on the way to their ship.

"I could use some food. Let's get off this moon and see what we can find on Oba Diah itself."

"Very good, sir."

Back on board, they checked their maps and found a likely spot on the planet that didn't look too sketchy. Within an hour, they were sitting at the bar of a cantina, surrounded by various species, including a few in beige mining jumpsuits that were covered in the same reddish dirt that coated everything back on the moon. He and RZ-7 got a few odd stares, but no one interfered with them when Karr ordered a slice of the local bread casserole that tasted like cardboard and the same weird fizzy soda Maize had bought the day before.

It wasn't good, but it made him think of her.

"Sir, you should be happy. You found what you were looking for—the veritable feather in a sandstorm though it might have been."

"You're right, Arzee. I just keep feeling there's gotta be a Jedi out there somewhere. Maybe not Sifo-Dyas, possibly Skywalker, but someone." He sighed dramatically and let his chin rest on the rim of his cup.

A man who was one part bartender, one part waiter appeared at his left with a pitcher of the soda—offering to top off Karr's glass.

Karr raised his head, accepted the drink, and said thanks. It wasn't tasting any better, but it was wet and he was thirsty. He'd been thirsty for ages, now that he thought about it.

The man with the pitcher paused. "Did I hear you say you were looking for Jedi?"

Karr refused to get excited. He was too tired, so he simply muttered, "Yeah."

"You're in for disappointment, my friend, because they're all gone. Been that way for a long time. Since the Clone Wars from what I've heard."

"Thanks," Karr said, with more than a hint of sarcasm.

"Of course, if you wanna hear a *crazy* story, you should talk to Nabrun Leids. He's one of our regulars who claims he saw one about thirty years ago."

"Thirty years ago?" Karr suddenly got excited. "That's long after the Clone Wars." He leapt from his chair to get closer to the bartender.

The bartender tried to keep Karr's expectations in check. "Don't get too excited, kid. As I said, he's a regular here. And I wouldn't be surprised if he was a regular in every cantina this side of the galaxy, if you know what I mean. Which is why I call it a crazy story.

There are two things you'll never find in these types of establishments: a low tab and an honest tale."

Karr spun around and scanned all the faces in the room. "Which one is he?" he asked, ignoring the bartender's warning.

The man sighed as he pointed across the room. "He's the Morseerian sitting over there."

Karr stared blankly. He liked seeming like an experienced traveler, but the truth was, he wouldn't know a Morseerian if he fell on one.

The bartender extended his finger farther. "The tall four-armed green guy wearing a gas mask."

As Karr approached the pilot, he wondered if he was scaring the Morseerian but then realized his species just had really big eyes. "Is it true you saw a Jedi once?" he asked pointedly.

The smuggler leaned back and siphoned a swig of his drink through a special tube that went into his mask. "As true as the hopeful expression on your face."

It was clear he was about to launch into a story he had told a hundred, maybe a thousand times before, but Karr couldn't even wait for it. "Where? When?"

"In a place not unlike this one, in fact. I was having a drink when this kid, not much older than yourself actually, comes sauntering into the place. Truth be told, I probably wouldn't have even noticed him except for the fact that he had droids with him that had the owner yelling. Anyway, I'm minding my own business when this same kid gets into an argument with an Aqualish smuggler I know named Ponda Baba. Next thing I know, out of nowhere, an old man in a flowing robe ignites a lightsaber. Now, I had heard rumors about Jedi before, and I always figured they were a myth, but suddenly, there in front of me, illuminating the place with his sword, this magical knight swings his weapon and cuts the arm of that smuggler right off. I'm telling you, it might have taken a second, it might've taken a day. All I know is that time stood still. And then, just as quickly as it began, it was over. Everyone went back to what they were doing, and the old man went off with the kid to talk to a Wookiee. I know because I couldn't take my eyes off them. A real Jedi. And I'll tell you what else I remember. Though he didn't use it . . . the kid had a lightsaber, too."

Karr's face was warm. Not from the heat of a vision but from the excitement of knowing he was closer to the Jedi than he thought. "And you say this was thirty years ago?"

Nabrun Leids took another sip through his mask. "Let's see, I've been smuggling for about forty years, give or take, so yeah, somewhere in there."

Karr almost couldn't believe it. This was the second bit of proof he had that the Jedi existed after the Clone Wars. And if that was possible, anything was possible. "Where was it?" he asked.

"Well, that's not so easy to say. See I've been all over this galaxy, and after a while one cantina starts to look the same as the next."

"Come on!" cried Karr. "You've got to remember something!"

Then Karr himself remembered.

"Let me touch your mask!" Karr excitedly ripped off his right glove and unconsciously threw it to the floor. But since they were in a bar and that gesture usually meant a fight, the Morseerian went for his blaster. Lucky for Karr, the amount of liquid in the pilot's system sloshed to the left and Nabrun Leids went with it, crashing to the floor.

"No, no. I wasn't going to hurt you," Karr insisted.

But the damage had been done. "I think you should leave!" the bartender yelled from across the room.

"N-no," stammered Karr. "I didn't mean anything

by it, I just—Were you wearing that mask when you saw the Jedi?"

Nabrun Leids crawled back into his chair. "No. That one's long gone."

Now Karr was getting hot from frustration. "Can't you remember anything about the planet?"

"Son, I'm asking you to leave!" yelled the bartender.

But Karr kept his attention on the Morseerian. "Not one single thing?"

"I—I don't know. There might have been . . ."

"Might've been what?" Karr demanded.

But the bartender had had enough. "Take your change and go," he insisted as he threw the credits across the room.

Instinctively, Karr reached up to grab the change.

"Oh, no," he mumbled as the pain rushed to his head. If there was one thing that had traveled from one side of the galaxy to the other and had witnessed all the important events life had to offer, it was currency. Wars, births, murders, negotiations, graduations, scientific breakthroughs, coronations—it all created a storm of cluttered and confusing images that left Karr powerless to exercise what little control he had learned, and he felt himself blacking out.

But not before he heard the Morseerian say, "There might've been two suns."

When Karr woke up, he was staring at a Chadra-Fan. It wasn't as nice as staring into Maize's eyes, but it was a friendly face nonetheless.

"You must be a lightweight."

"What?"

"I've been watching you, and it seems you passed out after having only one drink."

"I wasn't . . ." Karr didn't feel like explaining. "Yeah. I'm a lightweight."

"I also heard you talking to Nabrun Leids."

Getting his bearings Karr remembered the situation and frantically looked around for the smuggler. "Where is he? Where'd he go?"

"Relax, he's long gone. And from the look of our bartender over there, I'd suggest you head out, as well."

Karr thought for a moment. "You know of any planets with two suns?"

The Chadra-Fan laughed. "I'm sure there are many out there."

Karr lowered his head. So close and yet so far. At least it was something.

"Listen, don't waste your time chasing crazy stories. The Jedi are gone, but if you wanna chase their ghosts, you should go to Batuu."

"Batuu? I've never heard of it."

"It's on the edge of Wild Space—the sort of planet that folks mostly pass through, rather than live or stay. But there's a fellow there, Dok-Ondar. He's the finest antiquities dealer I know. The finest I've ever heard of. Tell him I sent you. My name is Qweek, and we were once acquainted. It's been many years, but he'll remember me."

"Thank you, I appreciate it. Really," he added for emphasis, shaking the Chadra-Fan's hand.

"Happy to be of service."

RZ-7 watched Qweek return to the bar. Then he said, "What do you think, sir? Is it worth heading to the edge of Wild Space?"

"Definitely. He was . . . very specific. And clearly the more we've traveled the more we've learned, so why stop now?"

"Perhaps because every venture has also brought us closer to Hutt hangouts, First Order stormtroopers and various criminal elements?"

Karr laughed. "That was a rhetorical question, Arzee. Besides . . ." He closed his eyes for a moment. "It's almost like the Force is trying to guide me. Every time I'm about to give up and say it's too much, we get another hint. Another lead. Another name, or another place."

Just then, a pair of stormtroopers entered the cantina, pausing to stop and interview a couple of men near the door. Karr's stomach clenched, thinking of how they'd taken Maize and wondering if they were coming back for him and RZ-7 after all.

"So we're going to Batuu, sir?"

He nodded, keeping one eye on the stormtroopers. "We are *definitely* going to Batuu."

Together, they slipped past the soldiers and out the door before they could be next in line for interrogation.

Later, on board the ship, they headed out to a stable orbit to rest for what should've been the night—if they'd still been on Merokia. Karr hadn't wanted to bother; he was content to stay camped on solid ground, but RZ-7 reminded him of the possibility of criminals or bandits.

Out to orbit they'd gone, with the droid controlling the ship's systems so Karr could meditate. Ever since his grandmother had taught him how, he'd tried to make a practice of it at least once a day. He figured it was one of the ways he could learn to do the things the Jedi could do. And it didn't hurt that it didn't hurt. His brain, that is. But despite needing a clear head, his thoughts kept going back to Maize. He pulled out the holocomm she had given him. He patched into the ship's holonet transmitter, plugging into the network that connected the worlds of the New Republic. It might have been a risk, but he decided it was worth taking a chance, so he called up his friend.

She answered right away. She was sitting on her bed—or what he assumed must be her bed, since he'd never seen her room—wearing pajamas and looking like she'd just had a bath. Her hair was up in a towel.

"How's it going?" she asked him.

"It'd be better if we had our rightful captain still flying this thing, but I haven't destroyed it yet!" he said with pride. "I landed it today and everything."

"Really? Where are you now?"

"Orbiting Oba Diah." He began to tell her about all that he had found, but she jumped right in again.

"Oh, wow—that's amazing! I'm sorry I missed it. Well, believe me. This planet still stinks just as much as it did when we left, and now I'm on house arrest." She sulked.

He was appalled. "Really? They arrested you?"

She shrugged. "Not technically, but I got suspended from school and I am extra grounded. They put an alarm on my door, Karr. Can you—ieve it—An *al*—"

Karr noticed the communication cutting out. "Hey, Arzee! What's happening out there? The transmission is breaking up."

RZ-7 tried to diagnose the situation but informed Karr that sometimes bad reception was just bad reception.

"Maize!" Karr yelled, trying to get her attention. "We're breaking up."

Then, suddenly, clear as a bell she said, "We are? Because I don't even remember us dating."

Karr laughed. "No," he said. "I mean I couldn't hear you and I wanted to tell you about what I found. I think the Jedi might still be alive. And I found a piece of a puzzle. Regarding a missing Jedi *Master*."

Maize's eyes went wide. But before she could respond, the transmission went dead. Too bad, he thought. So much to discuss. So much to figure out.

But he was sure he'd have even more to share with her after visiting Batuu. Karr settled in to call it a night, even though the bright star that fed Oba Diah and its attendant desert moon was pink on the horizon line. He turned off the lights and let himself drift off to sleep, inspired by the words of the missing Jedi Master: *Come find me!*

# CHAPTER 14

Karr and RZ-7 emerged from hyperspace. The star streaks shrank down to dots, the boy got his breath back, and the *Avadora* was hovering at the edge of Batuu's atmosphere. "There it is. This is about as far as we can go, before we hit Wild Space. And out there?" He shrugged. "Who knows what's out there, past all this."

"Let's not go out there, sir." RZ-7 locked the ship into a stable orbit, and they both sat back in their chairs. "Past all this."

"I'm not planning on it," Karr said with a grin.

"Good. In that case, let's not go down there, either," the droid said, pointing to Batuu's blue-and-green surface.

"What? Why? Is it something about Dok-Ondar's place?"

"Not necessarily, sir. But each time we've ventured out, I feel we've come closer and closer to peril."

"That's part of exploring, Arzee. You've got to get used to it."

"I'd really rather not, sir."

Karr waved his hand in front of RZ-7's faceplate and jokingly attempted to use the Force on the droid. "You *will* join me."

The droid thought for a moment and said, "All right, I will join you."

Karr's jaw dropped. "Wait. Did you say that because of the Force or because you're agreeable?"

"Which would make you happier, sir?"

Karr waved his hand again. "You will tell me the truth."

"Yes, I will always tell you the truth, sir."

Karr buried his face in his hands. Next time he needed to program a less congenial personality if he was going to get anywhere. "Find the location of Dok-Ondar's place, please."

"Oh, I've already found a location for it." The droid pulled up some schematics. "It's inside Black Spire Outpost."

"Sounds like an exciting place."

"It might be, but we should do our best to avoid excitement, sir. We don't need to attract attention. As I mentioned, you say 'exciting,' but I say 'alarming.' There's not a great deal of . . . shall we say . . . rule of law on Batuu. People come and go as they like, without the eye of the First Order. Or anyone else."

"There's no First Order on Batuu?"

"Not so far as I know, sir. As I understand it, the Outpost consists almost entirely of a spaceport, a cantina, a market, and a merchant row—so on the bright side, we can probably find this antiquarian without too much difficulty. He seems to be rather notorious at this end of the system."

"Here's hoping."

No one at the spaceport gave them any grief, and hardly anyone asked questions when they parked the ship and left it there like they owned the place. "Seems friendly," Karr whispered gleefully to RZ-7.

"Sir, it's much more likely that a young man with a very nice, private First Order ship is assumed to be on the kind of business no one cares to interfere with. As long as neither one of us blows it by telling the truth."

"I won't blow it if you don't."

The droid nodded, then said quietly, "You must pretend you're Maize, sir."

"What? I'd never pass for Maize—my skin's the wrong color, I'm the wrong species, and I mean, come on. I'm a guy."

"I don't mean you should pretend to *be* a girl, sir, and certainly not a Mirialan—but it'll be worth it to pretend that you come from money and privilege. Walk straight, with your head high. Ignore questions if you don't like them, and get offended when pressed for information. Behave as if you don't owe anyone any explanations. That's what I mean."

"Got it. That's a good point. I have to channel my inner Jedi."

"When you're not channeling your inner Maize, yes, sir."

Outside the spaceport, the world of Batuu was a bright blend of civilized and wild. The Outpost was surrounded by forests and hills, punctuated with the spires of giant petrified trees that gave the settlement its name. The sky was vivid blue, the forest treetops were brilliant green, and the market was a loud rainbow of stalls, squares, and alleys that held everything anyone could ever hope to buy. Legal or otherwise.

It only took a minute or two of asking around to learn that, yes, RZ-7 had been correct—Dok-Ondar was an easy man to find.

Or an easy Ithorian to find, as the case may be.

The gray-green fellow walked with a thick wooden

staff that he used to point when he spoke. His thin, angular neck bent up at a ninety-degree angle, into a stalk of a head with large bulbous eyes that were framed with long white lashes. He was speaking to a customer in a language Karr didn't understand while a dark-skinned woman with a clean-shaven head translated.

But when the customer was finished and had left, the shop was otherwise empty and Karr led RZ-7 inside. It did not feel like a junk shop so much as an overcrowded museum. The shelves were clean and dust free, and most items were affixed with labels that explained what they were, and where they'd come from, and what they were worth. They were not merely stored but on display.

The items themselves ran the gamut from tiny buttons and robes to statuettes, helmets, taxidermic animals, and more. It would have taken a thousand years to alphabetize it all in any language—which might have been why nothing was arranged that way. It was clustered at best, stacked carefully at worst, and every stray space was totally occupied in an orderly fashion.

The Ithorian spoke, and the woman next to him translated for Karr. "Who are you, boy—and what do you want?"

"Hello, sir, my name is Karr, and this is my droid, Arzee-Seven," he said, not sure at first whether to look at the woman or the Ithorian. "A Chadra-Fan named Qweek sent us. We've come a long way to see your store."

Dok-Ondar grunted and spoke again. "Everyone comes a long way, if they arrive at *my* door," the woman translated. "You must be looking for something special. How can I help you, if you have the money to pay me?"

"We have credits," he insisted. "We aren't asking for charity."

"Good thing, too. I am a fair man, but not always charitable. What do you seek?"

Karr bellied up to the counter. "I'm looking for Jedi artifacts. It's for a school project," he added, since that had worked before. It wasn't as much fun to pretend without Maize beside him, but he liked the idea of having a story anyway.

Dok-Ondar nodded, as if acknowledging Karr was in the right place. His eyes bobbed up and down. "Jedi. You don't see them anymore."

"Right. That's why I'm looking for artifacts. Things a Jedi might have used, or . . . or even encountered. Do you have anything like that in this shop?"

"You're going to have to be more specific," the

woman (*What is her name?* Karr wondered) said for Dok-Ondar.

The droid said, "Literally anything. It doesn't have to be in perfect condition, or expensive, or fancy."

"Thanks so much for narrowing it down," he said with enough sarcasm that Karr could hear the tone before the woman translated his words. "I might have something particular in the back room that will work for you, and since you have credits, I will check. Go ahead and look around, but don't touch anything you can't afford."

"Got it. Yes, sir. Thank you." Karr nodded his head wildly, excited because he knew he had to be in the right place this time.

"Sir, what are you doing?" asked RZ-7 as his master wandered off.

"Don't worry. I'm just looking. This guy is the real deal, Arzee. This isn't like Plutt's storage room at *all*." He took his gloves off and shoved them into his pockets.

"*Do* be careful, sir."

"I'm not going to break anything."

"I wouldn't dream of suggesting it."

Down one row and then another, he followed his intuition and a tingle in his fingertips that might or might not have been imaginary. From time to time he glanced down at his feet to make sure he wouldn't trip as he navigated the shelves that reached from floor to ceiling.

Soon he was standing before a mask.

No, a helmet.

It was the color of dry bone, with an abstract design on the face and two small slits for the eyes.

"Have you found something, sir?"

"Arzee, the tag says it's a Temple Guard helmet. Do you think the Jedi had their own temple? I have to touch it." Before the droid could dissuade him or the Ithorian merchant could return, Karr gently, lightly touched the pale blank face on the shelf. Lightning flashed behind his eyes.

A sea of white. No. A wall of white. Moving toward him.

He blinked hard.

Not a wall. Men. Troopers. Clone troopers marching in formation, but divided in the middle by something black. The men moved with purpose. With precision. More like a ceremonial procession than a battle. A parade, maybe? Or an exercise? Karr could only make out their movement. The colors were sharp and then dull. Karr focused hard, concentrating for all he was worth, and left two fingers on the mask—daring it to give him more and silently promising that he could take it.

The guard wearing the mask saw them approach. But there was no feeling of danger. There was only familiarity. Karr squinted to see more, but he couldn't. But the guard saw who led the troopers. The figure in black. The driving force. Somehow Karr knew that, knew also that the guard was confused. Under his breath, behind the mask and for only himself to hear—except Karr could hear it, too—the guard said, "Skywalker?"

Then all hell broke loose.

Skywalker ignited his lightsaber and cut the Temple Guard down.

Karr could hardly believe it, and he didn't understand it; he wanted to look away, but there wasn't time, not even in a vision. Skywalker, if that was him, moved too swiftly, his violence as baffling and brisk as a magic trick. Blasters fired. Lightsabers swished. Bodies fell. People screamed. It was so hard to focus on any given detail, any given moment. The whole scene was a jerky, pale watercolor blur.

Karr gasped and released the mask, stumbling back

into another shelf—but RZ-7 caught him and kept him from wreaking any havoc or ruining any of the pricey stock.

"Sir, are you all right? What did you see?"

"I don't . . . I'm not sure. It was . . . it was *bad*, Arzee. Something went wrong. Really, really wrong." He gasped and clutched the sides of his head, as if he could use the Force to calm the pain. Slowly, he got his breathing under control and the pain along with it.

Did it still hurt? Yes. Could he see without feeling spikes behind his eyes?

Also yes. Improvement all around. But was it worth seeing what he'd seen?

Dok-Ondar emerged from whatever back room or storage space he'd vanished into, holding a large glass case, the woman once again at his side. He barked at them, and the woman translated for him. "What have you done? Have you broken anything?"

The droid answered to buy his master a few extra seconds to gather his thoughts. "All's well, sir. We were merely exploring. Karr has found this fascinating helmet, and we were hoping you could tell us more about it. . . ."

"Ah, the helmet of the Temple Guards," the woman

translated for the Ithorian. "So you *do* know some Jedi lore."

Karr wasn't about to argue with him, so with all the composure he could muster, he said, "Yes, sir, I find it fascinating. Are you sure this came from the . . . Temple?"

"The Jedi Temple, yes. Or it came from one of the fellows who guarded it, at any rate. As I'm sure you're aware, the guards were rendered anonymous with these helmets and their ceremonial robes—but I do not have any of their robes to sell, I fear. Nothing to go with the helmets, I mean."

Karr couldn't believe he could be so rattled by something that happened so long before. He took a few more deep breaths and tried to remind himself that no one else in the room took the journey with him. And that he needed to relax.

"It's a shame," agreed Karr finally. His vision had almost settled down, and he was hardly seeing double at all anymore. *Seeing double!* he thought. It reminded him of the clue he got from Nabrun Leids regarding the twin suns. He thought for sure the Ithorian might know of the planet he was seeking. "Sir, do you—"

But the master collector was already on to another

thought. "Let me show you what I found in the back," he said through his human translator. "I've found something of interest to you."

Karr was polite but was also intent on getting his question out. "Do you know of any planets that have twin—

"Lightsabers," he said with a gasp as the collector placed his case on the counter. "You have lightsabers!"

In an instant, Karr forgot all about everything that came before and focused on what was in front of him. "Real lightsabers!"

"A number of them, yes," Dok-Ondar said, drawing his long fingers across the glass case with a lock on it. Inside the case on a bed of protective foam and fancy cloth, Karr saw at least half a dozen deactivated lightsabers, lying side by side. He pressed his bare hands against the glass.

"Please, can I see them?"

"That's what the glass is for," the woman translator said in as dry a voice as possible.

Diplomatically, RZ-7 said, "Ah, yes—but my friend would prefer to hold one, so he can examine it more closely."

"Please, sir?"

But the Ithorian shook his head; it bobbed back and forth on his long neck. "These weapons are precious and dangerous," the woman translated. "They are for serious collectors or those who wish to train in the old tradition . . . if they have the money to do so."

Karr tried to do as RZ-7 had advised and act both entitled and offended. "Sir! I have plenty of credits, I'll have you know! Do you always insult your customers this way?"

"Only the ones who arrive in off-worlder clothing, looking hungry and . . . smelling as if they could use a bath."

"I beg your pardon!"

The merchant said, "And I beg *yours*, but I'd prefer to see your credits before I let you see these swords. If you were truly a wealthy collector, you'd know that is standard." He stroked the glass case and stared at the boy thoughtfully. "Perhaps if you told me the truth about why you wish to hold these things, then we could come to some kind of arrangement."

Karr insisted, "I told you the truth—it's for a project at school. And . . . and I'm very interested in the Jedi and their teachings, and their traditions. I only want to learn, sir. That's all."

Dok-Ondar craned his neck so his narrow face hovered above Karr's head. "Just for knowledge, huh? So you do not wish to become a Jedi?"

Karr was taken aback. "It's not like that."

"Isn't it? Be careful, young man. These are complicated times. You must be wise about the world in which you are unleashing your desires. You do not want the weight of it upon you if you cannot withstand the pressure."

"I only want to learn."

"And yet you still have not shown me your money."

Thinking on his feet, sticking with his story, Karr said, "You haven't given me any prices."

The Ithorian laughed, his hands fluttering and his underdeveloped chin bouncing. "You think you're quite the negotiator, don't you?" the woman said for him. "How about this, then—I say the lightsabers are not for sale."

"But—"

"None except for this one." Dok-Ondar pulled out an oddly shaped saber hilt from beneath the others. "Which is broken. It's the only one I might be persuaded to part with, and only if you ask more nicely than you've asked so far. I know a ruse when I see one, and I know a farm boy from a lesser world when I see one, too."

"I'm no farm boy!"

"Not literally, no. Your hands have held something softer than a plow. But you know the sort I mean." The Ithorian held the broken lightsaber close to his chest. "Such deception may work on lesser beings, but it will find no quarter here."

"I told you, I *have* money."

Dok flicked his wrist. "If you had money, you would've shown it by now—which means you have less than you pretend."

Karr was beyond frustrated. He hadn't come so far just to be turned down because of the way he looked. He waved his hand before the Ithorian's face and said, "You will give me the lightsaber."

Dok-Ondar stared blankly at the boy. So did the woman beside him.

Karr couldn't tell if it was working, so he tried again. "You will give me the lightsaber." Still nothing. So he added, "At a reasonable price.

"Please," he interjected one more time with another hand gesture.

Dok-Ondar locked eyes with the boy, and Karr felt

like he was looking directly into the Ithorian's soul. He could see it wasn't working. But that didn't stop him from waving his open hand once more as he said, "You will forgive me for even trying this." By then Karr had waved his hand in front of Dok-Ondar so many times it looked like he was checking to see if the shopkeeper was blind.

The Ithorian sighed and spoke. The woman looked like she was trying to fight a smile as she translated, "I am going to let you see it. Not because of the ridiculous stunt you just pulled. But because of the difficult path you have chosen if my suspicions are correct."

That made Karr feel uneasy, but he said, "Yes, please." The collector released the saber from his grasp. Cold and dead, its handle was in two pieces—both of which the merchant set down on the counter.

"This lightsaber belonged to an Inquisitor," the woman said.

"Not a Jedi? What's an Inquisitor?"

"The Inquisitors were the weapons of the Emperor, sent out into the galaxy after Order 66 to track down and kill any Jedi who remained."

Karr's mind reeled. He had never heard of these Inquisitors and had no idea the Jedi were hunted even after the Clone Wars ended. That would explain why they seemingly disappeared.

"When assembled," Dok continued to explain through his translator, "this particular lightsaber could be used in one of two modes: crescent or disc. In crescent setting, it would produce a single blade. When used as a disc, a second blade would appear—and do tremendous damage if spun around at any speed. It was a terrifying weapon when it was intact.

"Here. Tell me what you think. How you feel. Is this perhaps within your price range?"

Before there was any chance of talking himself out of it, Karr touched the nearest chunk of the lightsaber's handle.

Fireworks erupted in his head, but they were familiar fireworks and he ignored them. He pushed them out of the way and listened, and watched, and struggled to pay attention to the scene that flashed through his brain.

Then he jerked his hand back and stared wide-eyed at Dok-Ondar.

Quickly, he grabbed the other half of the saber and clutched it hard in his naked fingers.

He saw a figure. A Jedi? Perhaps, but different.

Then another. This one was definitely a Jedi. The two faced off in battle. Lightsabers swinging, robes swooshing. Karr could feel the tension and the fear in the air. It reminded him of the scene he had just witnessed involving Skywalker. The vision hopped, skipped, and jumped. Fires burned. Men shouted. He saw the figure catch a break and cut the Jedi down. The knight fell to the ground, the light of his saber and the light of his soul both snuffed out in one blow. Karr's vision darkened. All that remained was the glow of the survivor's weapon. Was it Skywalker again? Karr focused on the lightsaber. Followed it down to the grip and up the arm of its wielder. He was getting better at this. No longer were the visions as blurry, and the crispness of the image allowed him to glide along the length of the figure until he came to focus on the face. But it was a face that struck fear into the young boy's heart. Because the face—was his own!

Karr gasped. No, that couldn't be him. But it was, wasn't it? In a fraction of a second, a fragment of a vision. Karr was again wielding the lightsaber, again attacking the Jedi who swung his own in defense. But whose fate would remain the same no matter how many times Karr saw it. And no matter how many times it replayed in his mind, Karr saw himself slay the Jedi. The vision fizzled. It sparked. It jolted him back to the present.

Karr dropped the broken lightsaber, and he must've looked as grim as death itself, because Dok-Ondar stared at him like he'd just set himself on fire.

"Sir, are you quite all right?" RZ-7 asked. You don't look like yourself at all."

The merchant agreed with the droid. "You're pale as a ghost. Does that mean you've found something you want—or something you wish to escape from?"

Karr struggled to find words, failed, then managed to nod. "I . . . how much do you want for this? I'll buy this. I'll . . . I'll take it. This should come with us." He pulled out his credits and dropped them on the counter like he didn't care how many the shopkeeper took. He retrieved his gloves and wormed his fingers inside them.

Warily, Dok-Ondar looked at the payment. He pushed it back toward the boy and then looked Karr up and down with those bulbous eyes. "If this is so important to you," the woman translated, "if you're looking for more, or even looking to run from something—you might try a friend of mine. In exchange for this lightsaber, broken and worth very little, if I'm being honest with you . . . I would rather have a favor than your money."

"A favor? What kind of favor?" Karr asked, his voice a little shaky.

"I have a package I'd like to send to a friend. On Takodana, you will find a pirate castle and its queen, Maz Kanata. Don't look at me like that—like a frightened mouse. She's no danger to you, so long as you appear before her with pure intentions. I have something for her, and I have not yet been able to send it. If you'll serve as courier, you can have the lightsaber. Is that fair?"

RZ-7 saw that his master was still flustered and trying to gather his thoughts, so he answered for them both. "More than fair, good sir. We would be happy to deliver your package to your friend."

Dok-Ondar nodded. "Very good. But you must go straight there. That is my one condition. No detours, no side trips. Can you promise me that?"

Karr wanted to speak for himself this time but was still reeling so only nodded.

"Good," Dok-Ondar grunted. "Give me a moment, and I'll prepare it for her. Stay here. There are many things in my shop that are dangerous, to those who aren't paying attention."

He and the woman disappeared back into his storeroom, and RZ-7 turned to Karr. "Sir, what did you see? What is it that's rattled you so badly?"

"Arzee, I saw more Jedi fighting. One of them killed the other one—and the murderer . . . the murderer was me!"

# CHAPTER 15

Back on board the *Avadora* with their package for Maz Kanata, Karr sat in the copilot chair while RZ-7 readied the ship for another hop across the galaxy. The boy was still stunned, staring straight ahead through the viewport as if he could learn something from the open space on the other side, but it didn't tell him anything at all except that the galaxy was made of so much darkness, with precious little light.

"Sir," said RZ-7, "there is almost certainly a mistake. You are not a Jedi, nor have you ever been one. You could not have seen a vision of yourself dressed as one, because you've never worn such robes. You could not have seen yourself killing a Jedi, because you've never met one. There is some other explanation. We simply don't know what it is yet."

"I know what I saw, Arzee. It was *me*. I was the one with the lightsaber, and its beam was so bright. . . . It was green, and I held it like I knew how to use it."

"Another problem, sir. Considering you've had no

training and, if you'll forgive me saying so, no idea how to use one." The broken one was stashed in a cabinet back beside Karr's bunk, next to the package they were carrying to the pirate queen.

"I know you're right, but I *still* know what I saw."

"Your visions have never shown the future before, have they, sir?"

Karr shrugged. "Sifo-Dyas said he saw the future. What if I can do the same? What if I've seen my fate and it's not to become a Jedi, but rather to become one of those Inquisitors? I've seen so many confusing images, Arzee. I don't know what to believe anymore. Were the Jedi good? I saw Skywalker cut down his fellow Jedi like they were made of shimmersilk. What if they were bad? What if they deserved to be taken down? What if—"

Arzee quickly cut him off. "The answers are out there, sir, but one thing I know for certain, we're not going to find them tonight."

"You're right. Let's settle in for the night, or for a few hours at least. We can run this package to Takodana once I've had some sleep. And something for my stomach. Whatever I ate in that market, it's not agreeing with me at all."

The droid brightened. "Perhaps that's the problem,

sir! Indigestion could have affected your abilities. I'm led to believe that it's a mighty distraction for your species, and your family in particular."

"Yeah, we've got to watch what we eat, and I've been . . . pretty adventurous lately."

"Well, you've been planet-hopping, and you've made do. All in all, sir, I'd say you've done remarkably well and accomplished a great deal. One bad vision on one bad day does not undo all your progress."

"Thanks, Arzee. I appreciate it."

Karr left the droid to manage the coordinates and set the course, and he retreated to his bunk to get some rest, but all he could do was worry. Had he seen his own fate? The fate of someone else, a Jedi murderer from long before? His visions were seldom crystal clear, but this one had seemed so very close. So very terrifying. More than sleep, he needed distraction.

First he tried to call up Maize on the holocomm, but she didn't answer and he couldn't think of anything he wanted to say in a message, so he disconnected. He wasn't about to tell her that he'd seen himself murdering a Jedi, after all. Maybe he could tell her he was headed for Takodana, but a moment of paranoia stopped him. What if someone was listening? He knew that his signal had to snake through multiple connections to reach her, and any one of them could be compromised if someone had the know-how.

He didn't care if Maize knew where he was headed, but maybe he didn't want the whole universe to know just yet.

He still needed the ship, and he had a mission to finish.

And after that?

He folded his hands behind his head and sank back onto the small pillow that was barely soft enough to work as a pillow at all. After the trip to Takodana, maybe he'd just go home. At home, the odds of him murdering any Jedi Knights were very low—virtually nil—and at home, there was no need to worry about getting caught with a stolen ship or getting lost somewhere at the edge of the galaxy.

Then again, home wasn't even going to be home much longer. It was going to be a trade school on the other side of the galaxy.

He didn't know where else to go. He didn't know where to find the Jedi Temple, if it still existed anymore, or even the planet with two suns—and he didn't know who the dead Jedi in his visions were. In some ways, he felt he was spinning his wheels, making no progress at all. Were the Jedi getting closer or farther away? Was he becoming a knowledgeable protector of the galaxy, or was he stuck as the small-town boy who knew nothing more than useless facts like "Never stare directly into a double-haloed Tatooine eclipse"?

Karr shot straight up, his head hitting the low ceiling of the bunk. "Double-haloed Tatooine eclipse!" he shouted. "That would mean—I mean obviously that suggests—" He couldn't even complete the sentence. "Arzeeeeeee!" he screamed as he leapt from the bunk. "How could I have forgotten that?" he said to himself.

"What is it, sir?"

"Tatooine!" he declared. "Tatooine has two suns!"

"Does it?"

"Yes! At least I think it does. A pilot—some guy I was trying to barter with on Merokia—handed me his goggles and said, 'They're pretty good, but mostly for glare and protection. You never want to stare directly at the sun with them. Certainly not during an eclipse. And definitely not during a *double-haloed Tatooine eclipse*.' And I've never forgotten that—I mean I did, until just now, but I remembered again. That could be our planet with two suns that Nabrun Leids told us about."

"Indeed it could, sir."

"Set a course for Tatooine!" he bellowed. "We're on to something!"

"But, sir."

"Maybe a Jedi still lives there. Maybe he could train me to use my powers so I don't become a threat. Maybe he can explain what I saw!"

"But, sir," the droid repeated, raising his volume three quarters of a decibel.

"What?" asked Karr.

"We promised Dok-Ondar that we would deliver his package to Maz Kanata directly."

"Yeah, but . . . Certainly he would understand, wouldn't he?"

"We gave our word, sir," the droid reminded him.

Karr exhaled loudly. He could think of nothing more important than following a Jedi lead, but he also knew Arzee was right. He desperately wanted to hone his Jedi traits, but not at the risk of forgetting his own decent human ones. "Okay, Arzee. We'll head to Takodana first, but then we are definitely heading to Tatooine."

"Agreed."

Karr went back to bed, but his thoughts were racing, and they kept him company until they became dreams about swishing robes and swinging sabers.

A few hours later, he shot awake. He didn't know how long he'd been out, but after taking a moment in the refresher, he staggered back up to the cockpit to find a blue-and-green planet on the distant side of the glass. It took him a moment to realize that it wasn't Batuu anymore. Was it?

"Arzee?" he began.

"I took the liberty of making the hyperspace jump to Takodana, sir. While you were . . . indisposed. It was a short hop, with clean coordinates and a clear path with no First Order or pirates to be seen. I hope you don't mind and the trip didn't bother you."

"No?" he said, accidentally adding a question mark. "No," he said again. "That's fine. That's good, actually."

RZ-7 headed him off. "Glad to hear it, sir. I know you were disappointed we didn't go directly to Tatooine, but we might yet find something promising at this pirate castle. From what I've been able to learn, it's a special place. Anyone can come or go, but everyone must get along or the pirate queen herself will toss them out. So it would be in our best interest to be polite to her. Perhaps forget everything I said about channeling your inner Maize. I believe we will get farther on Takodana by playing nice."

"Hopefully I'm better at 'nice' than 'entitled.' "

"Now, sir," the droid protested gently. "You *did* get something useful from Dok-Ondar. Eventually."

"It wasn't anything I wanted to see."

"No, but that's always been a possibility—that you'd find things you don't want, and learn things you don't like. No quest is ever guaranteed a positive outcome, sir. I daresay that most of them come to less than ours has already."

Before long, they were down on the ground again, parked at the rim of a pristine lake on the outskirts of the castle owned and operated by Maz Kanata, the pirate queen. It was more of a compound in Karr's opinion, and RZ-7 agreed with him. "Or else it's the kind of castle that's effectively a city of its very own," he added.

"Kind of old-fashioned, isn't it?" asked Karr, staring up past the walls at the hundreds of banners flying over the buildings. They waved and flapped in every color, every shape, and every size, like decorative confetti against the clouds.

The droid checked his databanks. "By all reports, the castle has stood for a thousand years or more—and its mistress along with it."

Karr let out a low whistle. "Wow. Well, old things *were* built to last."

"Some of them, it would seem."

"I've got a lot of books that are antique guides, back at home. There are a lot of antiques out there, that's all I'm saying. Old stuff has a way of sticking around."

"Do you have the package we're meant to deliver?"

He nodded and patted the satchel he carried across his chest. "Right here. Let's go find this lady."

It wasn't hard to track down Maz Kanata, since everyone knew her and everyone was a little afraid of her—and a little affectionate toward her. Never mind the giant statue of her that overlooked the castle. You couldn't miss it, not even for trying.

Everywhere Karr and RZ-7 went, the response to her name was the same, and directions to her likely location all pointed toward the heart of the castle itself.

Karr wanted to try the dining hall first but confessed that it was mostly his stomach talking. "Maybe she has an office or something," he proposed loudly, since a fair amount of raucous music spilled out of the bar and into the street. "Or . . . living quarters, I don't know."

"Me either, sir."

A tap on Karr's shoulder interrupted their

speculation. He turned around to see a copper-colored droid of significant height and considerable age. Never before had he seen anything quite like the feminized humanoid design or the yellow sensors. "You are looking for Maz Kanata, unless I am mistaken?"

The droid's presence unsettled him for reasons he couldn't put his finger on. He said, "We have a package for her. From Dok-Ondar on Batuu. He sent us."

The droid cocked her head to the side and said, "A package from Batuu?" as if she wasn't quite sure if that was the truth or not. "Entrusted to two travelers from . . . elsewhere?"

Her tone implied a prompt and a question, so Karr answered it. He gave her his name and added, "This is RZ-7. We've been on a quest to visit and collect Jedi artifacts. As part of a school project. We met Dok-Ondar and he let us see some of his stock, then traded us this favor for an item or two."

This time, it might be best to stick to the truth—or a near version of it. The longer he stood there within the castle walls, the more confident he felt that it was sacred ground of some kind. He could sense the Force in that place.

The droid nodded and said, "Very good. I am

Emmie-Eightdeenine, though I am mostly called Emmie by the locals—and you may call me that as well, if you like. Come along and I will take you to Maz Kanata. She will be interested to see what you've brought."

"Yes, ma'am," said RZ-7.

ME-8D9 led them past the cantina and down an alley, through a door and down some stairs. "You are welcome here, as is everyone," she informed them. "For exactly so long as you can refrain from violence. All fighting is prohibited. All fighters will be evicted."

"Sounds fair," Karr muttered, following along behind her.

Soon they reached a level just below the cantina band, or that was how it sounded through the floor. The music rose and swelled and tinkled and thrummed, and if Karr had been feeling better, he might've tapped his feet.

But suddenly, he felt the weight of the place above him and the weight of the place below him, too. He was sandwiched between two heavy spots, and he struggled to stand upright.

ME-8D9 noticed, and she stopped. "If you'll tell me what's wrong with you, perhaps I could assist."

"It's not like that. It's just . . . it's very . . ."

He was still hunting for a word when a small person

appeared at the end of the corridor where they stood. "Heavy," she said.

The woman was tiny, perhaps half Karr's height. Her skin was brownish and very tight on her skeleton; she wore big round goggles that distorted her eyes and made them look bulbous. She could've been a hundred years old or a thousand years old. ME-8D9 could've told Karr either one, and he would've believed her.

ME-8D9 nodded respectfully at the wee figure. "Maz Kanata, these two have been asking for you—all over the castle. I do not think they mean any harm, and they claim to have a package for you. From Batuu."

"Batuu?" She approached Karr and popped up her goggles so they sat atop her head. Her eyes were much smaller that way, and they stared so intently that he was half afraid she could hear him thinking.

Could she hear him thinking?

She laughed. "No, you silly boy. I can't hear your thoughts, but I am very old, and I have spent a very long time watching people. I know a lost child when I see one. And I know a fellow who can sense the Force, when I see him struggling in a place such as this. But I'm glad to see you," she concluded. "It's about time you got here."

# CHAPTER 16

Karr was confused. His head felt like it was stuffed full of wadded-up fabric. "I don't understand. Were you expecting us?"

"I always expect everything!" she said cheerfully, peering up at him with those bright little eyes. "But yes, in particular—I was expecting *you*."

Karr took her in for a moment. "Because of the Force?" he asked.

"No. Because Dok sent a message."

Karr gave her a look as if he'd just been had, but she continued. "About a droid and a boy with a passion for Jedi artifacts that practically knocks him off his feet!"

"He told you all that?"

"In not so many words, yes. You are welcome, as I'm sure Emmie told you—but I can see that you are not comfortable here." She walked away from them then, gesturing that they should follow. "Come with me and I'll tell you why. I might be able to help."

"Help with . . . what?" asked RZ-7. "Our only task is to give you a package."

"Ah, but your *quest* is quite different from your *task*, isn't it?" Over her shoulder, she gave Karr a wink. "You feel a connection to the Jedi, to the Force. It's very strong, I should think."

Vaguely but honestly, Karr said, "I don't understand what's happening. . . ."

She cackled. "Quite the understatement, young man." She led him into what looked like an office. There was a desk with no chair behind it and two chairs in front of it. She did not go behind the desk but sat on top of it and crossed her legs. "Thank you, Emmie. I'll take it from here."

Emmie bobbed her head and made a discreet exit.

Karr and RZ-7 took the seats. Even with Maz positioned on the desk, they were all nearly at eye level. The boy reached into his satchel and pulled out the package Dok had given him, then held it out to her.

Without even looking at it, she took it and set it down beside her knee. "I like your gloves," she told him.

"Thanks? My grandmother made them for me."

"A family that makes things, yes. A good family to

come from. But you don't wear them for the cold, or for the protection from callouses, do you?" Before he could respond, she answered her own question. "No, you do not! You wear them so you can be choosy about the things you touch. That's more like it, yes."

"Yes, ma'am," he whispered. His vision wanted to double up again, but he fought it. He focused on his breathing—one, two, in, out—until he didn't want to close his eyes anymore.

"Young man, do you know where we are?"

"In . . . in your castle. In your . . . library?" The room was about the size of a bedroom, lined with shelves that were overloaded yet somehow tidy. On one wall hung framed paintings, light sconces, and some plaques in languages Karr couldn't read.

"Close enough, yet insufficient. This castle, as they call it—it's been here for a millennium. Before that, it was broadly thought to have been a Jedi compound, with catacombs beneath. This was only a rumor, you understand. But that may be why you feel it. . . ." She peered at him. "Both coming and going. The weight of the Jedi presses down on you, and it rises up against you."

"Catacombs?" he squeaked.

"The Jedi dead must go somewhere. Why not here?"

He couldn't think of a good reason, and the idea that he was sitting in a room above a Jedi graveyard thrilled him so much that for a few seconds he completely forgot about his headache. "They're buried? In a crypt, right below us?"

She corrected him. "They're *interred*, my boy. Not buried. *If* they are here. All Jedi are cremated, if possible—so if you want to get fussy about it, you should call it a columbarium. So you maybe are feeling their presence above and below, that's what I'm saying."

"Do you . . . do you feel it, too? Because if you do, I have to know—how do you stand it? I can hardly *breathe* down here."

She shook her head. "Oh, I feel *something*, but it doesn't hurt me. Whether that's due to my age or my own abilities, I suppose we'll never know—the Force works in different ways with different people, understand?"

"Maz, are you a Jedi?"

Her rusty little laugh came back again. "Me, a Jedi? No way. But I've known more than a few, and I have . . . my own sensitivity. It's not an easy thing to explain, but you know this. You tried to lie, rather than explain. I'm not upset. I understand the impulse. Sometimes a lie is easier for everyone, and when it hurts no one—who can mind it?"

"I didn't tell the truth because . . . well, I didn't think your droid would understand, and I was going to lie to you because I didn't think you'd believe me. Besides, not everyone we've met so far has a lot of love for the Jedi."

"Oh, I know that's true. The universe is a darker place for it, too. The Force requires balance, and these days it seems like the dark side is the only side getting any traction. These are difficult times indeed, to favor the light."

Maz Kanata went on to explain—in a little more depth than Karr's grandmother had done—what the Force was and how it worked best when it was in balance. "But balance is hard to come by, these days," she finished with a sigh. "Now tell me, how does the Force move you, young man?"

"Like you guessed about the gloves, I touch things."

"Guess? I did not guess!" she objected, but with good nature. "I never need to guess. That's not all of it, though. You're not touching anything now except for your bottom on the chair—and that chair has never known anything of the Force, dark or light or otherwise."

"Oh. Right. Um . . . I can sort of . . . I get visions, when I touch things sometimes. Especially if they witnessed great events. The Jedi visions are the ones I like the best. But they do hurt me—they give me terrible headaches—and sometimes I don't . . . sometimes I don't like the things I see. . . ." He lost the thread, thinking about watching himself murder a Jedi Knight. He wanted to confess it to her but couldn't make himself speak those words.

"Oh, enough of your uncertainty. You're learning every hour, unless I'm wrong. And I'm almost never wrong," she assured him, thoughtfully tapping her finger on the side of her jaw. "When I first saw you, I thought you might collapse under the weight of your own pain. But now? You're uncomfortable, yes. But you're hardly dying."

She was right, and he agreed with her. "It still hurts, but . . ."

"But you're finding the balance, without even meaning to. You're finding the place that's level." On the desk was a clear glass filled halfway with milk. She picked it up and showed it to him. "Do you see where the surface lies? If I tip the glass to the left, the surface tips high to the left and low to the right. And the reverse, when I tip it the other way. But if I hold it still—even if I swish it a little first, like this!—you watch, and it'll . . . settle. It soon finds its level. Its *balance*. You're doing the very same thing, though I'm sure you couldn't explain it if I tried to force you."

"You've got me there. I don't know how it happens, or how to control it."

"But you're getting better at it, all the same. The Force is both a subject and a teacher. If you listen to it, you will learn a great deal. Now, I have a thought. I have . . . more than a few things which once belonged to the Jedi. I do not have the curated collection of my friend Dok-Ondar, but there are quality items to be found all the same! I will give you one to hold, as a test, and you can tell me what it says to you."

"How will you know that I'm right? Or that I'm telling the truth?" he asked.

"I will choose something with which I'm already familiar. I will give you something, but only if I know its history. One moment," she said. Then she hopped off the desk and disappeared into the hall.

When she was gone, RZ-7 said quietly, "Sir, you do

appear to be feeling better, if you don't mind me saying so. The color's come back into your face, and your heart rate is returning to a normal range."

"I don't feel great, but I do feel better. Sitting down helps."

Maz returned a minute later, holding something round on a wide ribbon. "Here," she said. "Take off your gloves."

Karr removed them and left them in his lap. He held out his hands.

"Do you feel it?" she asked him. "From there?"

She was still standing maybe three meters away. He said, "I don't know—I can't tell. There's so much . . . background noise."

"Fair enough. How about now?" She came closer by a few steps.

There it was, yes. He could feel that. It came off the object in faint, pulsating waves that sharpened his fading headache. "I can feel it now." He reached out farther with his right hand. "What is it?"

She hopped back up onto the desk, where she apparently preferred to sit. "It was entrusted to me for safekeeping, some years ago—by a man who couldn't pay his bar tab. You'll know more when you take it. Go on, hold it. Listen to it. Tell me what it says to you."

He did as she asked, jerking back reflexively when the first touch zapped him. He recovered and reached for it again. Maz Kanata dropped it into his palm, where the object felt thick and warm and buzzing.

"What is it, sir?" asked RZ-7.

Visions were brewing in his brain, but they didn't flare immediately to life—so he went with what he could see with his own eyes. "It's a medal? A big round medal with some symbols on it. It belonged to . . ." The vision smacked him hard upside the head. The room went white, and then it went black, and he fluttered his eyes trying to find the balance. He pictured the glass half full of milk. He imagined it sloshing around, back and forth, light to dark and back again. He thought of the surface, level and smooth.

Stay in the vision but stay in the real world, too. Find the level.

"Go on. Tell me. What do you see?" Maz asked.

He tried to obey. "Two men. One taller, with darker hair. One smaller and younger. This belonged to . . . it belonged to Skywalker." That name again! "It was put on his neck . . . around his neck. A woman put it there. She had dark hair, in a long braid. There was a battle, and he was a hero. It was given to him for bravery, and in thanks for his service."

Maz interrupted, "Wait. You say it was Skywalker's? Are you sure?"

Karr nodded and Maz laughed, deep and loud. She slapped the table beside her and slapped her thigh, and probably would've slapped Karr if he'd been sitting any closer—so great was her hilarity. "That bastard!" she said merrily. "That tricky bastard!"

"I'm . . . I'm sorry?" Karr said, not knowing what the right response ought to be. "Did I do something wrong?"

"No! No, you've done nothing wrong, and you've told me something I should've known in the first place! That scheming bastard Solo, always a cheater when cheating is easy. One day, that man will come to a terrible end—you mark my words."

He still had no idea what was so funny.

RZ-7 declared, "Words marked, ma'am."

"The medal was supposed to be a reward from Leia Organa to the man who became her husband—Han Solo, may you never be so unfortunate as to cross his crooked path," she said, but she didn't really sound angry. She sounded amused and as if she felt a little silly about having ever believed that man about anything, ever.

"Karr," she said, using his name at last. "What I'm trying to say is that the swindler swindled *me*. He told me that the medal was his own, but he gave me his friend's instead. They all fought at the Battle of Yavin and were rewarded together—along with a very handsome Wookiee who would *never* cheat me in such a fashion, nor would he allow it to occur if he'd been aware of it. We're very fond of one another, and he would not treat me so badly. Don't let anyone tell you different."

"No, ma'am, I wouldn't." Especially since he'd only ever seen a couple of Wookiees in his life and couldn't imagine the day he'd contradict one—or anyone who cared about one.

"That pain in the rear he runs around with, though." She shook her head. "Well, you have shown me what I needed to see. You passed my little test. Now this one should tell you even more, if you're correct—and I have no reason to doubt you. I knew what Solo was when I took the medal. I should've asked more questions, not that it matters in the scheme of things, I suppose. They were all identical, I believe.

"Here, let us try something for which I now believe you are ready." With that, she produced the package that Karr had only just delivered to her.

"I don't understand. . . ."

"I do. Dok-Ondar does. He sent you this package."

Karr frowned. "But he sent it to *you*."

"He sent it to *me* so that I could give it to *you* if I deemed appropriate. Try to keep up, boy. Look, this should tell you a great many things about the Jedi, if you're strong enough to see them, which I now believe you are." She snipped away the twine that held the package shut and opened it to reveal a large cylinder of rusted golden metal. She held up the bruised and dented object and asked Karr what he saw.

"Is that . . . ? I guess it looks like an arm." It began a few centimeters above the elbow joint, where the jumble of twisted connection wires suggested it'd been ripped free of some poor droid somewhere.

"Very good, yes. That's precisely what it is. Although how Dok-Ondar retrieved it from the belly of the beast that swallowed it is beyond me. He is a master collector, however, and when he sets his sights on something, he does not rest until he acquires it. You know the feeling, am I right?"

Karr nodded. His journey to find himself, to find out about the Jedi, was both fresh and old. Granted, he and Maize had only left Merokia days before, but he'd been obsessed with the Jedi since his grandmother called out his connection to them years before. Since she had given him hope that his headaches weren't so much a curse but rather a blessing that needed to be nurtured. And that if he could learn about the Jedi, he could learn about himself. He'd done his best, but sometimes the galaxy must also play its part.

"We have reached that moment," she said, pushing it toward him as if she had heard his thoughts. "I want you to touch it, but you must prepare yourself. I know the droid who wore this arm, and I know how much he's seen, and how much he knows. This old arm may have quite a lot to say."

Eagerly, as if he hadn't even heard the warning, Karr seized the old metal arm with both hands.

And the whole galaxy exploded behind his eyes. He struggled to keep up with the flashes of images, one after another, two at a time, ten at a time. Men and women, coming and going. Starship battles, lasers flashing. The Death Star! He knew it in an instant, watched it collapse into a fireball the size of a moon—twice even—while small ships streaked away from it. He saw Wookiees and space slugs. And tiny Wookiees. Or . . . not Wookiees? Something Wookiee-like, certainly a forested moon or planet with these hairy little tribes of creatures who looked like toys, carrying spears and shouting battle cries.

He saw holograms and droids, two in particular—one astromech unit and a shiny gold protocol number, almost certainly the original owner of the arm.

He saw great sweeping dunes with large and small sand creatures. He saw murders and marriages, near misses and fatal blows. But most of all, he saw Jedi Knights! Bold and strong and everything Karr had ever dreamed of.

Padawans and generals, men and women and everything in between, human and otherwise, every color. Thousands of them across the galaxy.

Older people, younger people. Troopers and smugglers. Learning and growing, embracing the Force and letting it guide them. He learned of Order 66 and of Palpatine.

He saw strength and honor.

He saw.

He saw Skywalker, a child in a podrace. A teenage

boy Karr's own age, apprenticed to Kenobi. He saw them both, generals and masters, trainers and trainees. Fathers and sons. He saw a young woman with elaborate hair and beautiful clothes, quiet and thoughtful and wise but anguished. He saw children, a girl and a boy, who were separated as infants and sent to different corners of the galaxy for their own protection.

From their own.

From.

From the knight in black, who would've killed them both. From their own father, warped into something appalling, turned more machine than man.

He saw.

He heard . . .

Maz Kanata's voice. "There's much to see, I know. Does it hurt you, this time?"

"It . . . hurts . . . but it also soothes?" he said vaguely, unsure if it was true at all. He could scarcely hear his own voice above the ruckus. "It's . . . it's so *much*."

She nodded. "Yes, that's closer to the truth. But you can take it, I know you can. You need to. This was *for* you, one way or another. This is the story you needed to see and hear, in order to understand." She placed a hand on his shoulder.

Karr hadn't even realized that Maz had left her perch on the desk, much less that she was close enough to touch him. Reality moved in fits and starts, jerking him back and forth between what he saw and what he knew, between what he was learning and what he was feeling.

Gradually, the visions faded, and Karr began to find his bearings. Suddenly, he was alive, right then, sitting in a chair in Maz Kanata's office between Jedi ruins above and Jedi ashes below.

Finding a place in the middle.

Finding his balance.

# CHAPTER 17

When the long, dramatic vision was over, Karr sat in the chair across from Maz—holding the golden arm in his lap and staring at his hands, as if perhaps there was more yet to see. His mind cleared up, and nothing was doubled, but his eyes were filled with tears. Tears of joy. Tears of loss. Tears of elation. It was exactly what his grandmother had said it would be: *wonderful!* And he felt her there beside him. He had felt her the entire journey, really, and he was happy they shared that experience just as they had planned. His heart finally quit racing, and he stopped breathing so hard. When he looked like he'd collected his thoughts enough to speak, Maz asked, "How was that?"

It was the kind of question that required multiple answers, but he only had the energy for one. "Helpful."

Maz Kanata was surprised. "Helpful? Is that all? You've been given the history of the Jedi—or a large portion of it, at any rate. And all you have to say is that it was helpful?"

"No," he admitted. "It was wonderful, too. All of it. I've been waiting so long. Trying to piece together who the Jedi were and what the galaxy was like when they were around, even what happened to them, and you've given me all the answers. You've filled in the gaps and showed me things I never knew. There were *two* Skywalkers!" he shouted. "Father and son! How could I have missed that? And Luke's sister, the princess! Plus the way the Jedi were killed—" He stopped suddenly, remembering the ghastly image of himself he had seen.

"What?" asked Maz. "You don't look very content, for someone who just saw a bounty of riches. Why are you still perplexed? What else did you see?" she asked him gently. She had climbed down from the desk again and was standing at his side.

When he turned to look at her, she was at his eye level. "I saw everything, except . . . except for the one thing I *didn't* see."

RZ-7 asked, "What's that?"

He handed the arm back to Maz. "I didn't see me."

She gave him a soft, friendly pat on the arm. "Ahhh. Well, that's because this isn't your story, my boy. I'm sorry if that confuses you, but it's not a bad thing. Your story is yours alone, and you must make of it whatever you will, and whatever you can. Whether or not you ever follow the Jedi path."

A lump formed in his throat as he processed her statement. It was the ambiguity of "whether or not" that scared him. For the longest time he had convinced himself that becoming a Jedi was his destiny. And that if he could just learn the truth about the Jedi he would become one. But there he was, having learned all he could, all there was to know about them, and yet he was still unclear. He wanted to tell Maz about the vision he'd had where he saw himself killing Jedi, but he couldn't bring himself to do it. It was scary enough when she *didn't* know the answers. Karr could only imagine how paralyzing it would be if she *did*.

With that, Karr thanked her for her time and even squeezed her in a hug—then he and RZ-7 left the castle through the dining hall.

Slowly, they made their way back to their borrowed ship. Karr looked around at the castle and its surrounding market. He saw the same things on the way out that he had on the way in—flags, statues, monuments—but now he saw them through different eyes. Through knowing eyes. In fact, he was pretty sure he recognized some of the symbols on those flags from some of the moments in his vision.

"I guess I should get used to this," he said aloud.

"What's that, sir?"

"I see things differently now, Arzee. I mean, I guess you can't expect to learn as much as I did in one afternoon and not have it change the way you view the world, right? In some ways I'm processing a lifetime of information."

"More than one lifetime, if I've understood what you've told me so far."

"True," he replied. "There's gotta be a term for that, wouldn't you say? *Crash course*, maybe?"

"I think the term you're looking for, sir, is . . . *maturity*."

Karr stopped in his tracks. "I don't think this counts, do you? It's not like *I* did all those things."

The droid pivoted toward his master. "Sir, I understand that you just experienced the journey of the *Jedi*, but do not forget that it was your *own* journey that got you here. Credit must be paid to that journey."

Karr took that in for a moment and realized he couldn't argue with it. There was really no telling what experiences would change a person. The important thing was to keep having them. "Thanks, Arzee. You're pretty wise for a droid."

"Don't thank me. Thank my maker—wink, wink."

Karr laughed. "You're not supposed to say the wink part."

"Well, you can take that up with my maker, as well. He's the one who left the eyelids off."

As they walked back into the hold of the *Avadora*, Karr saw the broken lightsaber that Dok-Ondar had given him in exchange for the delivery. The same one that had complicated his life from the moment he'd touched it. He had asked Dok-Ondar for it impulsively, because he didn't want anybody else to see his vision—not that anyone could—but now he was sorry to even have it on board. As he stared at it, brief flashes of his most recent vision flickered at the edge of his memory. Skywalker—two of them, Luke and Anakin—and Kenobi, and all the lives they touched and ended, and all the Jedi who had ever come or gone. He still wondered where he fit in all of it.

"I'm confused, Arzee. What if I'm not meant to be a Jedi?"

"Sir, your sensitivity to the Force would suggest otherwise."

"But that's what worries me. What if I'm not meant to be a Jedi because . . . because I'm meant to be something else?"

"I don't quite understand, sir."

"Clearly I have something, but Maz said I didn't appear in that vision because that wasn't my story. The Jedi aren't my story," he said emphatically. "So what if I'm meant to become one of these Inquisitors, instead?"

"I believe we've learned that they no longer exist."

Karr was beginning to get agitated. "But what if they come back? What if my vision was of the future and I become some sort of anti–Jedi Knight. We know now that the Jedi aren't gone completely. Skywalker survived, his sister married, and surely there might be others out there who feel a connection to the Force as I do. But if I've learned anything it's that history repeats itself. What if the Force awakens and there are those who want to snuff it out again? What if there are dark side users who are meant to do such a thing, and I'm meant to become one of them? Look at Anakin Skywalker. He didn't set out to be bad. He was a good kid who . . . had a rough childhood, lost his patience, and lost his way. How do I know I won't have a similar path? You've seen me lately, Arzee. I got impatient with Nabrun Leids, I acted without thinking in front of Dok-Ondar. How much darker can my path get?"

RZ-7 paused. He was a mechanical being who was programmed to, among other things, express empathy, but even he had his limits. "Sir, if you don't mind me saying so, that is a projection based solely on unsupported evidence. Maz herself is also in tune with the Force, and yet she does not seem tasked with the Jedi's demise."

"But she didn't have a vision of her killing Jedi, either!" he yelled.

The silence hung in the air until Karr realized he had misdirected his anger.

"I'm sorry, Arzee. See? There I go again. Let's—let's get out of here."

"And go where, sir?" the droid asked.

Karr wanted to give some epic answer, some command that would send them both traipsing across the galaxy in their stolen (no, borrowed) ship until the First Order caught up to them—then they'd go down in a blaze of glory, fighting the bad guys in the spirit of the Jedi, if only to reaffirm his allegiance to them.

But he didn't. Because it was pointless. So all he

said was, "I don't know. We're almost out of money, we're completely out of ideas. . . ."

"And we're nearly out of fuel, sir. I suppose I ought to mention it. We'll have to top off the tanks somewhere. This place doesn't seem to have a facility we can use."

"Great. Then we'll be *completely* out of money. But you're right, we should. Maybe . . ." He paused as he slumped down into the pilot's chair. "Maybe we could go to Tatooine. It played such a big role for Anakin and Luke—they both grew up there—maybe it'll spark something for me."

"That sounds like a plan, sir."

Karr appreciated the enthusiasm, but he knew he was grasping at straws.

Within the hour the two travelers were camping out in orbit while RZ-7 plotted a course for Tatooine.

Karr was about to try meditating on the plan when he saw that Maize had left him a message on the holocomm. It was almost enough to cheer him up, the idea that she'd thought about him—even when he wasn't standing directly in front of her. It might be a personal first!

The message was short and to the point: "Hey, laser brain, let me know what's up."

When he called her back, she answered right away. It was great to see her face, even if it was very small and transparent in hologram form. "Hi!" he said with a wave. He hoped it sounded cheerful. "How are things back home?"

It must not have worked, because she immediately frowned. "What's wrong?"

"What do you mean, what's wrong? Nothing's wrong."

"You look like somebody died. Is Arzee okay?"

He nodded. "He's fine. I'm fine. I'm just . . . tired, is all. I experienced something really big today, Maize."

"Tell me," she said eagerly.

"I don't know if I can."

She immediately got offended. "What? After everything we've been through, you can't—"

"That's not what I mean," he said over her protests. "It's just that there was so much. I came upon an object today that basically told me all of it!"

"All of what?"

"All the history, all the tragedy, all of it. I know all about the Jedi Knights."

She snorted. "Sure you do. A week on the hyperplanes, and now you know everything there is to know about an order of mystical monks with shiny weapons."

"But I do!" he protested. "And it was amazing, Maize. Their story is unbelievable."

"Really? That's incredible. I can't believe you know all about them now. So do you know how to finish your training? How to become one?"

"Well," he hemmed a bit, "like many answers, it . . . it also led to more questions."

"Isn't that always the way," she said in a light-hearted manner that made him realize she didn't fully grasp the weight of it all. But he was fine with that. In fact, he preferred it. For the moment anyway.

"What was the object?" she asked.

"The what?"

"What did you touch that gave you all the information?"

"Oh! It was the arm of a droid."

"Really? Weird."

"Not so weird," RZ-7 argued. "I find droids are full of information. And . . ." he added, leaning his body closer to Karr, "quick to lend a *hand*."

The silence that followed was deeper than space itself. RZ-7 righted his posture and headed for the cockpit, throwing back a pleading, "If ever I need reprogramming, sir, please adjust my humor levels."

Maize and Karr waited for him to leave before they both started laughing so hard they thought they might never stop. Eventually, Maize brought them back on track.

"That's really wonderful, Karr. I can't believe you learned so much. Where do you go from here?"

Karr knew she meant that question to be a figurative one, but he didn't have the answer to that, so he answered practically instead. "I'm not sure. Thought about heading to Tatooine since that played a big part in the vision I saw, but then again . . . I don't know? Maybe I should just come home and give the ship back, before I end up in real trouble."

"Oh, it'll be fine. My dad doesn't really care about the ship," she said, although that wasn't the kind of trouble Karr was referring to. "If he did, he would've mentioned it when he sent the troopers after me. So don't worry too much about that. You're bound for trade school, anyway. What else can they do to you?"

"Execute me at dawn," he joked.

She waved her hand to dismiss the thought. "Like I said, nobody cares about the ship. If anyone gives you any grief about it, I'll remind them that I'm the one who stole it in the first place. You didn't even know how to fly when we left."

"Yeah, I did . . ." he said weakly.

"We both know better than that, but it's nice that you've learned your way around the controls. Or did Arzee?"

"We, um . . . we share navigational duties."

She laughed, and even though she was laughing at him, he smiled in return. It was nice to spend time with her. "Yeah, well. Is anyone on fuel duty?" she asked. "I'm guessing you're gonna be running out of it soon if you haven't refueled already."

"We know," Karr said defensively, even though it was RZ-7 who had actually called his attention to it. "We're just figuring out where to stop." Which reminded him. "Oh, hey, how's your list coming?"

"What list?" she asked.

"The list of places you want to live, for when your dad asks."

She let out a little laugh. "Oh. Well, my trip got cut a little short, if you remember. But between the stench of Utapau and the heat of Jakku, I think I'll stick with Merokia for now."

He smiled back. "Yeah. I'm beginning to see the appeal."

"Although . . ." she continued, "I did hear my dad talking yesterday, and he mentioned a place called Kijimi. If it's not too out of the way, maybe you can stop there for fuel and check it out for me. If that's the next place he's gonna stick me I should know a thing or two about it. Or at least enough to argue why we shouldn't go there."

Karr saluted the hologram. "Aye, aye, Captain."

Maize smiled. "Great. Then get back here as soon as you finish up," she ordered.

"You know we will," he said, and ended the call with a cheerful, "Bye!"

After taking some time out for a brief rest, they made the jump to Kijimi and set down in the Kijimi City spaceport, high atop Mount Izukika. Even before they docked, Karr could tell that he was outside of his warm-weather comfort zone. And so far, there was nothing worth recommending to Maize. Maybe the whole planet wasn't an icebox, but Kijimi City was almost invisible between the mountains and thick white drifts of snow, except for its glimmering lights. The spaceport itself was nothing to write home about, but it had all the usual amenities—and Karr had just enough credits left to fill up the *Avadora* with fuel to get him the rest of the way home.

They wandered the city for a little while, admiring the ancient architecture that reminded Karr of pictures of old monasteries, and the wide assortment of goods available for sale, but soon Karr was both too cold to stay outside any longer and too unnerved by the number of disreputable-looking types walking about, so they returned to the service station. They sat in a lobby with small tables and chairs and tiny, insufficient heaters stashed in the corners. Self-serve drinks were available from a bar along one wall, and small packages of snacks for a variety of traveler species were offered for a couple of credits apiece.

Karr picked a bag of chips that tasted mostly like salt and silicon, but it was better than nothing. RZ-7 stood beside him, keeping one digital eye on the ship—which they could see through the large glass wall that separated them from the work going on in the spaceport.

Karr shivered and said, "It's freezing in here."

"It's freezing out there, too, sir, if you remember. But we won't be here long, and no one else seems to mind it much."

"Everyone else is dressed for it," Karr said, enviously remembering the Kijimi residents in their thick furs and animal hides. He dropped the mostly eaten bag of chips into a trash bin.

He closed his eyes and leaned his head against the wall behind him. "I hope Tatooine has answers, Arzee."

"I'm sure it will, sir. But if not, were there any other planets that you saw in your vision that might help?"

"Plenty, actually, but if we're gonna keep planet hopping, we should really save up for our own ship. Despite what Maize says, sooner or later the First Order will come looking for the *Avadora*."

The droid said, "Sooner, *rather* than later. Or so I fear. Sir?"

"Don't nitpick, Arzee. It's just an expression."

"Not nitpicking, sir. Trying to warn you."

But Karr was still leaning back with his eyes closed. "Warn me about what?"

"The ship, sir."

"What about it?"

"Sir, the ship is . . . not unattended."

Karr opened his eyes. There it was, the *Avadora*, right where he'd left it. But it was surrounded by about a dozen First Order stormtroopers.

He watched through the glass as the refueling attendant listened to the stormtroopers, looked up, spotted Karr and RZ-7 through the glass . . . and pointed them out.

Even though they were probably a hundred meters away, Karr held up his hands, and RZ-7 did likewise. This was way more troopers than the two who had picked up Maize. Minutes later, half a dozen soldiers joined them in the lobby area. Most of the stormtroopers stopped and stood at attention. A man in a black uniform seemed to be in charge. He stood in front of the boy and the droid with his arms crossed. He didn't say anything.

So Karr got the conversation rolling. "You caught us," he told them. "Here's your ship. We didn't steal it, we just borrowed it from Maize. I'm sorry, but I'm done with it now, anyway. Just take us home already."

The officer in charge shook his head. "Home? You're

not going anywhere. First, you're going to answer some questions."

"I am? I mean, I'll try."

"Good. Let's climb on board for a little bit of privacy, and have a chat."

Karr put his hands down, since no one was actually aiming any weapons at him, and besides, no one had told him he needed to do that in the first place. Furthermore, his armpits were starting to hurt.

As the troopers marched him through the spaceport and up the ramp (with RZ-7 bringing up the rear) . . . Karr again began to question the severity of his crime. What could these guys possibly want?

They had their ship back, for crying out loud. What else were they on this frigid planet for?

He and the grim-faced officer sat down facing each other in the tiny sitting area that was hardly big enough for the pair of them—much less the droid, who hovered at the entry until he was told, in no uncertain terms, "Beat it, before I turn you into a can opener and leave you here to open freeze-dried snacks for the rest of eternity."

Then it was just Karr and the officer. His face may not have given anything away, but his posture said plenty. He didn't want to be there, he didn't like Karr, he didn't like droids, and absolutely nothing had ever made him happy.

Which became clearer as he leaned in and said with a menacing tone, "Tell me what you know about the Jedi."

# CHAPTER 18

It took Karr almost an hour to relay everything he had learned about the Jedi that day. The golden droid's arm had conveyed so much, and it was all still fresh in his mind. But when he glanced up, the officer's expression was one of confusion, emphasized by his gaping mouth.

"What the hell are you talking about?" he said. "I ask about a Jedi, I get a history lesson?"

"You asked me about *the* Jedi," Karr argued.

"I was talking about Skywalker!"

"So was I!"

"That's ancient history!" the man yelled. "I'm talking about now!"

It was Karr's turn to be confused. "I have no idea where he is. Do you?"

The officer rested his face in his hands and took a deep breath. "Were you not on a mission to find Skywalker?"

Karr shifted in his seat. "I . . . guess so. Yeah. In a way."

"And did you not find a clue as to his whereabouts?"

"No," replied Karr.

The officer leaned in closer, if that was even possible, his exasperation giving way to anger again. "And that's the part I don't believe."

Karr protested. "Do you think if I had found Luke Skywalker I'd be sitting here with you? I'd be kneeling at his feet, begging him to train me!"

The officer tapped his fingers on a datapad that was sitting on the table in front of him, its screen glowing but obscured so Karr couldn't tell what was on it. "Let's talk about this message you sent from the Oba Diah moon orbit."

"What message?"

The soldier checked some notes on the datapad. "The one where you say, and I quote, 'I found a piece of a puzzle. Regarding a missing Jedi *Master*.' Do you remember this conversation?"

Karr thought for a moment and nodded. "Yeah, I was talking to my friend Maize that night, after we found the wreckage and the holoprojector."

"The holoprojector? Is that where the map was?"

"Map?"

"You didn't find part of a map? Or anything else that could point to Skywalker?"

"Skywalker? No. I told you, I found some pieces of a wrecked shuttle that belonged to Sifo-Dyas, a Jedi Master from long ago. There was an old, mostly dead holoprojector. I got it to play its last message, but there was nothing in it about Skywalker."

Skepticism permeated the officer's being as if he had just bathed in it. He told Karr to stand up and instructed a stormtrooper to search him. After a very rude and invasive pat down, the trooper reported, "Nothing, sir."

But the officer wasn't satisfied. He knew holoprojectors were small and that they could be hidden almost anywhere. "Take your gloves off."

Karr did and tossed them on the nearby table. The man looked them over, but the only thing they revealed was that J'Hara had been a skilled tailor.

"What next?" Karr asked. "You want me to stick my tongue out?"

The officer sat back and licked his lower lip. "Bring the droid back in!" he shouted to no one in particular.

But whoever's job it was knew enough to respond, because Arzee was escorted back up the ramp.

"Sir, may I be of assistance?"

"I'm not sure," Karr admitted. "I don't think so."

But the officer took command of the conversation again. "You two are pretty close, I hear."

"Of course."

"It would be a shame if you had to go home without him."

"Without him," RZ-7 said curiously. "That would never happen. I am devoted to my master and would never leave him or—"

But before he could finish, the officer unholstered his blaster, clarifying what he meant.

"Oh," the droid emitted. "Now I understand."

Karr tried to explain that there was a misunderstanding. "I'm telling you, I don't know anything about Skywalker's whereabouts. Or about any map. I only recently even heard of him!"

The officer slowly raised his arm and pointed the blaster at Arzee. Karr's words quickened. "I'm telling you the truth! I've told you everything I know. There's no reason to shoot Arzee."

RZ-7 interjected on his own behalf: "If I may, I can vouch for Master Karr. He is an honorable—"

But when the officer didn't lower his arm, Karr resorted to an old tactic. "Wait!" he yelled. "Don't do it! I have a condition. I get these headaches, and Arzee is the only medical droid who has the knowledge and the expertise to help me. Please! I need him."

The officer paused, finally lowering his arm. "I'm sorry to hear that, son. Because we both know he isn't really a medical droid. And that means you're a liar."

The blast that hit RZ-7 sent him across the room, separating his arm from his body. "Arzee!" Karr shrieked. Without a second thought for himself, he leapt out of his chair and dropped to his knees at RZ-7's side. "Why did you—How did you . . . know?"

The officer stood up from his chair. "We know a lot of things, kid."

He turned his datapad around and pushed it across the table. With a couple of taps on the screen, the officer brought up a holo—and it began to play.

Maize appeared. She was smiling and talking with her hands.

Karr seemed confused. "That's my friend Maize."

The officer smirked in a wicked way. "You sure about that?"

Karr kept watching, and the faint smile he'd mustered began to fade. Maize was in her house—he recognized the furnishings of the main living area. She was sitting on her couch, talking in an animated fashion about . . . him.

"He found something," she said. "Something about a missing Jedi Master. And I know he's orbiting Oba Diah."

The holo ended there. The officer pulled the datapad back across the table and turned it off. "Still want to stick with your answer?"

Karr could barely look at the man. Instead he spoke to the ground as his shoulders sagged with grief. "I told you already. The missing Jedi was Sifo-Dyas. I don't know where Skywalker is."

The officer exhaled heavily through his nose. "Let's get out of here," he said to the stormtrooper.

The trooper used his blaster to gesture over to Karr. "What about him?"

"Leave him. He's not worth anything."

As the intimidating men left the ship, Karr slumped

the rest of the way to the floor. All this commotion and still nobody cared about the *Avadora*. He might as well take it for good, fly to the other end of the galaxy and keep going. After all, what was left for him at home?

Karr tried to swallow, but his mouth was very dry. Maize had ratted him out to the First Order!

His stomach felt hot and his eyes felt hot and his face felt hot. He was embarrassed and angry. It'd been stupid, hadn't it? Stupid to think that the cool new girl at school was really his friend, and that she really believed in him and his mission.

He wanted to curl up into a ball and die, but he didn't have the luxury of that option. He had to attend to his droid.

"Arzee, you're still in there?"

"Nowhere else to be, sir," he replied, a whisper of static breaking up the words.

"You're going to be okay. You're going to be okay," Karr insisted to himself as much as to the droid. "I can fix this."

"Not to doubt you, sir, but the odds of fixing me with what you find on this ship are approximately two thousand eight hundred twenty to one. In fact, it's the first time I can say with complete conviction that I'd stake my medical reputation on it."

Karr gave a weak laugh, more for the droid's benefit than his own. "Arzee, I promise you're going to be okay, but I want you to know something."

"Yes, sir."

"You're my best friend."

If droids could smile RZ-7 would have, but instead his eyes just flickered on and off as if he was pleasantly taken aback by the announcement. At least, that was what Karr chose to believe. But he would not get the chance to confirm it.

The floor was covered with parts of his friend, and he knew that his only hope of rebuilding him was to collect them all. He was so overcome with emotion, however, that when he reached out to grab part of the droid's casings, he forgot he wasn't wearing his gloves.

A vision, sharp and loud, went pealing around in the space between his ears. He heard nothing else. He saw nothing else. Not RZ-7 or the interior of the *Avadora*, clean and bright and sterile.

He saw his parents. At home. RZ-7 was powered down and sitting in a corner like a discarded toy, and his parents were talking with the casually anxious ease of people who are worried about many things—but not being overheard.

His mother was at her sewing machine, which had been hauled out to the kitchen table for a large piece of work. She shook her head. "One day, he's bound to find out. If not from us, from someone else. Maybe we should just tell him."

"No," his father replied. "It'll only fuel his obsession."

His mother didn't quite sound cold, but she sounded tired when she said, "It's still our job to protect him."

"And that's exactly what we're doing."

The vision swam, and Karr missed a few words, but he caught the last bit. "What he doesn't know won't hurt him."

"True," his mother responded. "But it might just drive him mad."

The edges of the vision fluttered and melted, and Karr felt many things all at once. First he felt stupid. It had never dawned on him to touch RZ-7, because they were practically inseparable. What the droid saw, Karr saw, and what they didn't observe together they shared with each other. It hadn't even crossed his mind that RZ-7 could witness something without noticing it.

Second he felt confused. What were his parents talking about exactly? What would drive him mad? Did he have a tumor? But most important, he felt angry—angry that he was being lied to about . . . something. Something big. And he intended to find out what.

Karr's stomach was in knots, but his eyes became steely as he stared at the empty pilot seat. He had learned a lot in the past few days, but had he learned enough to pilot the ship home by himself? He sat in the chair and buckled himself in.

*Hell, yeah,* he thought. In fact, there were a number of things he was about to do that he had never done before.

# CHAPTER 19

The trip back home felt infinitely shorter than the trip that had taken Karr so far away from it, just a few short days before. There was no more hopping, skipping, or jumping from moon to moon, star to star—it was just a straight shot back to the little planet of his birth, his entire life so far . . . and possibly his future, too. He paced in the ship on the final ride, wondering if he was making the right decision, fearing that he wasn't, but knowing full well that his anger and adrenaline made it his only option.

As he maneuvered the *Avadora* back through Merokia's atmosphere, he thought about all the things that had changed since he left. About the boy who had set out with friends to follow a tale and the young man who was returning home alone to finish the story.

No one was around when Karr landed the ship on Maize's family's landing pad, just as no one was there when they had taken off. He wished RZ-7 could see the great job he was doing bringing the *Avadora* in, and decided to include him anyway. "Look at this, Arzee! We've come a long way from just being able to walk away from a landing. Owned it like a pro!"

Once the ship's landing gear was fixed firmly and he had powered everything down, Karr grabbed what he could of RZ-7's remaining parts and threw them into a bag. He grabbed the bulk of the droid's body around the waist, and the two of them exited the ship like old friends coming home from a party. Only Karr wasn't ready to celebrate. He was ready for answers.

When he finally got home, he slammed the door behind him and stormed past his brother, shouting "Where are mom and dad?" Not waiting for an answer, he made a beeline for the living room, where he found his mother measuring the waist of a clothing mannequin.

"What are you keeping from me?" he demanded.

Looway Nuq Sin nearly jumped out of her skin. "Karr! Where have you been? I have been worried sick about you."

Karr ignored her and repeated his question. "What are you keeping from me?"

"What? Nothing. I-I don't know what you're talking about."

"Don't lie to me!" he shouted. "Not anymore!"

Looway tried to calm him down the way people do when they're stalling for time. "Honey, you're upset, but I don't know what you're talking about."

"I'm talking about the secret you and Dad are keeping from me. The one that's for my own good. The one that might drive me mad," he said, quoting his vision.

That stopped her in her tracks, and Karr knew he didn't have to say any more. Feeling both vindicated and slightly apologetic for frightening her, he gently took her hands in his own.

"Mom, I have an ability. I didn't ask for it, and I'm not always certain I want it," he admitted. "But it's mine and it's real and I'm learning what to do with it. It hasn't been easy, and to be honest I'm still scared. But now that Grandma is gone, I could use your help. I have flown across the galaxy looking for answers, and I am tired. But I came home because I'm starting to realize that the answers I'm looking for might actually be in the same place I'm running from. Now what is it you haven't been telling me?"

Looway fought hard not to cry, but eventually gave in to it. "You've grown so much so quickly," she said. "But I need you to wait just a little bit longer. I promise you we will tell you everything, but your father had to leave for a few days to purchase some fabric and I want him here for this. You should hear it from both of us."

That seemed acceptable to Karr. After all, he half expected his parents to continue lying to him, so waiting was no big deal.

Maize called him on the holocomm, but he didn't answer. Not even when she tried again. The third time she called, he tossed the device out the nearest window. She was the last person on the planet he wanted to talk to. Whatever she had to say, he didn't want to hear it.

Days passed. He made sure to wear the gloves all the time, because he was too afraid of possibly experiencing any more visions. They were too strong, and he was afraid of what he might see.

What if he saw the future again? What if he killed more Jedi?

Was the future fixed? Could fate be distracted and avoided?

If so, Merokia was probably the place to do it. Much as he complained about it, the truth was his home planet was safe. Sometimes he pulled the Inquisitor's broken lightsaber out from under his bed and thought about, just one more time, touching it with his bare hands.

The thought of the dying Jedi Knights always stopped him. The thought that their deaths were his fault—or would be his fault—kept him from trying again. It was too hard to think about. It'd been hard enough to watch once. No, if he stayed home and went to school and took up tailoring like a nice dull citizen, surely there would never be any Jedi blood on his hands.

The thought of a trade school didn't horrify him quite as much as it had a week or two before. Now he could see the upside.

The trade school was a long way away from his parents, who barely knew how to speak to him anymore. It was a long way away from Maize, too, and he never wanted to see her again after what she'd told the First Order.

Karr sat on his bed and tinkered with the still lifeless body of RZ-7. The droid was almost back to his old self, courtesy of a new set of circuitry and a plate that didn't match the rest of his finish but held all his electronic guts securely where they belonged.

He was just about to switch the droid on when he

heard a scratching sound at the window. He didn't look to see what was making it, although he had his suspicions.

The noise continued until he heard a faint crack that suggested something small had broken. It was the latch on the window. Then a small click. His window opened with a sticky sliding sound.

Karr turned to face the window. A pair of hands was pushing it up. It squeaked in the frame. It slid far enough to allow a person to come inside. A small person.

A teenage girl, perhaps. Like Maize.

She heaved herself up onto the sill and squeezed inside hands and head first, then collapsed onto his floor. She stayed there, huffing and puffing like she'd climbed up a tower—and hadn't just toppled over a windowsill on a house's first floor. "For crying out loud!" she declared. "What's your *problem*, Karr?"

*His* problem? He had told himself that when this inevitable confrontation took place, he would remain calm and collected, but now that it had arrived, he decided it was just easier to yell. "*My* problem? What are you even doing here? *You* are my problem."

"Um, how do you figure *that*?"

He flung his feet over the side of his bed so he

could sit there and glare at her while he fumed. "You set me up!"

"Excuse me? If by 'set up' you mean, got you off this planet and helped you go on a quest to find stuff to touch, then, yeah, I guess I *did* set you up! And very well, I might add. Think of all the galactic sword swingers you would've missed learning about if I hadn't."

"That's not what I mean and you know it," he argued. "You knew I was desperate to find the Jedi, so you used me. Used my abilities to try and sniff them out so that the First Order could find Luke Skywalker."

"What?"

"Thank the Force I didn't find him. I would have led them right to him, and if he isn't already dead, he most certainly would be thanks to me." Karr paused, the image of him slaying a Jedi still fresh in his mind.

She stood up and faced him, hands on her hips and feet planted far apart. "What are you talking about? I didn't do anything like that."

"I saw it, Maize. I saw your holomessage to the First Order relaying all the information I had told you. About my whereabouts, about finding a clue regarding a missing Jedi Master. They even knew Arzee wasn't really a medical droid."

She glanced over at the refurbished robot and looked as if she was about to ask what happened to him, but stayed focused. "Karr, I never sent any messages to the First Order. The only messages I ever sent were to my . . ." She stopped as her mind caught up with her mouth. "Dad."

"Who works for the First Order," Karr said.

Maize stared at Karr, but really was staring through him. "They must have intercepted the message," she said. "Or hijacked it or something. I swear, I never would have told them about you."

"But why even tell your dad?"

She suddenly erupted. "Because you're my friend, Karr! I wasn't trying to tell on you, you big jerk. I was trying to tell my dad *about* you."

He paused. "You told your dad about me?"

"Eventually he wondered what happened to the ship, so yes—I told him about you. About the boy I met on this new planet who made me feel less alone. And who I didn't hate hanging out with. I was trying to tell him that you'd done a great job, and you weren't all bad, and that you wouldn't destroy the *Avadora* or anything like that. I told him that you were cool, and you knew what you were doing, and you'd come home on your own before long. I was trying to convince him that there was no good reason to send the stormtroopers after you."

He narrowed his eyes. "But he did."

She threw her hands up in exasperation. "That wasn't my fault! I don't even know if it was his fault. He might not even know they came after you."

"Don't stick up for him."

"Karr, did the First Order drag you home? I'm thinking not, because someone did a horrible parking job putting the *Avadora* back."

"Horrible? That was an awesome parking job!"

"You were so far out of the lines I assumed someone finally bought you a drink at one of those cantinas."

Karr started to crack a smile but wasn't ready to forgive her yet. There was too much he needed to digest first.

"Look on the bright side," she said. "You're home safe, you're not in any *real* trouble—and you don't even have to finish out the school term!"

"How did you know that?" he asked.

She sighed heavily and sat down on the edge of the bed. "Moffat told me, when she brought my homework over to the house. I can't go back to school until I'm ungrounded and unsuspended, but they're letting me keep up on my work so I don't have to catch up all at once. I asked how you were doing, and she said she didn't know—but that your parents had pulled you out of school. And then you wouldn't answer the holo-comm, and I got worried. Do you hear that? I was *worried* about you, even though you're being completely awful."

Karr was somewhat deflated. His anger still simmered, but mostly he was just unhappy. "Give me a break! You broke into my bedroom and caught me off guard. I've had a hard couple of days, you know."

"If you'd answered the holocomm, I wouldn't have had to surprise you. Why are you blaming me for everything that happened? You ought to be thanking me. I got you out of the house and into space."

Maybe that was the problem, he thought. Maybe he was better off not knowing anything. To quote his dad, maybe what he didn't know couldn't hurt him.

Carefully, sweetly, she patted him on the back of his shoulder. "I only promised you an adventure. I didn't promise you it'd all shake out just the way you wanted. I'm sorry you didn't find any intergalactic crime-fighting sorcerers to teach you, but you found evidence of them. You proved me wrong. That's got to be worth something, right?"

"Maybe," he admitted, with the barest hint of a smile. "But it's not enough. Can you just leave me alone, please? My parents have been lying to me for years about something, and I'm about to find out what."

She waited another minute or two to see if he'd change his mind. When he didn't, she gave him one last pat—a little harder than necessary, in Karr's opinion—and left the way she'd come in.

He went back to working on RZ-7. Despite the complicated mechanics required to bring droids to life, he found their relationships the most simple. He meant it when he told RZ-7 that he was his best friend, and he smiled at the thought as he switched the droid's power back on.

"And you are mine, sir," the droid said, responding to the last thing he'd heard before losing power days earlier.

Karr laughed for the first time in a while. "Good to have you back, pal."

"Did I miss anything important?"

Suddenly, the door to his bedroom creaked open

and his mother's perennially worried face peeked in. "Karr? Darling, your father is home. He and I would like to have that talk with you now."

Karr looked back to Arzee. "We're about to find out."

# CHAPTER 20

Karr joined them in the living area, where his mother had prepared a small spread of milk and cheese and crackers, as if she planned to host company. "What's all this?" he asked, gesturing around at the table, the food, the chilled beverages. "Is someone coming over?"

Tomar said, "No, it's all for you."

Looway added, "You've hardly eaten since you got back. You need to eat. You can't stay locked up in your room forever, and . . ." Whatever else she'd meant to say, she didn't get it out. Her voice faded away.

"Does this mean you're finally going to tell me the truth?"

His parents looked at each other, as if they didn't know how to respond.

Karr tried again, pushing a little further. "The truth you've been keeping from me?"

His father took a deep breath. "Let's all sit down, eh? Yes, there are some things we haven't told you. Things we probably should've told you a long time ago, but we've had our reasons. When you hear them—when you hear all of it—I hope you'll understand."

"What if I don't?" he asked, dropping onto the couch, daring them to impress him with their transparency.

"Then you can die mad about everything, I suppose. I'll lay it all out for you, and how you respond . . . that's up to you." His dad took the seat across from him while his mother hovered nearby, chewing on some reddish cheese that stained her teeth.

Not knowing what else to do, Karr took a couple of crackers and nibbled their corners. He swallowed the first bite dryly, and asked, "Am I really dying after all? Is that the big secret?"

"No, nothing like that, thank goodness," his father said. His parents shared another nervous look, as if deciding who would be the one to spill the beans. His mother bowed out by disappearing into the kitchen. While she opened cupboards and made other useful-sounding noises, his father cleared his throat and began to speak.

"We haven't been entirely honest with you," he began, fidgeting with his own piece of cheese until his fingertips turned pink. "We had this talk with your grandmother, a number of years ago. We had different opinions on the matter, but since you're my son she obeyed my wishes."

His mother returned from the kitchen, an extra glass of milk in her hand. Mostly, she was looking for something to do with herself—or that was the impression he got.

His father continued. "I don't expect you to understand, but your mother and I had your best interests at heart." Karr braced his hands against the seat cushions.

His parents shared another look. Karr couldn't keep track of all these looks, or what they might be in reference to. But he didn't like them. He was about to scream in frustration when his father said, "There's a Jedi in your family history."

Karr was stunned. It was fortunate he was sitting down, because otherwise he would have surely fallen down. "What? Who?"

"My grandfather. Your great-grandfather."

"Grandma's dad?" he asked, feeling a bit betrayed.

"Yes."

"I thought Jedi couldn't have families."

"Well, apparently this one did," his father said. "I'm not sure of the situation exactly. I think something happened and he left the Jedi, back before the Clone Wars.

After all the Jedi were killed he went into hiding."

"Why didn't Grandma tell me? Why didn't you tell me? I've been struggling for so long."

"We didn't think it was relevant."

"Not relevant?" Karr said incredulously. "What are you talking about?"

Karr's mother finally found the courage to chime in. "Your headaches were getting so severe, Karr. We needed you to take them seriously. And we felt that if you knew there was a Jedi in the family you might dismiss them, or claim they were signs of the Force instead of getting the proper care."

"But they are signs of the Force. I know it now. Grandma knew it then! Why didn't she tell me her father was a Jedi?"

"The answer is we asked her not to, for the very reasons we already stated. She wasn't happy about it, but she respected our wishes."

"Mostly," his mother added with the raise of an eyebrow.

"She agreed not to tell you about him, but she said she couldn't stand idly by and do nothing, either. So we made the agreement that we would each address this in our own way. Your mother and I would continue to have you tested by legitimate medical professionals, and your grandmother would do what she saw fit to nurture what she believed was the Force."

"Don't misunderstand, Karr," his mother said pleadingly. "We would've loved nothing more than to believe you had some mystical power instead of a terminal brain tumor, but we needed to be sure. We needed to exhaust every possible option. You're our son. And we need to protect you. Sometimes your blackouts were so bad, we honestly wondered if you were ever going to wake up. We needed to face facts, and telling you about some family member that may or may not have had something similar was only going to confuse things. We needed to know for sure."

"Grandma knew for sure."

His father leaned wearily back in the chair as if he very much wanted a drink of something much, much stronger than milk. "Well, maybe grandparents have that luxury."

Before Karr could question what his father meant by that, his mother stood up. "The point is we believe you now."

This hit Karr almost as forcibly as one of his visions. "You do?"

"Yes," she continued. "But that does not excuse your running off without telling us. You had us worried sick, Karr. You could've been dead for all we knew. Your headaches were getting worse and you just disappear? Did you ever once think of us?"

"I'm sorry," he muttered, knowing full well that he hadn't thought about them, and feeling guilty about it. "But what changed? Why do you believe me now when even Grandma couldn't convince you?"

Maize announced herself with a polite cough and poked her head around the living room entrance. She greeted him with a small wave and a shuffling of her feet.

"Maize?"

Karr's father crossed to Maize and put his hands on her shoulders. "This young lady filled us in on where you were and what you've been doing. I have to say, I didn't like it. It sounded reckless and rebellious. But when she explained to us how you were going about it and the results you were having, well, I guess I began to see things differently."

"We both did," Looway said. "Keep in mind, from where we stood those visions could've been hallucinations brought on by the pain. There was no proof of anything. But then Maize told us about how you used those visions to follow clues and found people to verify your findings. And that's not recklessness, that's determination. That's bravery. That's . . ." She struggled to find another word, but Tomar stepped in.

"Let's just say it's anything but weak."

Karr smiled, knowing his father could never allude to anything without using a heavy hand.

"Now, granted we weren't there to see all this," he continued. "But I'd have to say the thing that won us over the most was how convinced Maize has become. You've certainly made a believer out of her."

"Oh, really," Karr said with a slow turn of his head.

"Don't look so pleased. It took me a while," she said with a laugh. "If I'd known you had an actual family connection to all that mystical stuff, I might not have given you such a hard time. Are you mad? Please don't be mad at me anymore. I was only trying to help. I know you didn't want them to know where you were, but when I found out just how upset my dad was when I went missing, I realized it probably wasn't fair to torture your parents, either." She stepped farther into the room, looking nervous. "Then once I started talking about our trip, I guess I couldn't stop. I thought we had fun, up until the soldiers caught me. And I'm sorry you didn't find exactly what you were looking for but I was trying to tell them . . ."

Karr's mother nodded and gestured for her to join them. "She told us how important it was to you, and how determined you were, and . . . well. In some ways it seems you might have uncovered the news about your great-grandfather on your own. But I'm sorry we didn't offer it up outright."

Maize leaned into his line of sight. "So . . . are you still mad at me? I'm not leaving until you tell me you're not mad."

He thought about saying something clever, like telling her to pull up a chair and get comfortable, because she wasn't going anywhere for a while. But he couldn't do it. He'd never really been angry with her in the first place; he'd been angry with himself. And his parents, too. He was still annoyed by their betrayal, but they had finally told him the truth. Even if it came at his urging.

Karr finally had a real lead on a real Jedi. Maybe a dead Jedi, but a dead Jedi in his direct line of ancestry! He was the great-grandson of a Jedi!

Thinking back, he realized Maz Kanata had never said he wouldn't be a Jedi, just that those particular visions were not *his* story.

"What was his name?" he asked everyone and no one in particular.

His father said, "Naq Med. That was his name."

"Did you know him at all?"

He shrugged awkwardly, the forgotten piece of cheese still dangling from his fingers. "Not really. He was gone before I was old enough to care. In retrospect, I wish your grandmother had been willing to tell you about him. She knew him better than I ever did, of course." He sighed and looked sad enough to take away the last of Karr's lingering angry feelings. "She *did* want to tell you. I know she did. It's our fault, not hers."

His mother wiped away a single tear and blew her nose on a napkin. "It was never our intention to hurt you, Karr," she said, pointing at him with the damp scrap of soft paper. "We only wanted to protect you."

"Yeah, but you can't. Not forever," he told her.

His father mumbled, "Not even for as long as we hoped."

"Stealing a ship, honestly," Looway muttered through her sniffles. "I couldn't believe it, when they told me. I simply couldn't believe it."

Maize held up her hand. "Um, *technically* I'm the one who stole it. He couldn't even fly. Not until I showed him. I'm a terrible influence on him. You can go ahead and blame me for everything, if you want. My parents always do."

Karr finally laughed. "This is unbelievable. It's the most unlikely thing I've ever heard, and I'm hearing it right after the most unlikely thing that ever happened to me—with the weirdest person I ever met."

Maize grinned. "Aw, thanks, Karr. You're pretty weird, yourself. Oh, by the way. I've been in your kitchen, eating your food. This cheese is actually pretty great." She grinned even bigger, showing off her faintly stained teeth.

"Help yourself," he told her.

"*Way* ahead of you."

# CHAPTER 21

Karr and Maize went for a walk around the family homestead. It wasn't much of a homestead, really—just a smallish house with a large dirt yard, surrounded at a distance by other houses of a similar description. There wasn't much of a neighborhood to speak of, but they walked around it together regardless . . . purely for an excuse to get out of the house and have something like privacy.

"I'm sorry I didn't come right out and admit I told your parents," Maize said. "But I figured it was their place to let you know when they were ready."

Karr shook his head. "You just cannot keep a secret, can you," he joked.

"Look, I admit to telling your folks, but not the First Order. There's a big difference."

"And your dad," he reminded her.

"And my dad," she admitted. "Fine, you're right. I *cannot* keep a secret."

The two of them laughed. It felt good to have things

back the way they were, with nothing between them. Well, almost nothing.

Maize stared at the ground while she walked. The paths weren't paved, and the roads were mostly sand. Her expensive boots were getting filthy, but she didn't seem to care.

"The truth is, Maize, I haven't been completely honest with you, either."

"You told my parents that I have Jedi powers?" she said with a laugh, but Karr didn't join in. "What is it?"

He didn't know how to begin, so he just described it as he saw it. Like one of his visions. "When Arzee and I were on Batuu, I touched a lightsaber that belonged to an Inquisitor."

"A what?"

"An Inquisitor. They were Force-wielders who were tasked with taking out the Jedi. Wiping out all the survivors of what was known as Order 66."

"I don't understand half of what you just said, but they don't sound good."

"They weren't. But the thing is, when I touched the lightsaber I saw a vision . . . of myself. Striking down a Jedi."

"That's not possible," she said. "You can't see the future, you can only see the past, right?"

"Well, there was a Jedi named Sifo-Dyas who could see the future, and I'm worried that maybe I have abilities like him. Maybe I can see the past *and* the future."

She stopped walking. "Wow. No wonder you've been so out of it. That's pretty heavy stuff. Where do you even go with that?"

"Nowhere," he answered. "Which is the other reason I came home. I'm too afraid to touch anything anymore, or go anywhere or even move, really. How do I know every step I take isn't a step in that direction? So I figure if I just go to trade school and keep my head down, then I can't possibly become what I fear."

Maize gingerly reached for his hand. "But is that any way to live? Karr, when I met you, what I liked most wasn't that you could use the Force. It was that you had a spark. That's really what makes you special. I mean, sure, it's pretty cool that you share something with a legion of mystical knights who protected the galaxy, but if you deny that spark, what difference does it make? Good or bad, you won't be you."

He kicked at a clod of dirt. It shattered against

his shoe. "I appreciate that, Maize. But I know now that Skywalker survived. More Jedi could possibly rise again. And if my vision of the future is true, then I'm a threat to them. Where does that leave me? What can I do?"

Maize started walking again, briskly, and pulling him along. "We change your future, is what we do!"

"What?" he asked as he stumbled forward. "How are we going to do that? And where are we going?"

She suddenly stopped. "I don't know, I just got excited. But who's to say your future is set in stone. Why are you at risk of becoming one of these Jedi killers and these other possible future Jedi are not?"

"I don't know. Maybe because they'd have someone to teach them."

"So that's it. That's what makes the difference? Just a person to show you the way."

"You're making light of it," he said, "but I've seen the visions. I know what can happen. Light and dark live side by side, and without the proper guidance, the temptation to slip to the dark side can be great."

"So," she said, "we find your guide."

Karr couldn't help laughing as he shouted, "That's exactly where we started!"

"Yes, but now we know more. Wouldn't you agree that if Naq Med were still alive he would be your logical master?"

"I would hope so."

"So . . . let's go find where he lived and start touching things. Didn't your grandmother say life would be your master?"

"Yes."

"Then this is even better! You know she would've taken you to his place if your parents would've allowed it. She was practically telegraphing a message to you to look for it."

"She was?"

"Yes. . . . Possibly. I don't know. Think back. Knowing what you know now, did she ever hint at anything or suggest something in between the lines?"

Karr thought for a moment. "I don't think so. My grandmother was always true to her word. If she told my parents she wouldn't tell me, then she'd keep that promise as long as she . . ." The idea hit them both at the same time, but Karr finished the sentence first. "Lived."

Maize was getting excited. "Did she leave you anything special when she died?"

"Just my gloves." He waggled his fingers, inspecting them for any secret etchings.

"That's not what I mean." Maize shook her head. "I meant like family records, stories she wrote down, anything like that."

He paused and thought about it. "I don't think so, but we still have a lot of her things back at the house. She lived with us, until she died. Her room is full of stuff—but it's mostly bolts of fabric and sewing equipment. After she died, my parents just stuffed her things into the closet, and now we store custom orders there—until we get them finished and the client picks them up."

"So . . . what I'm hearing is . . . we could go digging around in the closet, and we might find something."

"I don't see why not?" he said, but privately the thought made him feel weird. The idea of going through his grandmother's things without her permission was strange and intrusive, even though she was gone. But he couldn't come up with a solid reason to protest, so he didn't.

"Great!" She smacked him on the back. "Let's go check it out."

Back at the house they found no one and nothing

waiting for them. His parents had gone back to work and his brother still wasn't home from school. It was just Karr, Maize, and RZ-7—who had parked himself beneath the landspeeder. It needed a tune-up, and that tune-up was within his skill set.

"Sir, do you require any assistance?" he asked, looking up from underneath the craft.

"Not sure, but you're welcome to join us."

"Where are you going, sir?"

Maize answered for him. "Grandma's room. We're looking for Jedi clues."

"Jedi clues?" Karr smiled. "I think that's the first time you've ever called them Jedi, and not laser space knights, or intergalactic sorcery monks, or something like that."

"I'm running out of euphemisms," she told him. Then to RZ-7 she said, "We're going to see if Grandma left behind any good hints about her dad."

"Ah, yes. Well, very good, sir. I'll be along when I'm finished here. My recent refurbishing has inspired me to do the same for these overlooked items. But feel free to summon me if needed."

They went inside, and Karr led Maize to the bedroom that once belonged to J'Hara and now belonged mostly to hangers, bolts and stacks of fabric, suits of clothing that were almost finished but not quite, sewing machines, scissors, and paper patterns for everything from socks to wedding apparel. Most of the floor space was occupied by racks and crates, but there was room to squeeze between them and climb over them.

Against the far wall—pushed into the corner—was a bed, still neatly made.

Karr made his way toward it and sat on the side—gazing around the room. "Most of her things are gone now. Some of them we sold off, some of them we donated to charity."

"Okay, but everything else is in the closet?"

"Um . . ." He scanned the scene, trying to mentally eliminate all the things that his parents had crammed into the space since J'Hara had died. "Yes. And that trunk at the foot of the bed, that was hers. My mom's been using it as a stand for her tailoring dummies."

Maize went to the closet and flung the doors open. Quickly and efficiently, she pushed the clothes around and looked for anything that might be promising, stopping to stuff her hands into assorted pockets and feel around with her fingers. She turned up nothing until she asked, "What about that case up there?" She pointed at the top shelf.

"That's just luggage." He'd moved to the foot of the bed so he could pop up the trunk lid and go digging around himself. "She used to travel a bunch, but by the time she moved in with us she hadn't been anywhere in a long time."

"Did she go visit her father? Is that why she traveled?"

"I have no idea. It turns out, nobody ever tells me anything. Not until it's too late to do me any good." He pushed aside nightgowns and slippers, stockings and sandals and gloves. Down at the trunk's bottom he found a couple of datapads, but they only held romance stories. He flipped open some holocubes he found, but they produced no promising pictures or documents. He put them on the floor beside the trunk and kept going.

Meanwhile, Maize dragged the case down from the closet shelf and opened it up. "Oh, hey, it's not locked."

"Neither was the trunk. Anything good in there?"

"Hmm." She held up a dead datapad with a crack in it. "Maybe?"

"Doesn't look like it."

"Yeah, I think this thing's garbage. What else . . . ?" she asked herself more than him. "A little bit of jewelry. Some of it looks pretty nice."

"Just put it back in there. If my mom wanted to wear it, she would've kept it out."

Maize smirked. "Maybe she wants to save it for her daughter-in-law, someday."

"Or that. Wait, what's this?"

She stopped her digging around and looked up. "What?"

He scrolled through another datapad folder full of receipts and other stray bits of ephemera. "There are important records in here . . . or they would be important, if she was still alive. Travel documents, that kind of thing. Nothing that helps me, though."

"Well, I've found something in this case. Looky here. . . ." She showed him another datapad that was probably older than both of them put together. "It still works!"

At least, it lit up and began projecting images when she pressed a button, and Karr's breath caught in his throat. "There she is," he whispered. His grandmother appeared in a flowing layered dress. She was perhaps thirty years old, and very happy—she spun around as if to show the pleats and folds. Her lips were moving, and he thought she was talking to someone just out of sight. But there wasn't any sound, and the image was terribly grainy. It fizzled out after a few seconds.

"It looked like maybe her wedding day? Was that a wedding dress?"

He swallowed hard, but it didn't fix the lump in his throat. "Yeah. She made that dress herself. Is that all there was?"

"Yeah, sorry. That's all that was in there. I'll keep looking."

He went back to looking, too.

Between them, they tore the place apart—until Karr flopped back onto the bed with a heavy, tired sigh. "There's nothing here," he proclaimed, folding his hands behind his head.

"There's plenty here. Just not anything that'll point us toward your great-grandfather."

As she said so, Karr felt something odd beneath his head. He rolled over and shoved his hand into the pillowcase, then pulled out a holocube that had somehow escaped his parents' repurposing of the room after J'Hara's death.

"Karr? What have you got there?" Maize asked suspiciously. "Share with the group!" she added, just like a teacher would say in class.

He tapped the cube and it began to play its message. An image of J'Hara appeared in bright blue-and-white light, with a soft flicker. She was older—the way Karr had always known her and would always remember her. She must have made the recording shortly before she died.

The image smiled warmly. "Hello, Karr," she said. "I assume you're the one who found the cube and you're the one who's playing it. If not, then I'd ask whoever pulled it out of my pillow to give it to my grandson, please. This message is for him."

Karr was too stunned to even gasp. He stared, open-mouthed, at his beloved grandma—or the shade she'd left behind, just for him. He cleared his throat, but that didn't help the lump at all. It filled the back of his mouth, threatening to make him cry at any moment. He did his best to breathe around it and only kind of succeeded.

"Darling Karr, by the time you see this, I'm sure I'll be gone. I've felt death creeping near, in these last few weeks. I haven't wished to say anything because I didn't want to worry or upset you—for death should not be upsetting. It is inevitable. We all leave one another, in time."

His nose was starting to run, but his grandmother always had tissues next to the bed. Maize handed him one, and he blew his nose.

"Once I'm gone, there will be no one left to teach you about the Jedi, and I suspect that your parents think it's for the best—but we haven't always agreed on everything, including this particular matter. You can't help being what you are, Karr. It isn't fair to ask you to live with your abilities without giving you any guidance as to what causes them, or how you can best navigate them. I know that my own teaching was insufficient at best, but I hope you believe me when I tell you that I've tried. I've tried so hard, but I fear that it hasn't been enough.

"Your parents and I reached a decision a few weeks after your headaches began. We would each be free to attend to you in the manner we felt best, but under no circumstances was I to tell you about your great-grandfather. This seemed particularly cruel to me, but in hindsight I guess I understand their fears. Not everyone is born with the clarity they need to see what lies before them. Nonetheless, I gave them my word that I would keep my promise until the day I died. Which brings us to today."

J'Hara smiled, a glint of glee in her eyes at the loophole she had discovered.

"I've often told you not to fear death, and that in many ways it can be perceived as a gift. Well, despite my penchant for speaking figuratively, today I give you a literal gift.

"My father's name was Naq Med. And yes, my dear boy, he was a Jedi. Which, I imagine, is why the Force is strong with you. Do not take this blessing lightly, for it is not necessarily a common occurrence. While my love for the Force is strong, it has not favored me. The abilities you possess were not passed down to me or your father. No one knows for sure if the Force is shared through family lines, because as I told you, a Jedi has no family. Or at least they were instructed not to."

His grandmother looked away for a moment. A wave of sadness seemed to wash over her, but she continued.

"From an early age my father's path was laid out before him. He was to become a Jedi Padawan and fulfill his destiny of being a Jedi Knight. But at some point, he began to question his fate. He struggled with the idea of blind allegiance when he still had so many questions. And so he took it upon himself to leave the Jedi Order. Not out of anger, or spite, but out of love. Love for his independence and eventually love for a woman. I am so grateful for his decision and for the family I have. I loved my father and cherished the time I had with him. But sometimes a person cannot escape their fate, and soon the shadow of the Jedi caught up with him. And although he had not been part of the Order for some time, he was being made to pay for their actions, and he felt it best to go into hiding. I never quite understood it all, but what I do know is that he did it to protect his family."

She wiped a tear from her eye. "Don't misunderstand me, I'm not crying because of his decision. I'm crying because I miss him. It has been so very long. We would receive messages from time to time to let us know he was safe and so he could hear of our lives. But after he learned that my mother died, he lost something of himself. He lingered long enough for me to tell him of my son, and my grandsons, but now that I am gone, perhaps we will be reunited again and we can share all the things that could not be conveyed in those messages. I do not have any of those messages to leave you, and I am sorry. I destroyed everything. It would have been bad enough if our family secrets were to bring him harm, but worse still if bad fortune or the Jedi's enemies were to take the both of you.

"The reason I tell you all this, Karr, is because I am the only person who knew where he lived, and I believe that if you find his dwelling there will be a treasure trove of artifacts that can guide you forward in the Force.

"The last I heard from my father, he lived in a modest home in a rural region of a largely uninhabited planet called Pam'ba—in some marshy grasslands around the equator. All I know is that there's a river that leads to an estuary, and he's built a little house on stilts to hold it above the water. I wish I could be more precise, but he refused to tell me any more than that. And most of it, he didn't say at all. I gleaned it from his messages.

"I have argued with myself a thousand times as to whether I should save this knowledge or share it with you. In the end, I have decided to trust you with it. It's your own destiny, after all. It belongs to you as much as the gloves I gave you, the brown eyes you inherited from your father, or the Force that connects you to your great-grandfather. If you do go searching, learn what you can from his possessions, glean what you can from his life, but then burn whatever you find. Leave behind nothing. Not even his ashes—throw them into the water.

"I love you, my boy. Your parents love you, too. I look forward to the day when I will see you again and we can discuss all that you've learned. Be safe. And may the Force be with you."

The message finished playing and went dark, and when Karr finished crying, Maize asked him what he wanted to do.

He composed himself and simply said, "I want to finish my training."

# CHAPTER 22

Maize was still technically grounded, so she headed home before anyone could accuse her of sneaking out—even though she'd done exactly that. Either the alarm on her bedroom door wasn't very good, or she was as sneaky about climbing out of windows as she was about climbing into them. That left Karr alone with his grandmother's hologram, which he played over and over at least a hundred times, trying to milk new information from every line.

Every word. Every smile.

Nothing new jumped out at him, and everything was both thrilling and terrifying. If he were to go looking for his great-grandfather's dwelling, he'd be taking his life into his own hands. And what would he find? A lightsaber? Bones to be burned? The remains of a small house that years before had fallen into disrepair and toppled into a marsh?

But what he was really hoping to find was answers.

Naq Med's story was a cautionary tale in itself. He

had tried to change his fate but in the end was tied to it. Could Karr change what he believed was his path to the dark side?

This was his grandmother's last act of love, the promise of a quest to find the answers that could help him.

If Karr could actually get off Merokia one more time and find the little lost planet with the little lost house. If only he had a ship that could take him.

Maize had ideas.

Maize probably always had ideas, but she *definitely* had ideas about Naq Med and how to find where he lived. At night, via the holocomm she'd found outside his window and returned to him, she spun wild tales of breaking loose and stealing ships—her father's or someone else's. She talked about cashing out the fund her parents had set up for school and buying a ship. Even a junk of a ship like that space freighter on Jakku would still have a little bit of life in it.

"Maybe we could actually buy it," she proposed. "I bet Plutt would sell it to us."

"I think Plutt hates us," Karr said. "I think he'd probably shoot us on sight."

"You're so *dramatic*," she said with an eye roll he

could see loud and clear, despite the projector's poor resolution.

"*I'm* dramatic? You're the one who wants to . . . somehow . . . go back to Jakku and test the patience of . . . of . . . a warlord, or a scavenger king, or whatever that guy is."

"He'd never shoot me. I have money."

"He'd definitely shoot me, because I don't. And you don't even know how to fly that kind of ship, do you?"

She shrugged. "Eh. The principle is pretty much the same, as long as you're talking about civilian ships. Fighting ships are different, and big transport cruisers are different, but all the ships that are kind of in the middle? They're all the same type."

He didn't believe her, not for a moment. She'd been able to fly the First Order yacht because her dad had taught her, but there was no way that every other ship of the same size and caliber was exactly the same from a controls standpoint.

But he was learning not to argue with her.

He sighed instead. "There must be some good way to get a ship again. We did it once, right? It's definitely possible."

Maize got very quiet. "I have an idea."

"Oh, no."

"No, seriously. Let me . . . let me plan some strategy, call a meeting, see what I can do. Give me a day or two, though. I'm going to try something I've never done before."

"You're scaring me, Maize."

She replied with a mock-evil laugh that sounded something like "Mwoohahahahaha." Then the holocomm went dead, and Karr was alone again in his bedroom with his thoughts, his hopes, and his grandmother's message.

As it turned out, Maize was as good as her word. The next day, she sat her parents down for a meeting—a meeting that surprised Karr from several directions when he arrived at her house and saw her parents together.

"Your dad's back?" he whispered from the side of his mouth.

Louder, like she didn't care if he'd heard her, she said, "Yeah, he came back for the ship."

Her father cleared his throat.

"And me! Probably. Since I managed to get us in such spectacular trouble, I mean."

The meeting was stiff and awkward, but rich people

were weird; that's what Karr told himself. He smiled anyway and tried to use his very best manners—and then his very best holding still and staying quiet while Maize did the heavy lifting.

Vroc Raynshi was tall and slim and cleanly shaven. His hair was black and his face was narrow and sharp; it was the face of a man who was either quite brilliant or a little cruel, and possibly both. Anaya was a small, pretty Mirialan woman with green skin, a rounded shape and the bleary eyes of a woman who didn't like to be out of bed so early in the morning—even though it was nearly lunchtime.

Everyone waited awkwardly in the living room while Maize began her sales pitch.

She stood up straight and took a deep breath.

"First, I want to thank you both for being kind enough to hear me out. Don't worry, I'll try to keep this short."

Her mother looked at her father and asked, "What's this about, again?"

He flashed her a look that was partly annoyed and a tad impatient. "I'm sure she'll tell us, if you'll listen. It's about her and her friend. The one she ran off with." They both looked Karr up and down, as if he was a strange new specimen their daughter had brought home as a pet.

"Right, right."

Maize absorbed the passing interruption with practiced ease and powered on through her little speech. "Yes, I'm going to tell you. For the last year or two in particular, I've been getting a lot of sit-down talks about taking responsibility for my actions and behaving in a more adult fashion. That's what I want to talk to you about. It's very hard to prove that I've learned anything, or to demonstrate any changes in my behavior, when I'm stuck inside. I can't prove I've grown if I can't leave the house."

Her dad frowned. "Is that what this is? Are you lobbying to have your curfew lifted? I'm not sure we needed all this formality for that conversation."

She pointed at him. "Yes, that's what this is about. Kind of. Let me explain how and why, though. Let me tell you what we need to do. *As you may recall*," she said with emphasis, in an effort to bring things back on track, "when I borrowed the *Avadora* and left the planet with Karr over there . . ."

He gave a small, uncomfortable wave.

"I was angry and selfish, and I shouldn't have

dragged him along with me." She shot him a look that told him not to argue—that she was choosing her framing of the situation carefully. "I got myself in trouble, and I got *him* in trouble, too. But! We also had a grand adventure where no one got hurt, and everyone came home okay. So it could've been worse, right?" Maize's father nodded so slightly that the motion could hardly be called a nod at all.

"I think we can agree that it worked out for the best. We're all alive and safe on Merokia, and now I owe a great debt to my parents and my school, and to my friend Karr." She gestured at him like she expected him to take a bow, but he didn't. He only sat there looking nervous.

"And to Arzee . . . Where's Arzee?" she paused to ask. "You didn't bring him?"

Karr said, "My dad needed him for something, sorry."

She shrugged. "Okay, with the help of Arzee, he managed to pilot the ship without me, and without breaking anything—mostly because I'm such a good teacher."

Her father cracked the faintest of smiles. "Are we here to listen to you pat yourself on the back, my dear?"

"No! Of course not. I'm setting the stage, that's all. Father, you like to sit me down and talk to me about growing up and conducting myself like a good citizen and a reliable adult. That's what I want, too! And I've been trying to figure out how to do it, and I have an idea—but I'll need help from Karr, and we'll both need everyone's permission."

Her mother squeaked, "Permission for *what*?"

Maize's eyes were warm and wide, but Karr knew one of her con jobs when he saw it. He tried really hard not to grin.

"Permission to become a better person. A less self-ish person. A person who takes responsibility for her actions and her promises. Karr has recently learned the whereabouts of his great-grandfather's home, and I want to help him find it. I feel terrible about all the trouble I got him into, and I want to make it up to him. I want to take the *Avadora* again, for one more trip."

Her mother rolled her eyes. Karr choked down a laugh. So *that's* where Maize had gotten it from. "This is ridiculous," Anaya said.

"We finally got a real lead on Karr's lineage, but it's at the other end of the galaxy, of course. Here's what

I'm proposing: You let us take the ship one last time. You can put a tracker on it, or a monitor to check my flying and make sure I'm not doing any crazy trick maneuvers. We'll bring Arzee, and he can record our every interaction for you to review upon our return. I'll call home three times a day, every day, so you know we're all right and staying out of trouble."

"This is the most unlikely thing I've ever heard," Maize's father said with a slow shake of his head.

Maize was on top of it. "Yes. I realize this is nuts. It's a ridiculous thing to ask, and a ridiculous thing to try. But I owe him, don't you see? I need to make it up to him." Her eyes were so big and so damp, and Karr thought it must be nice to be able to cry on cue—instead of by accident at inconvenient times.

By any metric, she was putting on a great show. Even so, Anaya couldn't help asking, "Have you lost your mind?"

But Maize stood firm. "No," she said with surprising weight. "But I have *found* something. I've found an answer."

Karr looked at her curiously, unsure where this was going.

Maize took a deep breath. "You both know how unhappy I am every time we move."

Vroc sighed. "Not this again."

"Yes, this again," she shot back.

"You've always told me that when the time was right I could pick wherever I wanted for us to live. And so I gave that some serious thought. I wrote a list. At the top of one column I wrote 'Things I Want,' and on the other column I wrote 'Things I Need.' Then I started with the wants—warm climate, access to technology, an arts district, major spaceport, an active social scene, a *respectable* library," she said, turning to include Karr on that one before continuing. "Fine restaurants, maybe a zoo . . ." By the time she was finished, it had been so long that her mother felt the need to reapply some mascara.

"That's it?" her father said sarcastically.

"Then," she said, ignoring his interruption, "I started the needs."

There was a pause, and everyone wondered if she had forgotten the needs because there were so many. But instead she said, "And that's when I realized there was only one thing on the list . . . a connection."

This was enough to make both parents straighten in their chairs.

"Dad, for so long I've tried to hold on to you. To keep you from always leaving, because . . . I worry you'll forget me. And I'll be alone."

Vroc bowed his head. Karr could see that Maize's words were reaching her father.

"And, Mom, you're here, too, but it's like you're not here. I know you miss Dad and you busy yourself with things to distract from your own loneliness, but that doesn't leave any time for me. And so then I get mad and treat you poorly, as well. And no home should be like that. In fact, it got me asking myself what exactly makes a home. And though it took me a while, I think I finally realized that a home isn't just a place. It's a feeling. It's a connection. When I was traveling with Karr, we stopped in hot places and dry places and scary places, but never once did I feel alone. Because I had a connection. I had a friend. And I know that if we spent more time together as a family I wouldn't feel so alone whenever you had to leave. Or if we had to move again, or anything."

The room was silent, and Karr realized that Maize

had been true to her word. She *had* done something she had never done before. Her big plan to win her parents over? Simply to tell the truth.

Maize's father was the first to speak. "Honey, I had no idea you felt this way."

"How could you?" she said. "You're always gone."

Vroc looked sad. "I know, honey. But I can't just stop working."

"I know," she said. "But maybe instead of having the First Order shuttle you back and forth all the time, maybe . . . maybe you'll let *me* fly you there."

Karr piped up: "She really is an excellent pilot."

Vroc smiled. "I have no doubt. And I love that idea. In fact, maybe we can find a position for you on my team. An internship or something so we can spend even more time together."

"Really?" Maize beamed.

"Why not?" he said. "The First Order can do many things, but they can't stop time. And pretty soon you might be leaving us!"

"Not if we have a real connection," she said, placing her hand on her chest.

Anaya whimpered.

"Mom, I know what you're thinking. That Dad and I are going to have a bond that you and I won't have, but that's not true."

"You say that, but it's unavoidable. You're too much alike," she lamented.

"Well, that's why I got to thinking. This trip with Karr is very important. It's about family, it's about fate, and it's about legacy. So when I come home . . . I'd like your help in getting a tattoo."

Anaya's eyes couldn't hold any more tears and she burst into a full cry. "Really?"

"Yes. Even though I tease him a lot about what he doesn't know, Karr has taught me a lot. About the importance of the past, and keeping a connection to the people we hold dear. I'd like to know more about our heritage. About our family. And I'd love for us to do it together."

When everyone was done crying and everyone had been hugged, including Karr, Vroc and Anaya gave the two their blessing.

"You'll have three days—no more than that," her father said, trying hard to project the stoic demeanor he was known for. "You'll take the trackers, make your calls, and meet every other condition you've laid out. I will watch how you pilot the ship from here on Merokia and judge your skills. I can't have just anybody acting as my chauffeur."

Not to be outdone, her mother said, "Start thinking of what kind of tattoo you'd like to get."

Karr couldn't resist joining in. "For the record, Karr starts with a *K*." They all laughed before Maize playfully punched him in the arm.

When Karr got home to relay the latest exciting development, his parents were appalled.

"Why are you leaving again?" his mother demanded.

"I need closure," he said. "Now that I know there was a Jedi in our family, it . . . it changes how I see my visions." He certainly wasn't as good at lying as Maize was, but he barreled forward regardless. "Maize's family already said she can go with me, and they're letting us take their ship again so that they can keep an eye on us with trackers."

"And where are you going exactly?" Tomar asked.

He hesitated. He hadn't told them about the hologram message. J'Hara had left it for him, not them. He made something up on the fly. "I've been practicing with the Force, and I think I can use it to find my future."

"Does the Force work like that?" his mother asked.

"This is how I'll find out," he said. "I know what I'm doing. And I'll call you, too. I'll let you know where we are, and what we're doing. I'll answer every time you try to reach me. You *have* to let me go do this. It'll be *so much* safer this time!"

Looway still wasn't convinced. "You want us to reward you for running away from home by letting you run away again? Are you insane?"

"I don't want to run away again, I want to go with your permission." Karr wasn't accustomed to sharing personal things with his parents, but in this case he thought it might help. "On my last trip, I was lucky enough to learn about the Jedi. About a family named Skywalker and how their lives touched countless others through the Force. It was a good story, and it was a helpful story. But it wasn't *my* story. I'd like to see if this trip can shed more light on my story."

He could tell from their expressions that this line

of reasoning did well, so he tried to land the ship once and for all. "Closure," he repeated.

The discussion went back and forth a few more times. But in the end, a deal was struck: Karr could go with Maize on one last trip if he'd swear on his grandmother's grave that he'd go to the trade school next month, as planned.

It was a devil's bargain, but from where he was sitting, he had no other choice.

He made his decision. He made his promise. And he made his plans to find a little planet called Pam'ba, which was covered in grass and water.

# CHAPTER 23

Karr and RZ-7 met Maize and her father at the landing pad where the *Avadora* was parked. It was right where they'd found it the first time, docked alongside similar ships—some of them belonging to the First Order and some of them merely fancy and expensive. His own parents had said their goodbyes at home. It was all too much for Karr's mother, who spent the day in bed with a cool rag over her eyes. It was too much for his father, too—but he holed up at the shop and performed the smallest, most tedious alterations by way of distracting himself from the doom at hand.

Karr tried to keep his own nervousness in check, but the stern version of Maize's father—whom he thought they had said goodbye to for good the previous night—was back.

"Hello, sir," Karr said hesitantly.

The greeting got him a lifted eyebrow and a nod of the man's head, and that was all. Karr was a little taken aback, until Vroc slipped him a quick wink.

After inspecting the ship and testing all the functions, checking fuel levels, and running diagnostics, Maize's father pronounced the craft space-worthy for another jaunt around the galaxy. He gave Karr and his cobbled-together droid companion a once-over, too, and concluded aloud that they were mostly harmless.

"Thank you, sir?" Karr replied.

"You're welcome. I'd tell you to take care of my daughter and be sure to bring her back safely, but I think we all know that the odds are better that she's going to take care of *you*. Did you really fly this thing back home? Unaided?"

Since RZ-7 didn't claim credit or responsibility, Karr said, "Yes, sir. Maize is a good teacher."

He murmured, "Quite a trick, considering."

"I'm sorry, sir? What do you mean?" Karr asked.

"Only that I've taken her flying a few times, but she's never had any formal training or instruction. She must have a real knack for it."

"You'll find out for yourself pretty soon," Karr said, leaning in. "And it won't hurt if you call her *Captain*." Vroc tried but failed to hide his smile.

"I don't know what he's telling you," Maize declared, appearing at his side. "But it was a joint effort. Look at this thing!" She slapped the side of the craft. "We brought it home without so much as a dent!"

"Yes, yes. I'm very impressed. Please do so again, darling."

She gave him a massive hug that he accepted uncharacteristically, responding with one of equal proportion.

With that, he wished her luck, then climbed back aboard the family landspeeder and drove away from the spaceport, leaving them alone with the expensive ship.

It hardly felt real at all.

"Are we really doing this?" he asked.

RZ-7 added, "Again?"

"We sure are!" Maize said proudly.

Karr was incredibly excited. And again he felt his grandmother's presence.

"Wait!" he said with alarm. "Your dad has this ship loaded with surveillance bugs, but my grandma asked that we keep Naq Med's location a secret. I can't just ignore her wishes."

Maize thought for a moment. "You certainly can't," she said. "And I know what I told my parents, but this is more important. Maybe one more *tiny* rebellious act is in order."

"Yeah," Karr replied. "Historians will say the great pilot Maize Raynshi was just getting it out of her system before committing to the straight and narrow."

Maize liked that. "First we have to sweep the ship," she said. "I overheard my dad's call to the tech support team. He ordered three surveillance bugs, one of which will be installed under the console—and I can't move that one, so we'll have to fool it. But that's no big deal."

"It's not?"

"Not if you know what you're doing."

He asked, "*Do* you know what you're doing?"

"Do you really have to ask? As for the other two bugs, I've got a plan."

"You do, Captain?" asked RZ-7.

"I do. You see that ship right there?" She pointed out a craft that was about the same size and shape of the one they were about to climb aboard. "It belongs to a friend of my mom's. She's going to the Chommell sector to visit her daughter. My mom spoke to her this morning. She'll be back around the same time we are. We'll just stick the trackers on her ship, go about our journey, and then, provided we time it right, stick them back on our ship when we both get home—and no one will ever be the wiser."

"What about the one under the console?"

She waved her hand. "When I get the other bugs back, I'll copy their data to that one so everything matches. I'm telling you, I've got this. Now help me look for the two bugs. I know they're in here someplace. We'll deal with those first, and we need to hurry. The other ship will launch within an hour. We might be cutting this close."

They did cut it close, but they got it done.

The surveillance bugs were each the size of Karr's thumb; one was stashed inside the back of a cabinet, stuck to the ceiling, and the other was spotted by RZ-7, who found it inside the docking gear. Maize collected them both and went to see her mother's friend on a pretend mission of "Fancy seeing *you* here."

When she returned, blushing and giggling and ready to go, she said, "I stuck one of them under one of the ramp steps and one underneath the emergency med pack. She'll never know about them, and probably wouldn't know what they are if she found them."

"But . . ." Karr broached, always the more anxious of the pair, "what if she *does* find them? What if she destroys them? What will we do?"

She shrugged as she stomped up the ramp and into

the ship. "It won't come to that, but if it does? We have options. We'll figure something out."

"Something like . . . ?"

From inside the craft she said, "Don't worry so much. This is going to be *fun*."

Karr looked at RZ-7, his entire face a mask of uncertainty. "What do *you* think she'll do?" he asked the droid.

"If I were forced to guess, I'd say she plans to blow up the ship or claim it was stolen by pirates, sir. Failing that, I'm confident that she'll pull some other plan out of thin air. She's quite good at that."

Karr trudged up the ramp behind her, RZ-7 at his side. "She's *scary* good at that. I'm just glad she's on our team and not somebody else's."

"Me too, sir. Me too."

They settled into the cockpit, Karr taking up the copilot's seat and the droid strapping in behind them. He told her, "I've been doing some digging, and I found out more about the planet my grandmother mentioned. It was mined for phosphates for a few decades, but it was such a miserable place to live and work that the mines eventually closed and mostly everybody left."

She frowned. "You can find phosphates in marshland?"

"In the area around them, maybe. I don't know. Anyway, it has a large continent with marshy grasslands near the equator. It's mostly hot scrubland and wet forests around the rest of it, plus a couple of big oceans."

Maize pulled up the nav maps, located the planet in question, and looked over the schematics. "It's kind of the far end of no place, isn't it? Not exactly Wild Space, but you can see it from there."

"All the more reason to pick it for a hiding spot," he said, with more confidence than he felt. He was desperately afraid that he was screwing this up, and if it didn't work out . . . then he'd sold his soul to the trade school for absolutely nothing.

He couldn't let it come to that. He had to believe in the balance. He had to trust the Force.

Everything was riding on it.

"Are we ready?" Maize asked him, her hands gripping the throttle.

Karr knew it didn't matter what he said. She was about to launch anyway. "Sure. Let's go."

Up they went, into high atmosphere—and then into hyperspace, to a strange corner of the galaxy with a planet no one liked, no one needed, and no one would ever want to live on.

Except maybe a very old man who didn't want to be found.

When they emerged from hyperspace, the planet Pam'ba was large and round before them. Its oceans were few and far between—dots of blue scattered among sandy savannas and dirty-green swaths of what must have been marshes. A brighter green around the equator probably meant jungles or rainforests, and here and there, patches of white speckled the lands between cold gray mountains.

Karr's head felt light, but it sometimes did when they emerged from hyperspace. He didn't know if he'd ever get used to it. But was that all it was? A little bit of disorientation from the travel?

He blinked hard and shook his head in an effort to clear it.

It wasn't that he could hear something, exactly. It wasn't that he could see it. It was more like he *knew* it, from the bottom of his soul—a sharp and distant warmth that felt like certainty. "This is it," he whispered.

"Do you sense something? Is the Force telling you anything? I don't know how this works."

"Neither do I," he said. "But we're in the right place. I feel like something is finally *right*. Does that make sense?"

She shrugged. "Not really. But I'm not stuck in my room surrounded by homework—so as long we aren't actually, literally violently murdered down there on the ground . . . I'm game to go check it out."

He frowned at her. "You don't think we're going to get murdered, do you?"

"Not if you're right and the planet is abandoned. If there's nobody down there to murder us, we're all good.

"Did you bring any weapons?" she asked.

"No! Of course not."

"That's a shame." She pulled up a scanner and started checking the planet's surface. "I tried to find something before we left, but Dad keeps everything locked up. I guess we're on our own."

"We'll be fine. What are you doing?"

She pointed at a set of coordinates that meant nothing to Karr. The numbers scrolled, rolled, and changed faster than he could read them. "I'm looking for someplace to set the ship down that's near the equator, near some marshy grasslands, and not likely to let the *Avadora* sink like a rock in a puddle."

"Oh. Good idea."

She said, "I know. Now pay attention. Let me know if anything jumps out at you. This is a big planet, and there's a *lot* of marshland to scroll through."

He thought about it hard and tried to be logical. "Look for signs of civilization."

"Why? Your grandmother said he lived alone in a house in the middle of nowhere."

"That's not exactly what she said."

"You know what I mean."

Karr rolled his eyes. That was usually Maize's signature move, but she was rubbing off on him. "He was a hermit, yes—but this planet has been abandoned for almost a hundred and fifty years. If he came here to live, he might've started out scavenging from what was left behind."

"Okay, I get it. If he lived in the marsh grass, he

might've needed a boat. It's easier to find one that nobody's using than to build your own."

"Exactly!" he said, pleased with his own deduction. "So we should look for small mining towns, or even mining equipment. Anything that a lone human might find useful, if he plans to live here for a while."

This was their hardest search yet. When they'd visited other planets before, they'd had an idea of a town, or a person, or a distinct geographical landmark. Finding a single dwelling on a large empty planet would be trickier.

Much trickier.

They spent an entire day scanning the planet, squinting at tiny landmarks, overgrown roads, and the scant remains of small communities that had been left to the elements generations before. Here and there, they spotted a large building or a set of silos to hold whatever the miners were dredging up from under the ground. Sulfates, phosphates, whatever-fates. Karr didn't know what they were for, or why anybody had ever wanted them.

Now nobody wanted them, not anymore. Not badly enough to live on Pam'ba.

Finally, Karr felt it: the twinge. The warmth, the

certainty. The sharp knowing that felt like a revelation. He held up his hand. "Wait. Hold on."

Maize paused the scan display. "What am I looking at? I don't see anything."

He closed his eyes and let his hand hover over the image. He pictured it in his mind—a squared-off map of dull green and brown, streaked with black water. Currents swirling. Local animals with thick skin and long faces, snaking among the reeds. Odd birds with very long legs and very small bodies. The collapsing remains of a pier and a brick-shaped building that might've been a store or might have been an office.

Beyond all that, a platform on stilts, raised above the wet grass.

On top of it, a featureless brown box. A door. A window.

A house.

# CHAPTER 24

The *Avadora* set down on a mostly firm bit of damp land, as close to the old pier and mining offices as they could get. The ship settled and squished into turf that was spongey and thick with long flat grass the color of dry moss. It was the best they were going to get, because beyond that little patch of land, the world of Pam'ba was very wet indeed. The mining office was lifted up on pillars so it stood above the murky water below—but when Karr and Maize tried to get inside, they found that the floor had rotted and fallen away. The building was only a shell, and anything useful that it might once have held had surely collapsed into the water years before.

RZ-7 waited for them by the pier, where he snooped around in search of boats or rafts. "Do you see anything, sir?" he called out.

"No!" Karr hollered back as he stomped and sloshed back and forth among various remains of the camp. Or town? No, a camp. There were only a few small buildings, and none of them looked like they'd ever been anyone's home.

Only one still had all four walls plus a roof and a floor. It was completely empty, with rows of vacant shelves and holes where windows used to be—their glass long since shattered and lost.

Maize looked over his shoulder, then shrugged and walked away. "There's nothing here, Arzee. It's all just old junk that's falling apart."

Karr agreed. "Nothing to scavenge except the wood, and most of that looks like it's gone moldy. Not sure what you'd do with it, if you took it."

"Build other stuff with it," Maize suggested. When she and Karr had joined the droid at the pier, she pulled out her datapad and checked it for inspiration. "Anyhow, the house we saw on the map is that way."

"I don't see anything, though."

"Sure you do. See that real tall grass? Where it's as tall as we are, at least?"

He nodded. "Yeah. Is it past there?"

"It's past there, sorry. And we don't have a boat, so . . . we're gonna get soggy."

The droid said, "Wonderful," in a tone that suggested he didn't think it was wonderful at all but he was along for the ride regardless. Better to be waterlogged than left behind.

Together they slogged through the water and grass, which was thigh-deep at worst and ankle-deep at best. Progress was slow and uncomfortable, plagued by mud that ate their boots and socks, and bugs the size of their thumbs that hummed, circled, and buzzed about. One tried to take a bite out of RZ-7. It didn't work.

"Now would be a great time to break out some Jedi robes, if I had any," Karr complained. "Everything on this planet bites!"

"Or stings."

"Or stings," he agreed.

"Some of them sting, and some of them bite, sir. I'm not familiar with the species that are common to this particular planet, but they aren't very pleasant."

"Like you care, Arzee. They can't suck any blood out of *you*." He slapped one of the smaller, shinier creatures into mush against his shoulder.

Maize smacked one against her neck. "Or shoot you up with itchy poison. This wouldn't be so bad if it wasn't so hot."

"Yes, it would. This is miserable. I totally understand why a guy who wants to be left alone forever"—he huffed and puffed and yanked his boot out of some thick, squishy muck—"would pick a place like this. You'd have to be pretty crazy to follow anyone out here.

"Are we still headed the right direction? It doesn't feel like we're making any progress at all."

"We're making progress," she assured him. "We ought to be able to see the house in a minute. We'll get there eventually."

"Eventually" didn't arrive for another hour, and by then all three explorers were completely exhausted—but when the little shack came into view, Karr felt a jolt of energy and a second wind.

"There it is! Come on, we're almost there!"

Maize groaned, and RZ-7 creaked, but they picked up the pace. Before long, they reached some sandy ground that wasn't exactly solid but wasn't as bad as slogging up to their hips through muddy water. Karr led the charge, breaking into a staggering run.

He tripped and fell, and caught himself on his hands—then picked himself up again. "Almost there," he gasped. "Almost there."

The house was elevated on thick wood pilings, sitting atop a platform. Against the platform rested a rough wood ladder that was held together with frayed brown ropes.

The boy stopped in front of it, his heart pounding and his legs burning. They hadn't come half a kilometer through the marshland, but it felt as if he'd climbed a mountain. Everything ached and nothing was dry, but he'd made it. He'd found the small house where his great-grandfather, a former Jedi Knight, had lived out his last days.

He steadied himself, forcing the hot, aching pain in his head to the side. With a deep breath or two—in and out, in and out—he grasped the ladder barehanded, for his gloves were stashed in his highest jacket pockets. There was a reaction, but it was only a zap. The wood buzzed beneath his fingers.

Maize came up behind him, RZ-7 at her side. "Well?" she asked. "Are you getting anything?"

"I'm getting . . . everything." The longer he stood there, holding the wood, the more his pain faded into something calm and understated. It was still present, but it didn't hurt anymore. It had become a strange sensation but not a miserable one.

"So get up in there. Let's go inside."

Karr began to climb the ladder. He went slowly and carefully, not least of all because he didn't want to pick up any splinters and he was thoroughly exhausted.

He paused, deeply tired from the trek through the water. He stayed there, in the shadow of the small house, staring out across the soaked grasslands. This was the view his great-grandfather had seen. And much like the connection he felt to Kenobi when he held the training remote on the ship, he felt a connection to Naq Med. Maybe even more so because he was family.

And just like before, a flash lit up the air and the hum filled his ears. Karr marveled at how well he had conquered his visions. The transition was seamless, he thought. Until he realized he wasn't staring into a vision. He was staring into a face with a very deep frown bathed in the green glow of a very intimidating lightsaber.

"What are you doing here?" the man yelled, causing Karr to nearly fall backward off the ladder.

"I'm looking for Naq Med."

"Naq Med? Who told you that name?"

"J'Hara."

The man took a step back, giving Karr a better view of his would-be assailant. What he saw was a very old man who was very thin—doubled over in a crouch, all the better to see who was coming up the ladder. His eyes were bright and deep set, and what remained of his hair was as light and gauzy as a cloud. Most of that hair could be found in his eyebrows, which were as wild and untamed as the wilderness around them.

Karr's heart almost stopped. He could hardly breathe, but he pulled himself together enough to say, "My name is Karr," with only the barest squeak of fear, or excitement, or whatever else he was feeling. Everything was a tangle in his chest. He wanted to scream, he wanted to cry, and he wanted to laugh, all at once.

The man said, "What's this about J'Hara? You know her?" Before Karr could respond, he observed, "You aren't alone."

"No, sir." His hands were getting sweaty, and his throat was completely dry. His tongue was like sandpaper and ashes, but he said, "They're my friends. They helped me find you."

The man extinguished his lightsaber and stood up straight. He was of average height, and he had the lean, sagging build of a man who was almost as old as the ruins he scavenged. He wore plain brown pants and a shirt that might've been white, once upon a time. His boots were caked in mud, and his coat hung loosely from his shoulders. "Why would you want to do that? Do you have a message from J'Hara?"

Karr swallowed a gulp and a gasp. Of course the man didn't know his daughter was dead. There was no one to tell him. Plus, up until moments before, they had all assumed he was also dead. "Sir, could I . . . could we . . . come up here? And come inside? I do have news, yes, but it's . . . my arms. And my legs. I'm really tired."

Maybe it was Karr's shaking elbows or his strained voice, but the old man agreed. He offered him a hand. "If you have news, all right. You can come up."

Karr was afraid to take the hand—afraid that the fragile old fellow would break if he touched him. But he thought it would be rude to refuse, so he accepted the help and climbed over the side of the platform. "You're Naq Med, aren't you?"

"I used to be," he said grumpily.

Karr called over his shoulder for Maize and RZ-7 to join him, but he could barely take his eyes off this ancient Jedi, wrinkled and withered and not especially happy to see him.

"Who are you, exactly?" the man asked.

"Oh! Sorry. I'm . . . well, if you're Naq Med, I'm your great-grandson. Karr Nuq Sin."

For a moment, he couldn't tell if the old Jedi believed him. The man didn't exactly soften, but he became curious. "Great-grandson? I thought you were . . ." he made a gesture with his hand that suggested a very small child.

Maize's head popped up over the side. "He's not exactly a giant, now. But at least he's—"

Naq Med cut her off. "Old enough to be flying around with another kid and a . . . some kind of medical droid?" he concluded as RZ-7 appeared.

"That's Arzee," Karr told him. "I made him. He's not exactly a medical droid—but he's my friend anyway. And this is Maize. She's my friend, too."

Naq Med gave them each a hard stare, one at a time, like he was deciding which one to eat first. But in the end, he sighed and said, "You'd better get inside, then. It's about to rain."

Maize looked at the sky. "Is it?"

Though it was clear and blue, a swift-moving line of gray appeared on the northern horizon. It hadn't been there ten minutes before, and it was moving so fast that it'd surely reach them in another ten minutes. Or less.

"Trust me on this one, kids. I've been here a long time." By the time he'd ushered them indoors, the first spitting drops of water were splattering down. They didn't fall hard, but they fell fast, and the sound of the small storm was a buzzing, humming patter on the metal roof.

"Wow, that was sudden," she observed, shaking her hair.

"It's always sudden. The weather here isn't too bad most of the time, but it changes in the blink of an eye. You may as well make yourselves at home for a few minutes, because you don't want to walk back in this."

"I don't want to walk back at all," Maize told him.

"I don't blame you. It was stupid to come on foot. You should've grabbed a raft or a dinghy." He went to the corner of the one-room building and lit a small fire on the stove. "You all look awful, like half-drowned swamp rats. I can't fix that—but I can make some tea."

She made a half-hearted effort to wring water out of her pant leg. "Thanks, I'll take some, and it could be worse. It could be *cold* and wet."

Karr was too distracted by the little residence to disagree with her. He didn't mind the heat, but the terrible stickiness of the humidity was surely more miserable than mere cold might have been. He was a child of the desert, and this semi-swamp made him feel like he was drowning in the very air he breathed.

But he was enthralled by the house, small and simple though it might have been. Perhaps the size of his own living room at home—or the foyer at Maize's house—Naq Med's quarters were clean but lightly cluttered. The floor was rough-hewn and covered with a rug that once might have been a curtain; along one wall an assortment of fishing gear was meticulously organized, and several pillows made of burlap sacks were set about the floor for seats or beds. Clean tins were lined up on a shelf above a makeshift sink, and there were two large barrels in one corner that seemed to hold clean water—for that's where the man dipped a ladle to collect water for tea.

Karr sat down on a cushion and crossed his legs, feeling the vibrations of the Force with his very soul. Every object in the room and the man who'd collected them all resonated with the same tone, buzzing at the same frequency.

This was the Force.

This was a man who'd dedicated his life to it, until he hadn't anymore.

"Give me this news of J'Hara, if that's why you're here," said the former Jedi, his back to the room as he tended the stove. "Don't just sit there and stare."

Karr didn't want to tell him the truth, but he was determined to be brave. His words only caught in his throat a tiny bit when he said, "I'm sorry to say, but she died."

Naq Med froze for a moment, his face an unreadable mask. Then he returned to the kettle. "Ah. That's . . . well. I'm sorry to hear it, but I thank you for telling me. I was afraid it might be something like that. I felt something. Not a shift in the Force, exactly. More like a hiccup or a"—he fumbled for the correct word—"burp. It wasn't . . . it wasn't violent though, was it? Or a terrible illness? I'd like to think I would have known if some horrific fate befell her."

"No, sir, nothing like that. Her heart gave out, that's all." It was hard to talk about and hard to even think about the way J'Hara's skin had been the color of old paper and cold to the touch.

"That's . . . good. As good a death as anyone could ask for. It's a tragedy, though. No man should outlive his children. What of her son? Your father, I suppose?"

"He's fine. Everyone's fine."

"You have a brother, too. Isn't that right?"

"Yes, sir. But, sir, I came all this way because I needed to talk to you," Karr tried, hoping to steer the conversation away from a painful family memory and toward something more hopeful and helpful instead. "J'Hara left me a message telling me to find you."

"Why's that? She and I, we had an understanding. She was safer without me. Your whole family is safer without me. You might well be putting them all in danger by coming here."

"The rest of them might be safer," Karr admitted. "But I'm not. See, for the last couple of years everyone's been telling me that I'm sick, but that's not true."

"It's not?"

"No, sir, I'm not sick. I am sensitive to the Force."

# CHAPTER 25

The tea was poured. Karr and Maize sat on the scratchy pillows, but Naq Med stood with a cup in his hand. All the cups were mismatched things—tin cans cleaned of their original contents. The heat from the beverages seeped straight through them, so the kids held on to them with the edges of their sleeves.

Either the old Jedi didn't notice the heat or it didn't hurt his hands anymore. He paced around the room while he spoke.

"I believe you. I should begin there, I suppose. I knew when I saw you . . . I knew who you must be, though I thought my eyes deceived me." He glanced over his shoulder at Karr, who was hanging on every word. "There's a family resemblance," he said with the faintest hint of a smile. "You might not believe it now, but I swear to you—it's like looking in a mirror, eighty years ago. You're quite a handsome young devil, aren't you?"

He'd never particularly thought so, but it was nice to hear. "Am I?" he asked modestly.

Naq Med shrugged. "Eh. The potential is there. Another five years, maybe. Another ten, and you'll wish . . ." He shook his head. "No, you won't regret your vows. You're not a Jedi, nor will you ever become one."

"That's what Maz Kanata said. I have the Force, but not enough to be a Jedi. Or not the right kind, I don't know. I don't understand, and there's no one to help me learn. J'Hara tried, but she didn't know enough to give me the education I need. That's why she suggested I seek this place out. She thought it might contain items that would help me understand, but I don't think she expected it to contain you."

"The Force manifests in many ways, in many different kinds of people. The kind that flows through you . . . it's not the energy of a warrior or a monk. It's something else. Something strong, but something different."

The old man shrugged again. "I cannot tell you what I do not know. But I can sense it about you. I felt it when you landed, and that's why I was waiting for you here. I returned to the house when I realized someone was coming and it was someone with the Force. I didn't know if you were friend or foe."

"What would you have done, if I'd turned out to be a bad guy?"

"Killed you, I suppose. Or you might have killed me. Who can say? I've lived longer than anyone had any reason to expect. Many days, I think it's a pity. Many days, I wish I'd followed my wife. It wouldn't have mattered to anyone, would it? You would still be here. Your father, too. My daughter. I'd done everything good I was ever going to do."

"That's a terrible thing to think," Karr protested.

"But no less true, for being terrible. Here, let me show you something." He put his can of tea on a tiny counter beside the bin he used for a sink. For a few seconds, he dug around in a box that he'd pulled down from a shelf. "It's in here somewhere, I'm sure. I remember it so clearly, that day. I was at the Temple and—yes! Here it is."

He retrieved a holoprojector the size of his palm and put the box away. He passed it to Karr.

When the hologram lit up, the boy gasped and slapped one hand over his mouth. He was holding a picture of a Jedi, a portrait on the steps of the temple he'd seen in his vision. The man was a bit older than Karr, maybe in his early twenties. Broad shoulders, flowing robes, lightsaber at his belt. And Karr's own face, wide with a big smile.

He jumped to his feet, holding the holoprojector by two fingers—like it might bite him if he brought it any closer. "That's . . . that's . . ."

"That's *me*," the Jedi said. "Many years before you were born. I told you, yes? The family resemblance is really something."

"No, but—you don't understand! I saw this! I had a vision, when I touched . . . when I held . . . when I saw . . ." He stammered wildly, trying to sync up the scene in his vision with the image in his hand. "I saw myself fighting! I killed another Jedi!"

Naq Med held out his hands. "No, that's not it. That's not it at all." He reclaimed the device from Karr before the boy could destroy it in his rage and confusion.

"I know what I saw!"

"What you saw might not be what occurred. The Force does not always work cleanly or clearly. What did you touch, when you had this vision of yourself murdering Jedi?"

"A lightsaber! A broken one. It was circular and in two pieces. It once belonged to an Inquisitor." His voice was shaking, like everything else. His hands quivered, his knees knocked. "I know what I saw," he said again. Then, with dawning realization he added, "I know what *you* did."

"No, you don't." Naq Med paused to think. He shoved the holoprojector back into the box. "Let me try to explain. When we discovered that I was Force-sensitive, it was decided that I would become a Padawan and study the ways of the Jedi. I trained tirelessly with my master. Such joy I felt just being in the Temple. But it was outside of the Temple, in the shadow of politics, that I began to have my doubts. A Jedi stands strongest in the light. He has no place in a bureaucracy. Even when approached by those in need of his abilities. And I thought how the Jedi were dealing with it was the wrong path. Perhaps it sounds cowardly or misguided, but you were not there, and you cannot say. After much deliberation, I left the Order. I chose my own path—and once upon it, I met your great-grandmother. We had a daughter, who you knew and loved. I will not say that I made the wrong choice."

Maize asked, "Where'd you go?"

"That's not important, except that a few short years later, I learned of Order 66. I heard Palpatine speak about the Jedi uprising. I heard what they did, and I was horrified. It was exactly what I had feared! By then, the Jedi were disbanded and scattered. They'd risen up against the Republic—I heard all about it when Palpatine sent out his report."

"Palpatine lied!" Karr insisted.

"No, young man. You may know what you saw, but *I* know what happened because I was there. In time, I was tracked down by the Grand Inquisitor, who pursued me as he pursued all who ever once were part of the Order. But I had a wife, you see? And a daughter. I was no longer any Jedi, and I refused to accept my fate—so I fought the Inquisitor. His lightsaber broke, I remember that much. That must be the one you found, the one you touched."

"Maybe?"

"Yes, yes. That must be it—but your visions, they're not perfect, are they? They're not always clear, and you can't always take them at face value."

But Karr wasn't sure. He repeated, "I *know* what I saw," like a mantra.

His great-grandfather knew things, too. "You see the truth, my boy—but you see more than one truth at a time. Yes, I fought the Inquisitor, and the Inquisitor fought Jedi, killed them, in fact. But when you touched the lightsaber, you combined the two visions. You're not lying and you're not wrong, you're just seeing too many things at once. In time, you might be able to tease them out and find more details, more clarity. Even though the Jedi turned on the Republic, I never harmed any of them."

"But they *didn't* turn on the Republic!" Now it was Karr's turn to share some knowledge. His head was light and his ears were ringing, but he was right and he was righteous.

"Then why else would they execute Order 66? Why else would I flee my family? Why else would I live in a place so far, so remote, and so awful? It was only to protect them. I don't have much longer to hide, for their safety. For your safety. My time is almost finished, and then you will all be free."

When he stopped talking, the fine rain shrieked and scraped against the roof. The shack shuddered in the wind, and shallow waves crashed against the pilings that held it all above the water. All Naq Med's questions had been the kind that didn't really seek answers, but Karr had some for him anyway.

"The Jedi didn't betray the Republic—the Republic betrayed *them*. It was all part of Palpatine's propaganda."

The old man whispered, "You don't know what you're talking about."

"But it's true! I saw it," Karr insisted. "I may not know enough about the Force to make me a Jedi, but thanks to my abilities I've seen some of their history. They were everything you once believed in—they were protectors, guardians, and helpers. They fought for the light, but the darkness won. I'm so sorry," he said, tears filling his eyes. "I'm so sorry you didn't know. I'm so sorry there was no one to tell you."

"It isn't possible." He shook his head, unwilling to hear this.

Maize had Karr's back. "It's not just possible, it's true. But the thing is, hardly anybody knows about it. Not anymore. The lie you knew became many people's reality. The Emperor poisoned the well for the Jedi."

RZ-7 agreed, as gently as he could. "Sir, you took such noble measures to protect your family—and those measures were successful. But there was no need to turn your back on the Jedi. They never turned their back on the Republic. Or you."

Naq Med sank slowly to the floor. His grip on the can he used for a cup loosened, and it fell—spilling its contents across the rug. "But if that's true, it was all for nothing. The Grand Inquisitor . . . ?" he asked of anyone who might answer.

Karr said, "A pawn of the Emperor. He turned on his own kind." He paused. In the back of his head, an idea gelled. He spoke slowly, putting the words in order as they occurred to him. "The dark side won. The bad guys won so completely that when they were finished . . . there was nobody left to remember the good guys. No one to tell their side of the story. No one to collect their history and write it down—not once the Temple was gone. They say history is written by the winners, but it should be written by those who remember. Those who care about the facts."

The old man settled in a loose cross-legged position, his arms at his sides, his hands lying limply in his lap. "It was all a lie. My whole life, everything I lost . . ."

Karr scrambled to his side and picked up the rolling cup. He dabbed at the spilled liquid with the cuff of his sleeve, then gave up in favor of supporting his miserable host. "Grandfather," he said, taking one of Naq Med's hands and holding it—trying to compel him to make eye contact, but failing. "You did what you had to do. You did everything as right as you could. Your family survived. I survived."

His great-grandfather shook his head and closed his eyes. He was deflating, becoming smaller as he closed in on himself—as if he would sink through the floorboards if only he was able. "You *did* survive. J'Hara survived, and she lived . . . a long life. A happy life?" he asked.

Karr nodded, even though his great-grandfather couldn't see it. He squeezed the man's hand between his own. "She was very happy. She ran the family shop until a few years ago, and was known all across Merokia for her fine clothing. She took pride in it. And in her son, and . . . and me, I think. It was a good life," he concluded.

"Then it wasn't for nothing." When he opened his eyes again, they overflowed. "But it's a shame that it cost so much, and it took so long. So much was lost."

Maize tried hard to pretend that she wasn't getting

sniffly, but her words were thick when she said, "So much was saved, too."

"That's true," Karr said. "For a long time things were bad for the Jedi. But then a Jedi came along who brought balance to the Force. Palpatine eventually lost. And the days of hunting Jedi came to an end."

Naq Med sighed so deeply, so heavily that Karr thought it was the very last of his soul leaving his body. He sank even deeper into his oversized, scavenged clothes. "That's good, yes. Very good. Then my job is finally done. I kept my family safe. And now I can rest."

"Yes," Karr confirmed. "You've done all that you needed to do."

Naq Med smiled. "Tell me something. Have the Jedi been redeemed? Do people know the truth?"

Karr lowered his gaze. "Not exactly."

The old man's smile began to fade. He slumped forward, his head hanging so low that his chin tapped against his chest. "A pity. Soon there will be no one left to remember."

Karr was quick to respond. "I'll always remember!"

Naq Med lifted his head, but this time it was only his eyes that smiled. He reached out his other hand

and grabbed Karr's in his own. Then with one more breath, let out slow, he sank down farther—folding in on himself until he appeared to have no bones at all. He was still and quiet, his scraggly head resting on his knees and his back bowed, elbows jutting left and right. "If only people knew . . . the truth."

Karr touched his shoulder. It collapsed, as light as matchsticks. "Great-grandfather?"

Maize left the cushion and crawled a meter across the floor, where she pulled Karr back, first by his arm—and then she pulled him into a hug. "He's gone. He's already gone."

Karr could hardly breathe and barely speak. "He *can't* be gone. I just got here. . . ."

"I know." She rocked him back and forth, pulling him away from the corpse of the old man who looked so very small. He could've been a child or a small mannequin. A ghost made of kindling and cotton. "But he left because you allowed him to. You gave him what he needed. You helped him. You *saved* him."

# CHAPTER 26

They wrapped Naq Med's body in the curtain-turned-rug that took up most of the floor in the shack he'd called home for decades. He hardly weighed anything at all, and when he was wrapped in the makeshift shroud, the kids placed him at rest on the pillows he'd made out of bags he'd found at the mining camp. They were stuffed with sawdust and straw, so Karr knew they would burn.

"When the rain stops . . ." he started to say, but ran out of words.

RZ-7 picked up the thread. "When the rain stops, we can honor your grandmother's wishes—as she spelled them out in her message."

Maize nodded. "Leave them nothing to find. Not even ashes. We should burn the whole thing. He might have things inside that could point back to your family."

The boy stood baffled and restless, looking for something to do with his hands. "It'll be like he never existed."

"No," she argued. "You're living proof that he

existed. When the rain stops," she started again, "we can dump a little fuel on the house as we leave and hit it with a plasma beam. It'll be a great send-off. Your grandmother would be satisfied, and he would be proud."

The droid was ambling around the little cabin, poking his hands into baskets and bins, drawers and shelves. "But while the rain holds, sir . . . perhaps we should look for items to add to your collection. It's grown quite extensive, but you should save something of your great-grandfather's—for yourself, if no one else. Your father might want something to remember him by, too."

"He's got a point, Karr. You've collected Jedi artifacts from every corner of the galaxy. It'd be a shame to leave your great-grandfather's place empty-handed. He'd want you to take something."

He tried to keep from staring at the body, laid out on the cushions. "You don't know that," he said, but he couldn't really argue. The small house was flooded with the Force, accumulated over a long lifetime—whether or not the old man had renounced his vows. The Force didn't go away just because you were no longer pledged to it. And it didn't only touch those who'd made pledges in the first place.

It stayed.

And it touched many people who weren't committed to the light or the dark. Sometimes, it touched people like Karr.

"Look around," she pressed. "Hold out your hands, feel the Force, or whatever it is you do. There must be something in here that calls to you. Try it and see."

He held out his hands and scanned the room thoughtfully, trying to ignore the black hole around his great-grandfather. He felt the Force in all four corners, and in the rafters, and under the floor.

Under the floor.

In the back corner, behind some shelves that held folded rags and a tin of tea that the man had either found or collected and dried himself. Karr pushed aside a canister that looked like it might have held trash or compost and found a hatch cut into the grain of the floor. There wasn't any lever or handle to open it with, but he pried it loose with a rusted knife blade he'd found in the sink.

Maize joined him. "What have you got there?"

They both stared into the hole while RZ-7 craned his metal neck to get a look for himself. Down under the floorboards, hanging in a net above the water—tucked tight beneath the house so no one would be likely to see it, or find it, or open it—was a box about the size of a suitcase.

Karr hauled it up into the house. It wasn't heavy, but it was bulky and hard to maneuver; he pushed it into the middle of the floor so he'd have more room to work and tweaked the latch until it popped.

"It's not locked?" asked Maize.

He lifted the lid. "Nope. Oh . . . oh, *wow*."

"Is that . . . ?"

RZ-7 let out a soft digital whistle.

He reached inside and pulled out a neatly folded bundle, tied with twine. With the same rusty blade he'd used to pop the latch, he sliced the twine and unleashed a pale, wax-colored robe. He held it up by the shoulders and rose to his feet—measuring it against himself and his own shoulders.

The robe was made for a bigger man, but not that much bigger. It was made for a man with wider shoulders, but not that much wider. In another few years, Karr would be big enough. His shoulders would be wide enough. But this robe was not for him to wear, and he felt it in his bones—every bit as much as he felt that it now belonged to him.

The Jedi might be dishonored rogues, if any of them remained alive to care, but he knew the facts and he could remember them. He could collect the robe, and archive it, and save it for future generations.

If the Force was as eternal as Karr believed and history did, in fact, repeat itself, then more Jedi would come, and they would need to know the truth. They *deserved* to know the truth.

He held the robe up to his face and sniffed it deeply. It mostly smelled like mildew, and he loved it. For a split second, he wondered if they ought to dress his great-grandfather in it before they set fire to every shred of evidence that he'd ever lived there—but no. He understood his role now. He was a collector, and he would collect.

"Can I see it?" Maize asked.

"Sir? Don't forget about this. . . ."

Karr passed the clothes to Maize and turned his attention to the droid. "What is it, Arzee?" But he saw it before the droid could answer—Naq Med's lightsaber. It remained on the table where he'd left it, looking as unobtrusive as a teacup without the Force of the Jedi behind it.

He ran his thumb up and down the metal cylinder

until he found the switch that turned it on. A bright green column shot out, startling them all. It buzzed and hummed, glowing with power.

Karr held it with terror and awe, aiming carefully at the middle of the room where no one stood and no one could be hit or hurt. "A lightsaber," he gasped. "I'm holding a real lightsaber. Not a broken one, not a piece of one. A *real* one."

"And your head didn't explode or anything!" Maize said, clapping her hands and laughing. "Does it hurt?"

"It feels . . ." How did it feel? He didn't have the words. It felt like electricity and pressure between his ears, but it didn't feel like a hot spike. It felt like hyperspace. It felt like the Force. "It feels . . . good."

"Good? That's all you've got?" she asked, but she was grinning from ear to ear.

"It feels light, not dark. It feels like I've finally found the balance."

RZ-7 asked, "In the Force?"

He nodded. "And in life. I don't fear the future anymore. It'll be whatever I make of it. Good? Bad? Jedi? Tailor? Collector?" A light went off in his head, and almost to himself he said, "Maybe I'll even be a . . ." But his voice trailed off, and he replaced the last word with a smile. He took another admiring look, then turned off the lightsaber.

"What are you doing?" she wanted to know. "Swing that thing around! Get some practice!"

"No, it isn't for me to use—it's for me to hold. That's where the balance is, see?" He put it back down on the long strip of cloth and rolled it up. "I spent so long trying to figure out how to be a Jedi, and how to master the Force . . . but I've been looking at it all wrong. Maz Kanata knew. That's what she was trying to tell me with the milk. I'm not the milk."

"You're losing me, Karr. I don't get it."

"That's okay," he told her. "Because I get it, finally. I'm not the milk. I'm the glass. I'm the one who sees the past, and the truth about what happened there. I'm the one who holds the memory."

"Why you, sir? Why now?" asked the droid.

"Because there's no one else to do it. This is where I fit," he said with real confidence. Real certainty. "This is what I'm meant for. I get it now. I'm ready now."

When he stopped talking, he realized that the sky was quiet. The rain had stopped. The storm was over, and they had everything of value there was left to take. His great-grandfather was dead, and he was going to leave for a trade school in a month—but that was all right. He understood that part now.

"Let's go," he told them, tucking the case with the robe and the lightsaber under his arm. "We still have some tracks to cover when we get home, right, Maize? You have to switch the transponders, and all that stuff?"

"It won't take me twenty minutes, but sure."

"Arzee, do you see anything else we should take with us?"

"No, sir, I don't."

"Then let's head home."

Down under the house, they found a shallow dinghy tied to a post. It wasn't much, but it made the trip back to the *Avadora* that much less miserable. When they got stuck, bogged down in the thick grass, they took turns getting out to tow the other two passengers—and the hike back to the ship took half the time.

Maize made them all clean up, or make a token effort to do so. "It's my dad's ship. If we get mud all over the interior, I'll never hear the end of it. He's already going to wonder about the fuel we're leaving behind. Let's give him one less thing to gripe about, huh?"

So they swabbed themselves off, removed their boots, wrung out their jackets, and hung it all up in the bunks to dry. They buckled themselves into their seats wearing little more than their undergarments. It was awkward at first, but mostly because of habit. Everyone was covered up enough to be decent, and their wet clothes were gross and uncomfortable.

RZ-7 found a hand towel and used it to wipe himself down, afraid of rust.

When the engines were ready, Maize took the ship up and out, flying low above the marshlands, the dark grass, the swirling water, and the remains of the mining community that had no one else left to scavenge them. "If we had enough fuel, I'd burn it all down for fun," she declared. Karr gave her an unhappy look. "But we don't. So I won't."

She saved it for the shack on the platform. She calculated how much they could spare, dumped it right on the roof, and pulled the ship back.

"Any final words you'd like to say?" she asked Karr, who stared at the little building with a mix of emotions that he couldn't have untangled to save his life.

"I can't think of anything except . . . thank you. Thank you to the Force, for keeping Naq Med safe—and thank you to my great-grandfather, for doing everything he could to keep me and my family safe. He wasn't all wrong, he just didn't know the whole story. He has inspired me to fix that for other people, in the future."

"By collecting the Force?"

"One piece at a time. Go ahead, Maize. Do . . . whatever it is you have to do, but burn it all down and let the ashes wash away. It's the last thing I can do for him."

"Very well, Mr. Copilot." She aimed the small forward cannons and pulled the trigger. An instant later, the house was reduced to flaming rubble that sizzled and sank and disappeared into the marsh.

They waited, hovering over the water, until it was completely gone except for a couple of straggling, scorched piers.

"Sir, if you'll excuse me for asking, what do we do now? Should we head home, or have you decided to dodge your tailoring fate once more?"

"Home," he said decisively to the droid. "I'm not dodging anything anymore. No path is set in stone, but the fun of it will always be that next step. Because they'll be my steps. My story. All right, Captain. Bring us back to Merokia."

"You've got it."

Hyperspace engulfed the *Avadora*, and with one more jump, they were back in their home orbit. Then back on the ground, where Maize was as good as her word—and she swapped out all the fiddly technical things that would hide their trail, even though there was no one left to protect on a big abandoned planet called Pam'ba.

It was the principle of the thing. Like J'Hara had said in her message: leave them nothing—not even ashes.

"We'll tell them we didn't find anything," she told him. "We'll say it was a bust, and we lost some fuel so we gave up and came back. My dad might not believe it, but he probably won't ask too many questions. I don't think he'll care that much, as long as I make it back safely. So what about you?"

"What about me?" Karr asked, unsure of what she meant. He sat on the ramp, eating a piece of fruit and waiting for her to finish tidying up the ship to her personal satisfaction.

"What are you going to do now?"

RZ-7 clarified with his own version of the question. "I think she means about the trade school, sir. Do you intend to keep your word?"

He nodded. "Sure. Why not? Being a Force collector won't pay the bills. I'll need something to fall back on. Something to pay for new collectibles, at any rate."

"Well, thanks a lot," she told him. "You're leaving me to finish out school on my own?"

Karr took another bite, crunched up the fruit, and swallowed it. "That place isn't so bad. Besides, I've still got your holocomm. You can call me and yell at me whenever you want."

"Promise?"

"Promise. Arzee, you're coming with me, right?"

The droid said, "But of course, sir. I doubt your parents want me lurking around listening in on their conversations anymore."

Maize laughed. "I'll keep you right here always, Arzee." She placed her hand to her chest.

"Hey, what about me?" Karr asked.

"You're out of luck, I guess," she said. "Oh, hey. I know I told my mom she could help me pick out a tattoo, but you want to see the one I've got my eye on?"

"Sure."

She took out her holocomm and projected an image.

"Wow," he said. "That's beautiful. Does it translate to anything specific?"

She looked at him sideways. "You mean like *Karr*? Fat chance." She laughed.

Karr turned red. "No, I didn't mean that. I meant—"

"I know what you meant. And yes, it does translate to something. It means . . . 'friendship.' "

Karr smiled, and Maize smiled back. Then the two teens hugged, eventually making room for a protocol droid disguised as a medical droid—and went their separate ways for the time being. Maize went home to talk to her folks about family, and Karr went home to share his findings quietly with his own.

Even his brother was impressed—a little bit, anyway—when Karr produced the lightsaber and turned it on. The little house lit up green, and it hummed with electricity. It sizzled with the Force.

And at night, when everything was put away and all Karr's collectibles were cataloged and sorted and stashed on their shelves . . . he pulled out a datapad. A Force collector's job was more than just collecting. It was also explaining. His job was to remember. To share the stories. And he couldn't wait to begin.

He called up a blank document, cracked his knuckles, and began to type.

*A long time ago . . .*

# ACKNOWLEDGMENTS

This book could not have happened without the continued enthusiasm of Mike Siglain, the guidance of Jen Heddle and Story Group, and the constant support from my own personal Jedi Council: Scott Shinick, Karina Green, Jen Carta, Stephen Wacker, and my wonderful wife, Eileen. All of them listened to me talk about *Star Wars* far longer than I'm sure they expected to after offering up the innocent query, "Would it help to talk it through?"

Also thank you to my parents for always nurturing my obsession with things found in a galaxy far, far away.